THE SOWER COMES

BOOK THREE IN THE SOLAS BEIR TRILOGY

MELISSA ESKUE OUSLEY

Renton, Washington

Cover Art by Aaron Cheney.

Edited by Laura Meehan, S. C. Moore, and C. E. Moore.

Published 2015 Castle Garden Publications,
an imprint of Gazebo Gardens Publishing, LLC.
www.GazeboGardensPublishing.com

978-1-938281-39-6 (hardcover)
978-1-938281-40-2 (paperback)
978-1-938281-37-2 (e-book)

Library of Congress Control Number: 2015937221

Printed in the United States of America.

For my Father:
if You are for me, who can stand against me?
And for my niece and nephews.

TABLE OF CONTENTS

ACKNOWLEDGMENTS	III
REVIEWS	IV-VII
MAP OF CAI TERENMARE	VIII
CHAPTER ONE: THE WASTELAND	1
CHAPTER TWO: BLACK RAVEN, WHITE RAVEN	24
CHAPTER THREE: TRIALS AND TRIBULATIONS	45
CHAPTER FOUR: YAKEZ	78
CHAPTER FIVE: STRIFE	99
CHAPTER SIX: PLAGUE	126
CHAPTER SEVEN: NUREN	149
CHAPTER EIGHT: TIERNEY	171
CHAPTER NINE: THE NORTHERN STRONGHOLD	194
CHAPTER TEN: GIANT'S HELMET	222
CHAPTER ELEVEN: THE PROPHECY	237
EPILOGUE: THE CEREMONY	263
GLOSSARY OF CHARACTERS	270
MAP OF CAI TERENMARE	274
GLOSSARY OF PLACES AND TERMS	275
ABOUT THE AUTHOR	277

ACKNOWLEDGMENTS

Many thanks to Shelley and Caitlyn Moore of Gazebo Gardens Publishing for everything you've done to bring *The Solas Beir Trilogy* to fruition. I appreciate all you've invested in my writing, and I'm grateful for your incredible help, mentoring, encouragement, and friendship. My gratitude to Aaron Cheney for another beautiful book cover. You do amazing work.

Thank you to Laura Garwood Meehan and Indigo Editing and Publishing for editing the manuscript. Laura, you are so brilliant. I can't thank you enough for your wonderful advice, friendship, and sense of humor. I'm so glad I got to work with you and the fabulous folks at Indigo!

My gratitude to my family and friends who joined me on this journey. I truly appreciate all the ways you've shown support, from your kind words to spreading the word about my work. My thanks especially to Chris, for all the sacrifices you've made, and to Aiden and Elliot for being my biggest fans and letting me read to you. Knowing that you love these stories as much as I do means the world to me. Special thanks also to my dear friends, Jessie Antonellis, Justin Cunningham, and Marian Rose for being some of the first people to read this book. Your encouragement and friendship have meant so much to me.

Thank you to the many fellow writers who have been so supportive of my work: DelSheree Gladden, Christine Finlayson, Kate Dyer-Seeley, Nancy Slavin, Brian Ratty, Paula Judith Johnson, Honey Perkel, Gloria Linkey, Mary Fryling, and Kay Kjemhus. My gratitude to Karen Emmerling of Beach Books and Lisa Reid of Lucy's Books for your amazing help in hosting me and spreading the word about my books! My appreciation to the many booksellers and bloggers who have also shared about *The Solas Beir Trilogy*. Thank you for all you do to help me and other authors.

And finally, my appreciation to all the readers. I can't thank you enough for adventuring with me in Cai Terenmare. I hope you enjoyed your time there and have returned unscathed. Thanks for reading!

REVIEWS

Melissa Eskue Ousley's first book, the Young Adult novel, *Sign of the Throne,* Book One in *The Solas Beir Trilogy,* received positive reviews from readers and fellow writers, and won a 2014 Eric Hoffer Book Award and a 2014 Readers' Favorite International Book Award.

The Rabbit and the Raven, Book Two in *The Solas Beir Trilogy,* also received praise from both readers and fellow writers, many of whom mentioned their anticipation of the third and final book in the series, *The Sower Comes.*

"Series rarely wrap up with as satisfying an ending as *The Solas Beir Trilogy* does. All the heart rending agony and joy readers experience in the first two books comes to a beautiful conclusion in *The Sower Comes*. This series has a permanent place on my bookshelf."

—DelSheree Gladden, USA Today Bestselling Author of *The Aerling Series*

"This long awaited conclusion to *The Solas Beir trilogy, The Sower Comes,* truly fulfilled my expectations. Opening to the first page, I was swept away into a world I had come to love. As I read this book, I found myself so wrapped up within the characters and their adventures, I wanted to strap on a sword to help them fight, and to embrace the light with them. I highly recommend this book. The romance is age appropriate for teens and has enough of the frustrations we have all felt as youths to help them appreciate, love has its ups and downs, but can be victorious in the end."

—Deborah, *Goodreads*

"The final installment of *The Solas Bier Trilogy* does not disappoint the reader! Setting the foundation with relatable characters and wonderfully descriptive prose in *Sign of the Throne*, seamlessly continuing the narrative in *The Rabbit and the Raven*, and concluding this wonderful fantasy/thriller series with *The Sower Comes*, elevates these books to the top of my favorites! Melissa Eskue Ousley has shown herself to be one of the premier writers of this genre, and the series' appeal extends beyond the young adult market.

The Sower Comes' stays true to the nature of the characters, and the plot continues seamlessly. The internal and external conflict between good and evil, rages within each villain and hero while they battle each other. The author is able to portray this clash of weakness and strength, resistance and compliance so artfully—the reader can establish relationships that make the characters come alive.

All three volumes held my interest from the first page to the last, and I look forward to her next book, or books. I highly recommend this series to anyone who is a fan of this genre—no matter their age."

—Signe Hill, *Reviewer*

"Melissa writes YA fantasy beautifully. Her attention to details and her characters shine through. I have read all three books in *The Solas Beir Trilogy* and watched her characters evolve. I do enjoy her villains. She writes them well. Tynan Tierney is a great villain, and Lucia, even though she is a villain, can also make you feel other emotions toward her. *The Sower Comes* is a fitting end to this wonderful YA fantasy trilogy."

—Michelle Auricht, *Novels on the Run*

"All too often, the final installment of a series turns out to be the final wheeze from the author who has somehow lost the concept somewhere along the way. A series, which started out brightly, is met with a discordant sigh of relief when the reader turns the last page and closes the book. This reviewer is happy to report that Melissa Eskue Ousley has avoided that fate, and done so quite handily. Her writing is as fresh and as riveting at the end of *The Sower Comes,* as it was in the opening pages of *Sign of the Throne.* Ms. Ousley built upon that early momentum in *The Rabbit and the Raven,* and maintains it superbly throughout this final installment.

Adolescence is a time when young minds begin to stretch themselves and wander through both strange and familiar realms of possibilities. *The Sower Comes,* and its predecessors, place the Young Adult reader in the heart of a marvelous and chilling adventure that may very well seem as real as life itself. Is the plot of this story, and the situation it presents, a metaphor for the life and choices we must all face at one time or another? It is up to readers to determine this for themselves. It cannot be denied, however, that Ms. Ousley's books are among the best in contemporary Young Adult Fiction."

—Howard Parsons, *Parsons' Rant*

"Yet again, another of Melissa Ousley's books that demands to be read in one sitting. This was truly the perfect ending to the perfect series, and a trilogy I will be reading many times over.

I cannot thank you enough, Miss Ousley. Such writing talent is rare, and you use your talent to bring suspense, humor, and beauty to the world. I love the meaning behind this story, and it fills me with Light. Beautiful, beautiful series everyone should read. I love these books!"

—Cyndi, *Goodreads*

"This book has everything fans of the series want. There is action, romance, tension, humor, and redemption. There are scenes to make you smile, scenes to make you hold your breath, and scenes where you are willing things to go the way you want. It is not slow in any way, keeping a fast pace and giving you enough back story to add to the plot, without burying you in things you don't need to hear. The story is always moving, delivering through action scenes and emotional character interactions, which are beautifully written. It is an excellent piece of writing and a fitting end to the series."

—Reviewer, *Chuckles Book Cave*

"Perfectly entwined and written urban fantasy fiction. *The Sower Comes* does justice to the other two books in the series. The unpredictability of the story and the suspense lasts until the end. It teaches us there is a bit of Darkness in all of us, and we have to deal with it and not let it dominate and control our decisions. And there is Light in all of us too. Which path we choose depends entirely upon us.

A message in this trilogy is, there is a bit of magic in all of us. We just have to believe in ourselves and discover that hidden power. The author has woven in the emotions and feelings of the characters very commendably. It's a beautifully written book about love, affection, loyalty, sacrifice, responsibility, and having faith and believing in oneself. I'll miss the characters and the kingdom of Cai Terenmare."

—Simmaron, *BFF Books are Friends Forever*

"Full of twists and turns, humor, love, suspense, and hope, I could hardly stand to put this book down! It was well worth the wait. Melissa Eskue Ousley is an author worth keeping your eye on."

—Susan Crabtree, *Reviewer*

CAI TERENMARE
N
E
W
S
HOUSE OF THE NORTHERN ORACLE
THE GAUNTLET
ICE MOUNTAIN TERRITORIES
HIGHLANDS
NORTHERN STRONGHOLD
NORTH FOREST
GIANT'S HELMET
WESTERN SEA
EYE OF THE NEEDLE
YAKEZ
CAISLUCIS
NUREN
THE BARREN
CITY OF THE EASTERN ORACLE
LONE TREE ISLAND
SOUTH FOREST
GREAT PLAINS
THE EMERALD GUARDIAN
THE CLIFFS
RAINFOREST
ISLAND OF THE WESTERN ORACLE
SOUTHPORT
VILLAGE OF THE SOUTHERN ORACLE
THE BLOOD ALTAR
RED RIVER
EASTERN SEA

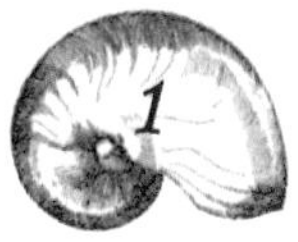

THE WASTELAND

The girl sat beneath the cobalt sky, cupping the scarlet sand in her hands. She mumbled the numbers to herself, counting, counting, counting. She remembered nothing but her name. Sometimes she was called Abigail, and sometimes she was called Abby.

Casting his net into the bay, the fisherman surveyed the inky expanse of water. He'd been working all day and most of the night and still had nothing to show for his efforts. All of the other boats in Yakez were already docked—his small wooden craft was the only vessel absent from the marina. He wondered how the other men had fared, if they'd had better luck than he had. Perhaps when he pulled his net up this time, he'd finally have a catch and be able to row back and get some rest.

But for now, sleep would have to wait. With the cupboards in his tiny cottage nearly empty, his children were depending on him to provide. What, if anything, had they eaten for dinner? Another bad day like this one, and they'd be relying on the generosity of their neighbors. The fisherman felt a glimmer of hope as he noticed something tug at the net. He held his breath, waiting, hoping the thick threads hadn't simply gotten caught on the rocks and weeds at the bottom of the harbor.

There it was again—a tug—stronger this time, as whatever he had caught struggled to break free.

Excited, he checked that the anchor was set and then began the arduous process of pulling the net into his boat. The weight of his catch added to the difficulty, but he didn't mind. A heavy net meant his family wouldn't go hungry.

The net was halfway in the boat when the fisherman felt the strongest tug yet. He lost his hold on the net and had to scramble to grab it before the whole mess slipped out and into the water. He grinned—he'd caught a fighter. He wondered how big it was. He laughed, imagining the looks on his children's faces when they saw it, the looks on the faces of his fellow fishermen. By the way it pulled and fought, making the boat tip dangerously toward the surface of the water, this would be the biggest fish he'd ever caught.

Then, without warning, the net went slack.

"No," the fisherman moaned. No—he hadn't lost it, had he? Frantically, he pulled in the net, distraught by how easy it was without the weight of his catch. "No, no, no!"

Focused on the net and the loss of the fish, the man barely registered the vibration as something bumped the underside of his boat. When it happened again, he froze. Hands full of netting, he peered over the side of his craft, into the dark water. It was a cloudy, starless night, and he could barely see the edge of his boat, much less what swam underneath the placid surface of the Bay of Yakez.

Securing the net around a metal cleat, he lit his lantern. When he fished at night, he preferred the darkness, believing the harsh light scared away the fish. Now that he'd lost his catch, however, that didn't matter.

Directing the lantern's beam out over the harbor, he glimpsed a black shape slicing through the water toward his vessel. He gasped—was that what had been in his net? No wonder he had struggled pulling it aboard.

He was only seeing the back of the fish, and that was huge. He tried to calculate how long it must be. He frowned. There was probably a gaping hole in his net, which meant time lost on repairs. His hopes for feeding his family had been dashed, and now this. He studied the way the fish circled his boat—it was clearly a predator, and likely the reason fishing had been so poor of late. He'd never seen anything like it, but he'd have to report it to the others. Yakez would suffer competing against a predatory fish.

The fisherman didn't feel frightened until the beast began to rise from the water. That was when he understood how big it truly was, and that it wasn't a fish.

Hands shaking, he almost dropped the lantern into the water. Gingerly, he set it down beside him. Keeping a fearful eye on the creature, he grabbed the oars, intending to row back to shore. He never got the chance. He didn't even have time to scream.

David Corbin was trapped. Lost somewhere between waking and sleep, he remembered everything, especially the last thing, the part when he had heard *her* voice telling him to heal Lucia, even though that was the last thing he wanted to do. After all the lies, all the betrayals, he had wanted to see Lucia die.

But the healing wasn't for Lucia. It was for her, the one he'd lost. Now Lucia had no more pain. He had taken it all. A part of him savored the agony that twisted his broken body—he was drowning in pain, but it helped him forget Abby's eyes. The problem was that he would heal eventually. He always did. Before long, the pain would fade. Then he wouldn't be able to forget. And then he would have to face Lucia. Already, she had been calling for him.

Lucia had been staring at the floor of her cell for hours, waiting. The other cells in the dungeon were empty—she had woken up alone, in the dark silence of the underground.

She suspected the other prisoners had been removed out of fear that she would bend their will to serve her own. Even the guards had kept their distance, afraid she might somehow infect their minds, reducing them to serve as her minions.

The thought that she was so feared was amusing, considering her mind was still clouded from a deathlike sleep. But there were benefits to having a bad reputation; she preferred the solitude. There was only one person she wanted to speak to.

Lucia looked up, out into the dungeon's dark, narrow corridor. Someone stood there, speaking her name, but it wasn't him. No, he was too broken to come to her just yet, but he *would* come, and soon. She reached out to him again with her mind.

She had awakened with no pain at all, which was strange, because the last thing she remembered was falling to her death. She should have died. She remembered seeing rage in Tierney's dark eyes and then coming to the realization that he had finally decided to end her. She remembered the tender, incongruent tone that remained in his voice, even as he grabbed her with strong, unforgiving hands and dropped her over the side of the balcony.

The King of Blood and Shadows had held her gaze the entire time she was falling, as if he truly *was* sorry it had come to this—as if he were sad, so sad, that he'd had to do it. As if it were her fault. He'd said as much, hadn't he? That she had betrayed him, that she'd broken his heart. What he didn't say was that he had no choice but to end her—that in her betrayal, she had taken away his other options. But Lucia understood his meaning. She knew him well enough to know that was how he thought of it. Just as part of her had always known it would end this way.

She simply hadn't wanted to face the fact that he would eventually kill her. It was so much nicer to cling to the hope that perhaps he did still love her enough to overlook her *indiscretions*, as he called them—that he might understand why she hadn't killed the boy. Lucia had hoped he loved her enough to keep her by his side when he took the throne, as he had promised so long ago. But when you are falling down the side of a cliff, truth overrules denial, at least until you hit the water and everything goes black.

Now Lucia had no memory of how she'd gotten here, to this place she had once called home. She looked up into the face of the young woman who drew closer, speaking to her. It was a face she almost recognized.

The girl was explaining that Lucia had been pulled from the water by the Western Oracle. Lucia knew that couldn't be true; the Western Oracle was dead, had been dead for years.

The *new* Western Oracle, the girl clarified in response to Lucia's murmur of disbelief, the daughter of the Sea King. The mermaid called Nerine had retrieved Lucia from the bottom of the Eastern Sea and carried her home using the system of underground rivers. They had woven through the honeycombed caverns spanning the vast continent of Cai Terenmare, bringing her here, to Caislucis, the castle on the western shore.

But there was something else, something Lucia had said as the Western Oracle transferred her to the custody of the Solas Beir. It was important, the girl was saying, vitally important, that Lucia remember what she had said.

"I remember nothing," Lucia mumbled. "I said nothing."

Her mouth felt dry, her tongue numb. It was difficult to form words. Her vision was hazy, and the sound of the girl's voice echoed as though Lucia's small cell had stretched into a long tunnel. She held her head propped up in her hands, trying to focus on the girl standing outside her iron cage.

"But you *did* say something," the girl insisted. "You said the Sower was coming. Right after the Solas Beir healed you and took your wounds. You opened your eyes and said it."

Lucia shook her head, waving the girl away as though she were a nuisance. "I do not remember that—I only remember pain."

"Fine," the girl said, throwing up her hands up in frustration. She looked disgusted. "*Fine.* You can stay here until you remember. Or until you rot. After everything you did, that's more than you deserve." Turning on her heels, the girl stormed toward the exit.

As the fog clouding Lucia's mind lifted, she rose and walked to the edge of her cell. She placed her hands on the bars and craned her neck to see the girl starting up the stairs, gesturing for the guards to resume their posts at the door.

"Wait," Lucia whispered. She coughed and tried again, speaking louder. "Wait, Marisol Cassidy."

The girl hesitated. Lucia wasn't sure if she would turn around or not—maybe the girl didn't know herself.

"Do you remember?" Marisol asked, as she approached the prisoner hesitantly.

Lucia's dark eyes glittered, and Marisol found herself shocked by the lucidity in them. Minutes before, Lucia's eyes had looked dull, like she was half-asleep or drugged. The change was startling and a little terrifying. Marisol took a step backward, thankful there were bars between her and this woman.

"No," Lucia said. "I do not remember speaking, and I do not

remember how I got here. But I do remember *you*."

"Oh?"

Lucia nodded firmly, all signs of frailty gone.

Marisol wondered if the weakened version of Lucia had been an act, and her fear of the woman was replaced by anger. She and her friends had lost so much during their battle at the Eye of the Needle, a rock spire on the eastern edge of the desert known as the Barren. Lucia's alliance with Tynan Tierney had cost them dearly.

They'd fought against the Kruorumbrae, monsters who served the Darkness. One of the Blood Shadows had nearly killed Cael, the closest thing Marisol had to a father in this world.

David had managed to save their mentor, but not Abby. She was taken by the Daughters of Mercy, winged mercenaries who looked like angels and fought like demons. They had herded Abby into their cave at the top of the spire, and she hadn't been seen since. Marisol suspected they'd killed her.

With her hand clenching the hilt of her sword, ready to draw it from its sheath, Marisol raised an eyebrow. "And what do you remember about me?"

"You were there, at the Eye of the Needle. The boy—he surrendered himself to save you," Lucia answered.

"Yes. His name is Jonathon Reyes." Her stomach roiled with a mixture of hope, fear, and disgust in having to speak to the woman who had taken Jon away from her.

During the battle, Malden had grabbed Marisol. He was a beast straight from her nightmares, a bogeyman who lived to torture her and then feed on her fear. She still remembered the feeling of his sharp claws pressed against her throat.

When Jon saw her in the creature's grasp, he had offered himself as hostage to Lucia. Marisol could only watch, helpless, as the boy she loved was shackled and taken away by the Kruorumbrae. But Jon had to be okay. She couldn't bear the thought that he wasn't. "Is Jon still alive? Please, I have to know."

"He *was*," Lucia replied, "before Tierney tried to kill me. Now...I do not know."

Marisol felt her blood run cold. Thinking about what might have happened to Jon filled her with dread. That Lucia couldn't give her a definitive answer terrified her. The only way to help Jon now was to ask questions Lucia could answer.

Marisol took a breath to steady herself, and then asked, "Why did Malden want to take me?"

Lucia smiled—it was a cruel smile. "You are marked. You are his."

Marisol's mouth dropped open in shock. She thought about it, the little things Malden had said to her about being his to torment. She shuddered, recalling images from childhood nightmares.

She had convinced herself the monster living under her bed was a figment of her imagination. She had been wrong about that—her personal bogeyman was real. Still, just because Malden thought she was his didn't make it true. She felt her fear of him fade, replaced by revulsion. "What do you mean, I'm marked? I'm not marked. And I am *not* his."

"Your grandmother. She was a *bruja*, was she not?" Lucia asked.

Marisol crossed her arms. "A witch? Maybe. How do you know about that?"

Lucia ignored the question. "Your grandmother had great power, but it came with a price. Who do you think gave her that power, and why do you think your mother ran away from home when she was still a girl?"

"My mother never ran away from home. She traveled the world—for her job," Marisol insisted.

"Oh yes, she traveled," Lucia said quietly, almost to herself. She returned her gaze to study Marisol's face. "Your mother used to tell you stories—she tried, in her own way, to warn you.

I knew your mother. She was haunted by the same mark you have."

"What are you talking about?" Marisol demanded.

"I'm talking about children bearing the sins of their fathers—or mothers, in your case," Lucia explained. "Malden has gone by many names. *La Malogra* is one of them. It means the monster that ruins, a creature that haunts crossroads, waiting for prey. He tricked your grandmother. She did not know the price of her deal with him would be her daughter—or her daughter's daughter. Your mother moved frequently, did she not?"

Marisol nodded.

"He followed her. She thought she would be protected in Newcastle Beach—that you would be protected. But he found her. She did not even know of the portal's existence, but it called her. The same force that drew her there also drew him. That is why she left you. She thought if she was far enough away from you, he would seek her and you would be safe. But that's not true, is it? Malden wanted both of you, and your mother's efforts to protect you were fruitless. "

"Yes," Marisol said bitterly. "He found me. And Jon took my place. What is he planning on doing with Jon?"

Lucia smiled again—that cruel, haughty smile. If there was any good in this woman, Marisol couldn't see it.

"I doubt it is Malden your friend needs to worry about. I have a feeling there are bigger plans in play than his."

"Tierney."

Lucia nodded. "For now, your friend may be safe from the likes of Malden, assuming Tierney sees some value in keeping him alive. He knows the boy is close to the Solas Beir, so perhaps that knowledge will work in his favor."

"Tell me how to rescue Jon," Marisol pleaded. "If we act quickly—"

Lucia laughed. "Go to the City of the Eastern Oracle, and

you might as well kill your friend yourself. Malden will get his hands on you, and the sacrifice Jonathon Reyes made will be for naught. I told you—you are marked. That city is no place for a marked child."

"What is this mark you keep talking about? I don't have any mark on my body." Marisol's patience was wearing thin, and she hadn't had much tolerance for this woman to begin with. Lucia was just like the monster Malden—nothing but riddles and games and a sick sense of humor.

Lucia narrowed her eyes. "It is not a physical mark, silly child. Do you really think it would be? Some kind of special birthmark designating you as the chosen one? Please. The creature has your scent—he can smell the essence of your very soul, and it doesn't matter how far you run. He will find you. You are his and there is no escaping that fate. He will destroy you as he destroyed your mother."

Marisol stared at Lucia, as shocked as she would be if the woman had reached through those bars and slapped her face. "But my mother is still alive."

"For now." Lucia stepped away from the bars and sat on the wooden bench lining the back wall of her cell. The shadows fell across her face, but Marisol could still see Lucia's eyes, eyes that were much too black to be human, burning into hers. "Malden has always been rather sentimental about his girls—he was never one to snuff out a life quickly, not if the life belonged to one of his marked ones. He likes to savor the process, to let his beloveds fade like a flower after its glorious bloom—"

"Stop it," Marisol said, her anger now just a flimsy cover for her horror. Her hands were shaking. She gripped the iron bars of Lucia's cell to steady herself. "Stop talking like that."

Lucia shrugged. "You asked the question."

"How do I save my mother?" Marisol asked. "How do I get rid of the mark on me?"

"Kill the wretch."

Marisol eyed Lucia suspiciously. "Why would you want me to kill Malden? I thought the two of you fought for the same side."

"Not at all," Lucia smiled. Her black eyes glinted in the darkness like hard, shiny stones. "I want you to kill him because I want him dead even more than you do."

"If that's true—if it's true that you are no longer fighting for Tierney, then tell me about the Sower," Marisol said. "Don't say you don't remember. I know you know something."

"When do I get to speak with the Solas Beir?" Lucia asked.

Marisol frowned at the change of subject. "As soon as he heals. Assuming he will actually *want* to talk to you. I wouldn't blame him if he didn't. Not after what happened to Abby."

"That girl?" Lucia spat.

"Yes, *that* girl," Marisol replied. "You know, the one David was in love with. The one who is dead because of you and your kind."

Lucia's eyes blazed angrily, and her jaw clenched.

Marisol took a step backward when she saw Lucia draw herself up and hold out her palm, generating her signature electric-blue orb. She kept her eyes on Lucia's and got ready to leap out of the way should Lucia shoot the fireball in her direction. There was nothing Marisol could use as cover in the dungeon's narrow corridor, but if she could dodge the orb and make it to the stairs, she might escape Lucia's wrath unscathed. Then, to Marisol's surprise, the orb flickered and sparked on Lucia's palm before fizzling out.

Lucia studied her palm, seemingly as surprised as Marisol, and then lowered her hand to her side, composing herself, the strained look on her face becoming oddly tranquil.

"Well, then, I will save my thoughts regarding the Sower until the Solas Beir comes to speak with me personally. Be a dear and let him know." With that, Lucia sat back down on her bench, her eyes obscured in the darkness of the cell.

Marisol studied Lucia's silhouette for a moment and then turned to ascend the dungeon steps. There was nothing more to say. Until the Solas Beir made an appearance, it was obvious that Lucia was done talking.

In the middle of the counting, the girl who had come to call herself AbigailsometimesAbby became aware of a rhythmic pecking sound. A sharp pain had crept into one of her hands, the one cupping the scarlet sand. Her disconnected mind slowly associated the pain with the pecking, and she absently brushed away the thing doing the pecking. Then she returned to her own rhythmic plucking of sand from her open palm, naming each grain with a number and letting it drop back onto the ground beside her crisscrossed legs. She was counting. She couldn't be bothered with anything else.

AbigailsometimesAbby began again, scooping up a fresh handful of sand, methodically mumbling the numbers to herself. The pecking began again too. It went on for some time before she noticed that the sand in her cupped hand had grown darker, a deeper red than before. She let the sand fall through her fingers to the ground and held her hands out in front of her face, studying them up close as if they were foreign objects.

Her hands, both of them, were bleeding. Rivulets of blood ran down her palms to her wrists. There were stray grains of sand caught in the blood. With dismay, she realized she had dirty hands. This would not do. She wiped her hands on her dusty dress, leaving long red stripes on the grimy white fabric.

She bowed her head to scoop up more sand, but then saw that drops of blood had fallen to the ground, creating a series of miniscule red craters, wet sand with the consistency of paste. She could not count this sand. It was dirty, impure. She shifted her body, scooting over to find a clean patch of sand so she could scoop up a fresh handful, and begin once more.

She felt another sharp peck, this time on her cheek. Annoyed, she swiped at her injury with the back of her hand. To her astonishment, she found that a fresh batch of red had bloomed on her hand, somehow connected to the pain in her cheek.

She wiped her hand clean on her dress and raised her head. A large, jet black raven stood in front of her, his wide eyes looking directly into hers. She cocked her head to the side, trying to make sense of the vision before her. Beyond the bird, scarlet dunes stretched to the horizon. Didn't this intruder understand that there was counting to be done? She couldn't just stop—there was much to do, so much more sand to count. She would never finish if she was continually interrupted like this. And she had to finish.

The raven blinked his gold-rimmed eyes and cocked his head as well, mirroring her. AbigailsometimesAbby stopped counting and let the sand fall through her red fingers. She knew this bird.

Marisol knocked on David's door, and Obelia answered.

"Come in," she whispered, silently ushering Marisol into a room that was as hushed as a hospital ward. Or a crypt.

Marisol looked around the bedchamber. David lay still in his bed, his skin ashy, his eyes closed tight. His mother, the dowager queen, was fast asleep in the chair next to David's bed, her hand covering his.

Eulalia had stayed with David all night again, praying her son would awaken from his deep sleep of pain. Marisol could see that the queen's long, sleepless nights had finally caught up with her.

Erela, the last Daughter of Mercy, stood at the foot of

David's bed, keeping vigil over her Solas Beir. Her features looked harsh, as though carved from stone; her white wings were extended slightly, as if shielding him. The warrior woman was bathed in a shaft of morning light that shone through the beveled diamonds of the leaded glass window behind her. The soft feathers on her wings almost seemed to glow, a contrast to her statuelike stance.

Branded as a traitor, Erela had been banished by her sisters, which was how she came to be in the service of the king. It was a good thing she had fought for David, or the losses at the Eye of the Needle might have been far worse. Marisol doubted they would have made it back to Caislucis without her.

"Has he awakened?" Marisol asked softly.

"Not yet," Obelia whispered. The head of the Solas Beir's court council looked as tired as the queen. Her worry was etched on her face. "What news of Lucia?"

"She is awake," Marisol whispered back, "and uncooperative. She refuses to speak about the Sower until the Solas Beir meets with her himself."

"I cannot imagine he would wish to," Obelia murmured. "Perhaps the queen should give it a try. Lucia may be more responsive to her sister. I will ask Cael to escort Eulalia to see her when he returns from meeting with the castle guards."

"I'm not sure that will help," Marisol countered. "Lucia was adamant about speaking with David."

"Her cruelty has no bounds, it seems," Obelia mused, gazing at David with sad eyes. "She will hurt him more than she already has."

"Probably," Marisol agreed grimly. "But on the other hand, he may be the only person she has ever truly loved."

"I will speak with her."

Marisol looked up to see that David's eyes were open, and he was pushing himself up into sitting position.

In a few quick steps, Marisol left her place near the door

and was at David's side. She took his hand. "You're awake. Finally."

"Yes," he smiled weakly. "Finally."

"Are you in pain?" Obelia asked David.

"No. My body has healed itself," David said. "I am relatively whole again."

"Relatively?" Erela asked. "What remains broken?"

David met her eyes. *Dear Erela,* he thought. *Always the literalist.* "Nothing much," he replied. "Just my heart."

Erela cast her eyes downward, and David wished he could take back what he'd said. It wasn't just that sarcasm was lost on her. He had forgotten that Erela was no longer the stoic warrior he had first thought her to be. With the loss of her sisters, she had softened, and was now so gentle with him, so protective, as if she could feel his pain acutely. Maybe she could. Loss had a way of generating empathy.

"I'm sorry, Erela. That was just a little joke. Sometimes I use humor to deal with emotional pain, but I should not have done so at your expense."

"I understand," Erela nodded.

David wasn't sure if she *did* understand. Did Daughters of Mercy possess a sense of humor at all? He wouldn't think so. But then again, Erela had always been a bit different from her sisters, and she had changed since becoming the last of her kind. Maybe she did understand humor now.

"Well I should warn you then," he said, giving her a smile. "There's a rather large hole where my heart used to be. I'm going to be pretty funny from now on."

"Perhaps, in time, even that wound will heal," Erela said. She didn't smile back, but her effort to connect with him was a vast improvement over the emotionally flat responses she used to give. He just had to remember that she wasn't human and it wasn't fair to expect a human response.

"Perhaps," David said. "Although I have a feeling it will be hard to forget about Abby so long as I have Lucia around to remind me. Probably best to go deal with her and sort out this Sower business."

"Solas Beir," Obelia said, "I do not wish to burden you when you have only just awakened, but regarding Lucia—"

"It's fine, Obelia," David insisted, waving off her concern. "If the Sower is a threat to our safety, we need to get the information from Lucia as soon as we can. I'm fine—I can handle her."

"I have every faith in you," Obelia asserted. "But...there remains the matter of what to do with Lucia once we have the information we need."

David shrugged. "She can remain in the dungeon for all I care."

Obelia nodded. "Yes, Your Majesty, that is a possibility. For crimes against the kingdom, however, it is traditional to hold a public trial. Your people will expect that she be held accountable for what she has done, starting with the assassination of your father."

David frowned. "A trial? That hardly seems necessary. We already know she's guilty."

"It is not the same as the world in which you were raised," Eulalia said.

David turned to her, surprised. She had been asleep when he woke but was now sitting upright in her chair, staring at him, a look of relief on her face. How long had she stayed by his side? How long had he been asleep? He remembered hearing her voice in hushed conversation, but in the midst of his pain, he wasn't sure how much of that had been real.

His mother reached for him hesitantly, as though she wanted to hold him but was afraid to hurt him. He gave her a reassuring smile and opened his arms. Eulalia held him tightly for a long moment, and when she released him, her eyes were damp.

She wiped her eyes and then took his hand in both of hers. "It is not a trial to determine guilt," she said, resuming her explanation. "It is a public statement of her crimes by witnesses and the court council. You will be expected to deliver a statement in response, regarding her sentence. And if you decide she should be sentenced to death..." Eulalia seemed hesitant to complete her thought, but, staring into her eyes, David realized what she hadn't said and why she looked distraught.

"Oh," he said soberly. "I'll be her executioner."

"So says the law," Obelia said.

"It is a law with which Lucia is familiar," Eulalia added quietly. "She did serve on the court council once."

The raven hopped away, and then stopped a few feet from where AbigailsometimesAbby sat watching him. He turned back and looked at her, cocking his head as if beckoning her to follow. Then the raven began hopping again.

Halfway across the dune, he stopped once more to see if she had taken the hint. She rose to her feet, blinking as if she were taking in her surroundings for the first time. Above her, a cobalt blue sky arched over the world. Where it met the horizon, it bled, becoming the scarlet sand that stretched in every direction as far as she could see. There was nothing else, only the sand.

She looked down at the sand at her feet. It was calling to her urgently, reminding her that she had a responsibility. She almost sat down again, compelled to count, but the pull of the raven was stronger than that of the sand.

AbigailsometimesAbby began walking, following the raven. He continued on his way, stopping his insistent hopping now and again to look back and make sure she was coming. She was.

Jonathon Reyes shivered in his dark cell. It was a wonder he felt so cold, considering how hot and dusty the city above him was. His prison lay somewhere beneath the City of the Eastern Oracle, the bustling trade center straddling the cliffs along the Eastern Sea and the edge of the Barren, the vast desert that had swallowed up so much of this world.

There was a heaviness in the dungeon, as if the air itself had weight. Perhaps this was a remnant of events past, the collective despair of all whom had dwelt in this netherworld before Jon's imprisonment. He hoped that was the case, because he had seen other things that could make air grow heavy—hellish creatures that fed on despair. The thought of one of those things sharing a cell with him chilled him to the bone.

Even so, he would have welcomed such a cellmate if doing so had guaranteed Marisol's safety. Where was she now? There was no telling how much time had passed since he'd volunteered himself as hostage at the Eye of the Needle and freed Sol from the clutches of that monster. Day and night were the same in this dark place.

His unwashed hair hung in his eyes, slightly longer than it had been when he was tossed into the cell. How fast did hair grow? He didn't know, but surely, by now, Sol should have made it back to David's castle on the other side of the Barren. Of course, by now, Jon should have been dead. Malden had been very clear about his intentions toward Lucia's hostage. She must have convinced Tierney that Jon was worth something. Otherwise, he *would* be dead.

He'd seen neither Malden nor Lucia since the Kruorumbrae guard had brought him to this cell. At present, there were no other prisoners. He had overheard the guards talking about a girl who had been imprisoned for a short time, possibly the one Abby had tried to rescue from becoming a courtesan. But Jon hadn't seen a little girl. The Blood Shadows had caught her, so she was probably either dead or sold to the highest bidder. He wasn't sure which was worse.

The unending night of Jon's new world was pierced by a shaft of light. A pair of Kruorumbrae guards marched down the steps of the dungeon, dragging someone between them. A third guard followed, holding a set of skeleton keys. This guard gruffly ordered Jon to the back of his cell. Jon made no reply, but took several steps backward. He had learned quickly that Shadow guards expected immediate compliance. He did not want to get on their bad side again by moving too slowly.

He had also learned the hard way that they had no patience for a retort, no matter how witty or well timed. The guards seemed to be suffering from a serious lack of humor, but it seemed prudent not to bring that to their attention.

The guard with the keys opened the cell door, and the other two threw the new prisoner to the floor of the cell. Then the guard locked the door and proceeded back up the steps without another word, his fellow Kruorumbrae following him.

Jon rushed to the front of the cell to catch a glimpse of the man's face before what little light that remained was extinguished by the closing of the dungeon door.

The man's eyes were closed, but he appeared to be conscious. His face was a swollen mass of bruises and lacerations. Jon imagined that the rest of the man's body bore similar wounds. The man looked familiar, though given the severity of the beating, Jon couldn't be sure.

The prisoner's long, sandy hair was matted with blood and dirt, and his beard was beyond scruffy—clearly personal hygiene had been the least of this man's recent concerns. The door closed, and the light winked out before Jon could see more, but he thought he knew the name of his new cell mate.

"Hedeon—is that you?"

The knight groaned, and in the darkness Jon heard the man push himself up to sit on the floor of the cell. "A rather bloody version of me," he spat. "And you are?"

Jon sat down on the other side of the cell. "It's me, Jonathon Reyes. I met you when I was in the city with the Solas Beir."

"Jonathon Reyes...fancy meeting you here. Why are you not with the Solas Beir? Did he make it back to Caislucis?" Hedeon asked, his voice hoarse.

"I don't know," Jon said. "I was taken prisoner at the Eye of the Needle. As far as I know, the Solas Beir headed west across the Barren. You haven't heard anything about my friends in the Eastern Oracle's court?"

Hedeon laughed, and then fell into a fit of coughing. It was a while before he could speak again. "No—I have not been to court of late. After I left the Solas Beir at the city gates, I was summoned. I thought I was being called to search for an escaped prisoner, but apparently my presence was required in the torture chambers. I am afraid my loyalty to the Solas Beir has come to light."

"How?"

"A little maggot by the name of Malden," Hedeon explained. "Before we left the Eastern Oracle's court, he snuck into the Solas Beir's carriage and wedged himself under the seat. He heard every word."

"Oh, I *hate* that guy," Jon said, muttering a curse under his breath.

"I take it you have made his acquaintance?"

"Several times, unfortunately," Jon said, nodding in the dark. He stopped when he realized Hedeon couldn't see him.

"He's the reason I'm stuck in here. Will they execute you for your loyalty to David?"

"Oh, quite likely." Hedeon laughed again, his voice cracking. He cleared his throat. "Until then, you and I have the pleasure of sharing these dismal quarters."

"Well, you seem to be in awfully good spirits about it."

"Gallows humor, my friend," Hedeon said bitterly.

"I don't think humor is appreciated here," Jon said.

"So I noticed. But I am afraid that is all I have left in the way of dignity. The rest was taken by the comrades who tortured me. Not that I had all that much to begin with." Hedeon sighed.

"What do you mean?"

"Any honor I had was surrendered the moment I turned against your king. Not that I was truly against him, you understand, but the things I did…misdeeds for the sake of the greater good…I believe I was rather mistaken in thinking I could make a difference." Hedeon's voice sounded strained.

In the blackness of the cell, Jon could only imagine what his face would express. Guilt? Regret? "You did make a difference. You helped us leave the city," Jon insisted.

"And a fat lot of good it did *you*," Hedeon scoffed. "How did you get here again?"

"We made it to the Eye, but Lucia and her cronies attacked us while the Daughters of Mercy ambushed David and Abby in the air. We held our own for a while, but Cael was injured and Malden took Marisol captive. I offered myself in her place, so Lucia brought me here. But she left for the city before I found out if we beat the rest of the Daughters. I don't know if Cael made it or not—his wound was pretty bad."

"I am certain that if there was any way your Solas Beir could heal Cael, he did," Hedeon replied.

"I hope so," Jon said. "I hope they made it home okay. Not knowing is killing me. Of course, there could be other things killing me soon enough."

"If they wanted you dead, you would be," Hedeon asserted. "The fact that you are still here means you are still valuable."

"Yeah, but for how long?"

"Long enough for us to escape, I hope," Hedeon said.

"How?"

"*That* I am still working on. But have no worry, my friend."

Jon could picture Hedeon grinning in the dark; with his face so mangled, it probably hurt to smile.

"I would like to think the knowledge I gained as the right hand of the Eastern Oracle may help," Hedeon said. "I would also like to think my getting tossed in here with you is a sign from the Light that we may yet leave this place intact."

AbigailsometimesAbby shuffled after the hopping raven. Ahead, gleaming like a gem on the scarlet sand, was something that sparkled sapphire. As her stumbling steps brought her closer, she could see the jewel's form wavering in the heat, becoming a shallow pool. Water.

For the first time she became aware of her thirst, and once she was aware, her thirst grew, blistering her throat. The desire to drink grew stronger than the force that had pulled her to her feet to follow the raven, more compelling than the counting that had held her in the grip of a trance for so long. How long, she did not know. Perhaps she had counted for a day, perhaps for a thousand years. There was no time here. The sun, forever frozen in place, remained at its peak in the cobalt sky.

She knelt at the edge of the pool. The water was strange—a dark blue, almost as dark as the sky, but murky, so she could not see the bottom of the reservoir. Gold particles drifted through the depths as though silt at the bottom had been stirred, but she could see no fish, no signs of life.

She cupped her hands, intending to draw up a drink to quench her miserable thirst, when she felt a hand on her shoulder. In the reflection of the water, she could see that the hand belonged to a man.

"Stop," he said. "Do not touch the water."

Startled, she whipped her head around to identify her visitor. There was no one behind her. She rose to her feet, scanning the endless sand bordering the water. She was alone, except for the raven standing by her side. The bird stared up at her and then glanced down at the pool. She followed the raven's gaze and realized he was casting no reflection, though she and the man were mirrored on the water's glassy surface.

"Where are you?" AbigailsometimesAbby called. "Why can I only see you in the water?"

"Because," the man explained, "the water is only an illusion. It is the ghost of something that once existed. As am I."

"You look awfully real to be a ghost," she replied simply.

The man smiled. He was tall, with dark, unruly hair. He reminded her of someone, someone who only seemed to exist on the edge of her memory. Someone who used to be important to her. But there was something different about this man—his eyes were darker—a deep brown. She wished she could remember the other one, the one with the blue eyes.

"Sit, child," the man said. "Hear my tale, and return home with haste. Hear me well and learn, for your Solas Beir is about to commit a grievous wrong."

BLACK RAVEN, WHITE RAVEN

"My name is Ardal, and I was once heir to the throne," the man said. "That was in the time before the closing of the portals, the time when my father ruled as Solas Beir. I wished to be a wise king, a Solas Beir worthy of my people's trust. I searched the ancient texts for wisdom, but there came a day when Gorman, my tutor, told me I had exhausted the resources at hand. To gain the wisdom I sought, I needed to leave the sanctuary of my father's house and travel. With my father's blessing, I crossed from my world, the old world, into a new one, a place you once called home.

"It was there I first saw the monsters, the shape-shifters called the Kruorumbrae. I was aware, in theory, of their existence—there was much written of them in my beloved books. But I could not truly fathom their evil. I understood why my teacher bade me leave home. I had great knowledge, but I was woefully unprepared to be king.

"Your world was so much bigger than my own, with its vast oceans and many lands. I daresay my first impression was that it was a realm with limitless resources. Unfortunately, that was also the perspective of the Kruorumbrae. They saw the human race as a never-ending source for their insatiable bloodlust. I tracked them, and I saw brutality beyond measure as they slaughtered humans as though they were nothing more than livestock to be harvested. And then I met Eve."

"Eve?" AbigailsometimesAbby asked. The name sounded oddly familiar. Images from an old story came to her mind: a woman, a serpent, and forbidden fruit. "You can't mean...?"

"No my dear, not *that* Eve," the man chuckled. "'Twas not so long ago as that, but still, it was long before the year of your birth. My Eve taught me more about being a just king than any of my books.

"I found her after one of the Blood Shadow raids. She was a young girl, a terrified young girl. Her family had been killed and eaten before her eyes. Then they burned her home, a small cottage in a meadow. The tall grasses caught fire, and everything within the circle of that meadow was licked up by the flames. She saw what was left of her parents' bodies consumed by the fire. The Kruorumbrae responsible for the murders of her mother and father had marked her as his own and planned to take her back to my world to be a blood slave. I stopped him, and he fled.

"I crossed back over with her, thinking I could protect her, that she would find refuge in my father's house. I was wrong. My father was angry, so angry, that I had soiled his threshold by bringing a human into the castle—particularly one marked by Darkness. Worse, the anger directed at her was my fault. I had fallen in love with her, and he knew it.

"He commanded me to take her back and forbade me from ever seeing her again. I told him she had been marked, and that if he sent her back, the Blood Shadow would find her again. He so loathed the idea of a human as queen, he would not listen.

"I had no choice but to give up my right to the throne. How could I ever be Solas Beir with her blood on my hands? I left with my Eve, and we made our way in her world, finding peace in a land far from where tragedy had befallen her family. I lived as a human since I did not yet have the powers of a Solas Beir.

"I still carried with me a little of the magic of Cai Terenmare, a kind of luck that aided me in my dealings with the traders who passed through our forest. I was still able to take the shape of the white bear, as well as being skilled in the way of the sword. I was more than able to protect my Eve, should the Blood Shadow return to claim her.

"We were happy. She began to forget the horror of the night that changed her life, and I began to forget my old world. I had no wish to return. How freeing it was to shake off the shackles of my father's unbending rules, to escape his demands for unquestioning compliance! But alas, it seems my rebellion was not without consequences.

"Early one morning, when I went to hunt for game, the Kruorumbrae returned. He had her scent, you see. I was wrong to think we could hide from him. He was single-minded in his desire to retrieve his prize. I returned to find him feeding on her. He was not trying to kill her, only to ensure that she could never be with me.

"For that I took his head—but it was too late. He had damaged her beyond repair. His poison was in her veins, and because I was not a Solas Beir, I could not heal her. I went back to my world, vowing I would return home if only my father would heal her.

"He refused. He said I needed to see for myself what my act of defiance had wrought. When I returned to Eve, she begged me to end her life. She could not bear the thought of the Kruorumbrae's poison changing her, transforming her into the kind of monster that had killed her family. I told her I would look after her, that I would keep her from becoming such a creature. I stayed with her for many months, watching as she slowly lost her mind.

"Finally, who she had been was gone, overtaken by some feral creature that knew only the desire to feed, a kind of human and Kruorumbrae hybrid that knew no reason. It was then that I gave her what she wanted and ended her life. I promised myself then that I would return and become Solas Beir, but I would never be without compassion as my father was."

David slowly made his way down the steps to the dungeon. His legs felt like they were made of stone, stiff and heavy. Perhaps he had not yet healed completely. *No, that's not it,* he thought. He felt fine, physically. Strong even. It was the thought of facing Lucia that filled him with dread, that made him want to turn around and run back up the stairs. It wasn't that he feared her. No, he feared what he would do *to* her once he saw her face.

He stopped just in front of her cell. Lucia was sitting well away from the iron bars, on the low wooden bench that served as her bed. She sat with her back against the wall. Her face was masked by shadows.

She rose and stepped into the light, approaching the bars of the cell with trepidation—as well she should. "You came," she said.

"You knew I would," David replied.

"I had my doubts."

"So did I," he admitted. "But I'm here now." He studied her face. It was void of emotion, stony, not unlike Erela's, but for a much different reason. He hesitated, suddenly unsure of himself. He couldn't let his emotions get the best of him—he had a job to do. But it was hard not to get lost in a whirlwind of conflicting feelings.

It had been easy to hate Lucia when he thought about all the pain she had caused, but now that he was here, standing face-to-face with her, he couldn't help remembering the woman he'd once known in the form of Aunt Moira. He had cared for her once, before she had hurt him so deeply. He had to stay objective, professional. That was the way to get through this.

David gathered his thoughts and cleared his throat. "You should know that this is not a social visit. I'm here in my official capacity as Solas Beir. You know there will be a trial?"

"Yes." She looked down at her feet.

"Good. Then you must also be aware that as Solas Beir, I will hear from witnesses and the court council before deciding your fate. If I determine that your crimes merit execution, I am required by law to put you to death. Do you understand this?"

Lucia nodded. "Yes. I understand." Her voice was flat, almost robotic.

"Wonderful." David narrowed his eyes. He felt frustrated. He wished that he could sense what she was feeling, that she would show some sign of regret. He didn't want to be her executioner, but she wasn't helping herself. It was like she wanted to die. Maybe she thought she was out of options and had already resigned herself to her fate.

He sighed. "Then you also understand this is your one chance to redeem yourself. If you help us, I may not have to kill you. So tell me what I need to know." She looked up at him, and her dark eyes glittered, but he couldn't tell if they were full of hope or deceit. "And don't play games with me," he added, for good measure.

"I won't," Lucia assured him. "The time for secrecy is over." Suddenly she reached through the bars and grabbed his wrist. "David."

He stepped back, surprised. "Yes?" He braced himself for a jolt of electricity, but there was none. Instead she was staring at him intently, as though she could see what he was thinking. She let go of his wrist and stepped away from the bars, avoiding his gaze.

"Thank you. For healing me," she said. "I know you didn't have to do it. And you probably didn't want to."

Her gratitude surprised him. It wasn't quite an apology,

but it was a start. Maybe there was still something left of the woman he had known. She wasn't Moira. She didn't look anything like Moira. David only needed to look at her young face and long blond hair to remember that.

But her eyes...they were darker than Moira's had been, but they *were* Moira's somehow. And her soul was the same, assuming of course that she actually had one and wasn't just toying with him by putting on an act.

"You're right. But I didn't do it for you. I did it because Abby wanted me to." He corrected himself, remembering that Abby's voice had only been in his imagination. "I mean, *would* have wanted me to."

"Nevertheless," Lucia said softly.

"Yeah. Nevertheless." David wanted to ask her if there was a chance Abby was still alive—to hear Lucia say he was wrong in the certainty he felt that Abby was gone. But he couldn't talk to Lucia about Abby. He wouldn't allow her to see that pain, allow himself to be that vulnerable in front of her. Not yet anyway. He changed the subject. "Tell me about the Sower."

Lucia raised her head, meeting his gaze. "I will. But first I must tell you about your father."

"What does my father have to do with it?"

"Everything," she replied. "Your father once made a deal to protect the kingdom. That deal was a terrible mistake, a mistake which now threatens us all."

"When I returned to my world, my father made me prove my worth to regain my place as heir," Ardal told the young woman standing before him. "He threatened to appoint another if I did not. He was so angry with me, that although he still loved me, he was willing to sacrifice our family claim to the throne if I did not obey.

"I was sent to the northern border of the Barren to fight in the war against the Kruorumbrae. It was there, many years before, that Tierney had begun his assent to glory.

"He originally fought for our side. As a reward for his valor, he was appointed Southern Oracle. But then he changed. Perhaps the war drove him mad. Or perhaps there was always darkness in him, a greed for power and blood.

"My father gave me the throne when I returned from the war, and serving as head of the court council, bore witness to my coronation. Before he was called by the Light to transcend to the higher realms, he urged me to take a queen, to sustain our bloodline. He asked my forgiveness for his threat to disinherit me. He said he had been angry and rash, and if his actions had given me cause not to marry, he regretted them. Time has a way of softening even the hardest heart. I felt my resolve waver and made a promise to find a queen.

"The most likely candidate was a young woman who had grown up close to the throne. Lucia was beautiful, graceful, and intelligent—a brilliant leader. Indeed, she had already made a name for herself serving on the court council. People far and wide sought her wisdom. But like my father, she had no compassion when it came to humans. She was at ease with the Kruorumbrae preying on them. It kept them from preying on us. Better, she argued, that lesser beings were sacrificed than our own people. On all other matters we were in agreement, but on this one subject, I could not budge. Neither could she.

"Although we seemed a good match, and she believed I would ask her to be my queen, I simply could not marry someone who would have me compromise a value that defined me. I loved her as a dear friend, but I could never love her as a wife.

"I suppose I should have foreseen her reaction when I asked her younger sister to be my queen instead. I did not mean to slight Lucia, but I could not pretend to love her. Love is not logical. Reason does not determine with whom you fall in love.

"Eulalia had been a child when I had last seen her, but when she came to court after my father went to the Light, my world changed. Although I could not forget the woman I had once loved, Eulalia was gentle, compassionate—everything that Lucia was not. She understood my reasons for wanting to help humanity. I knew she even understood my hesitation to love another. And her dark hair...she reminded me so much of Eve.

"I discovered that though she was honored to become my wife, she too had a first love. I sensed he could not elevate her rank the way I could, and I admired her choice, her commitment, to love me instead. I knew she gave me her heart, and it gave me strength. She made me want to be better than I was. How could I not love her?

"I did not know that my decision had set Lucia on a course for revenge. I had hoped that, given her wisdom in other matters, she would understand my choice for queen. Instead, I sent her straight in to Tierney's arms.

"During the wedding feast, she stole away, meaning to find solitude. She wandered down to the labyrinth on the edge of the castle's gardens. There, she met the man who began poisoning her against me.

"I had learned of his tyranny against mankind when I was crowned Solas Beir. It was then that I had removed Tierney from his position as Southern Oracle—to do anything else would have been to dishonor the memory of my beloved. That was when he took control of the Blood Shadows, and the conflict between us began. Because of this, I knew Tierney coveted the throne, and I expected that at some point, he would hatch a plot to assassinate me. I just never expected that my executioner would be a trusted friend.

"Eulalia became pregnant with Artan, who now goes by the name David and reigns as Solas Beir. With the increasing attacks on our kingdom, I feared I might soon meet my end, and if that happened, that Tierney would also kill my wife and son. I was desperate to protect them. I simply could not bear the thought that they could share Eve's fate."

AbigailsometimesAbby nodded absently, staring at the man's reflection. There was something familiar about the story he was telling. She had an odd feeling that she'd heard part of it before.

"Secretly I crossed into your world, using the portal on the Buchan estate," the man continued. "Samuel Buchan, the man who lived there, possessed a magical hand mirror, one capable of transporting me to someone who could help. Samuel had an unfortunate addiction to the mirror's charms, and at my request, his sister, Adelae, had taken possession of the treasured object to keep him from breaking his promise to cease traveling to other worlds. I feared the mirror's darker tendencies would corrupt Samuel and send him to a dangerous place, somewhere even I could not rescue him.

"I asked Adelae to let me borrow the mirror, and I transported myself to meet with the Western Oracle at her island home. She was waiting for me on her marble throne, a goddess in a temple of her own making. The Western Oracle was powerful—more powerful than any of the other oracles—and I hoped she could help me find some way of protecting my child and my kingdom.

"She assured me she had something that could protect my kingdom, but she could not guarantee the safety of my child. And such protection as she could offer would come with a heavy price.

"Disheartened, I asked her what she could do.

"The souls of Tierney and the child would be intertwined, she explained. If Tierney killed the child by his own hand, he would die as well, and my people would be saved from his tyranny.

"I pleaded for my son. There had to be something else,

something that would keep him safe. But the Western Oracle said she could do no more.

"I reluctantly agreed to her proposal. 'It shall be done,' she swore. 'Now, what shall I receive in return?'

"I offered her my life, but the Western Oracle only scoffed, 'Soon enough you will meet your end. Why should I take the life of a dead man as payment?'

"I offered her the Sign of the Throne, but she derided me. 'Foolish man. Do not think you can trick *me*. I know you would ask me to protect your sacred sigil regardless—that is not payment,' she chided.

"I was puzzled. What else could I give her, if not my life or one of the greatest treasures of my kingdom? Was there some other object she desired?

"The Western Oracle was not only known for being powerful, but also for being beautiful. But hers was a terrible beauty, one that could destroy those who became enraptured by her charms. I quickly discovered that she hoped to seduce me, but she found me guarded. I would not be swayed so easily. So, she robbed me of my innermost thoughts and showed me the one face I could not resist. Not the face of my wife, but that of my first love.

"Wearing the countenance of my Eve, she attempted to beguile me. I knew it was an illusion, and I refused her. I told her I would not betray my queen.

"The Western Oracle drew me into her arms. 'And if your queen dies at the hands of the Kruorumbrae? Surely this is a trifle compared to that,' she argued.

"And so I betrayed my wife."

The girl who called herself AbigailsometimesAbby studied the man's face, the deep pain in his eyes. His reflection wavered as though he were trembling. He was silent for a long moment, and then continued his tale.

"I returned from the island of the Western Oracle to find

that Lucia had followed me to the Buchan estate, and then to the Western Oracle's island. She had seen everything. Lucia was so angry with me, and I assumed at the time it was because I had betrayed her sister. Now I think she was angry because I had chosen a monster over *her*.

"I feared she would tell Eulalia what I had done. Instead, she regarded me with cold civility and kept her silence about my deeds. However, I believe my pact with the Western Oracle caused her to agree to my assassination.

"I died the night my son was born. I held him and then took my leave so my weary queen could rest. Lucia found me and asked to speak with me privately. I agreed and invited her to dinner in my chambers. She apologized for her behavior and asked if we could find some peace between us, now that we had a shared joy in the birth of my son, her nephew. I happily agreed. She was dear to me, and I was sorry there had been a rift between us. Then I started choking, and she made no move to help me. As I collapsed on the floor, gasping for breath, she stood over me.

"She told me she had poisoned my food with silver powder. 'It works quickly, does it not?' she asked. 'But do not fret, my king. When Tierney takes the throne and *I* am queen, I will protect your child as though he were my own.'

"I reached for her, wanting to beg her to help me, to think of her family and how they would suffer at Tierney's hands, but I could not speak. She took my hand, kissed it tenderly as I passed from life into death, and left the room. Since I had retired for the evening, no one found my body until the next morning.

"As a mere shadow of myself, wretched wraith that I am, I followed Lucia. I watched her make her way to the labyrinth where she had met Tierney so often. I saw his pleasure at her news and heard the promises he made to her. I heard his plans to overtake the kingdom, *my* kingdom.

"I visited my wife in her dreams, warning her of Tierney's

pending attack on our home. Thankfully, she heard me and had the foresight to warn Cael, the man who could stop the Kruorumbrae. It was not until after my death that I realized it was Cael who was my wife's first love. Now I am glad, for had he not cared for her, he might not have believed in her visions. His love for her made him a great champion, and he fended off the attack and imprisoned Tierney.

"With Tierney banished to the Wasteland, Lucia feared her part in the plot would be discovered. She became a recluse, and it was rumored that she was ill, since she rarely left her chambers.

"My poor wife never suspected her sister and visited Lucia with my son, trying to cheer my murderer. Lucia bonded with the child. I said before that you cannot help with whom you fall in love, and this is as true with a child as it is with a lover. Lucia did love the boy as if he were her own. She began to question her decision to kill me and her loyalty to Tierney's cause. I think she would have fully repented had it not been for what happened next.

"Tierney's army of Blood Shadows waged war against the kingdom in the absence of their leader. Lucia woke one evening to a tapping at her window. One of the Kruorumbrae had come through the portal at the center of the labyrinth to seek an audience with her.

"Even she knew better than to allow the creature access to the castle, so she spoke with him through the glass. He told her she was the key to Tierney's freedom—that she must bring the heir to the throne to Tierney's disciples so that their master would be released. She refused. She was horrified at the thought of the baby in the clutches of the Kruorumbrae.

"The creature left her but came back the next night, and the next, tormenting her, trying to weaken her resolve. Every night, just as she went to sleep, she could hear the monster knocking at her window.

"Lucia was strong, and she was able to withstand the endless harassment of the Blood Shadow for a long time. Confronting the creature did not work, so she tried ignoring him. But he knocked on the glass every night, all night.

"Finally, with the same desperation that sent me into the arms of the Western Oracle, Lucia crossed over to the new world and used the silver hand mirror to visit the Western Oracle to try to make a pact of her own. But the Western Oracle only laughed and said she could not protect the child. Instead, she told Lucia to flee and take Artan to Samuel Buchan's world, where he would be hidden from the Kruorumbrae.

"The Western Oracle also made a prophecy. She said there would come a time when Tierney and the child would meet face-to-face, and Lucia would be the one to decide who lived—the man she loved, or the child she longed to protect. She was once again destined to become someone's executioner. For Lucia, this was not just a prophecy—this was her curse.

"She returned to Cai Terenmare, but she could not warn her sister of the danger Artan was in without revealing her own guilt. So, she killed the creature that had tormented her and burned down the labyrinth, closing the portal that led to the Kruorumbrae stronghold. Then she stole the child, crossed into the other world, and destroyed that portal as well. She set an ancient curse upon the boundaries of the Buchan estate, thinking it would imprison any Blood Shadow that came looking for the child. Instead—she imprisoned her sister.

"When the Kruorumbrae in your world found Lucia, she lied to them. She told them that in Tierney's absence, they had to submit to her authority, for when Tierney returned, she would be queen. When she learned of her sister's imprisonment, she did nothing to free Eulalia. She thought that if the Blood Shadows believed she had betrayed her own sister to help Tierney, they would not question her loyalty to him.

"Lucia recruited her own army of Kruorumbrae, and

unbeknownst to them, used them to protect the child she had hidden from both his mother and Tierney. She thought that if the child were to remain in the human world, Tierney would have no need to seek the boy's death once he was released from his desert prison and took the throne. Lucia assumed if Tierney believed she had been working to find a way to release him, he would be true to his promise to make her queen, and she would be able to influence his decisions as Solas Beir.

"She thought I had been too soft a king in my compassion for humans, that in closing portals to prevent their destruction at the hands of the Kruorumbrae, I had upset the balance of my world and made my own subjects the prey of the Blood Shadows. Lucia intended to rectify my mistakes and restore that balance. She lied to herself in justifying her actions, but her lies have been her undoing."

"Your father was blinded by his desperation to save you," Lucia told David, finishing her version of the story about Ardal's bargain. "He was so blinded, he could not foresee the consequences of his pact with the Western Oracle. From their union, the Sower was born. Now he will come and challenge you for the right to the throne. He is, after all, Ardal's firstborn."

David was confused. "How can that be? If my mother was already pregnant with me, wouldn't I have been born before the Sower?"

"You are thinking of time in human terms, assuming that those who live in Cai Terenmare have the same life cycles as those in the world in which you grew up. But neither your mother nor the Western Oracle were human. Had you grown up in this world, you would still be a young child, but you aged like a human, did you not?"

David thought about it and frowned. "Yes, of course—I

keep forgetting that things are different here. What *is* the Sower, exactly?"

"A monster, like his mother," Lucia spat, her face twisted in disgust. "I imagine, though, that he has some of your father's traits as well. He may well appear as one of us when he comes. I do not know what he looks like. What I *do* know for certain is that Tierney plans to use him to take the throne from you. There is a prophecy that the Sower comes to sow the seeds of strife. I fear this prophecy will come true. And I fear the Sower will destroy us all if he is as bloodthirsty as his mother and sisters. The sirens were ruthless, and they weren't above making a meal of the Shadows. But Tierney swears he can control him, that the Sower is loyal to him."

"And what about you?" David asked, searching her face. "Are you still loyal to Tierney?"

Lucia laughed bitterly, her eyes hard with anger and defiance. "Not anymore. I'm none too happy about him trying to kill me."

David caught himself smiling. A lesser person would have been undone by Tierney's betrayal, but not Lucia. She always came out fighting. He could almost believe this was the woman he knew, back when she was still Moira. The memory was bittersweet. "Why did you kidnap me?" he asked.

"You must believe me—everything I did was to save your life," Lucia explained. "When I learned of your father's deal with the Western Oracle, I tried to make my own. The Western Oracle wouldn't help me. She just told me that if Tierney killed you, he would die. And vice versa—if you kill him, you will die. So I ran away with you. I knew I had to keep you separated from each other."

"You loved him."

"Yes," Lucia answered. "And I love you. As if you were my own son." She reached through the bars to touch his cheek and then stopped herself, looking pained. She withdrew her hand

and stared down at her feet. "Despite what you must think of me, my love for you was never a lie. I thought I could give you a life where you would be safe from him."

"But it wasn't a real life," David objected. "It was just a faery tale you sold me to keep me from the throne. So *he* could have it."

Lucia looked away and didn't answer. That was answer enough.

David crossed his arms. "What you really wanted was for Tierney to be Solas Beir, and for you to be his queen. It had nothing to do with me at all."

Lucia turned to meet his gaze, her eyes flashing angrily. "That's not true. I really did want to protect you. And I did keep you hidden." She scowled. "Until that girl came along and unraveled everything."

David was taken aback, remembering the argument about Abby he'd had with Moira the night of the Autumn Ball. It felt like that night had existed in a different lifetime. In a way, it had. The anger he'd felt that night reignited in his chest. "That *girl* has a name. It's Abby," David snapped. "And just so we're clear, I love her, and I asked her to marry me. Then the Daughters of Mercy stole her from me and killed her. And why did they do that? Because of Tierney. And because of *you*." He was furious. After everything that had happened, was this what it boiled down to in Lucia's mind? Was she actually blaming Abby for what had happened?

"I *am* sorry," Lucia murmured. "I know you are hurting—"

David cut her off before she could finish. "Hurting doesn't begin to describe it." He gripped the iron bars of the cell to keep himself from doing something he would regret. He could feel his hands growing warm. He was afraid that if he let go of the bars, he might unwittingly unleash a volley of fire, incinerating Lucia where she stood. He was enraged, but he didn't want to hurt her.

He fought to control his fury. "After everything that's happened, you still think what you did was for a good cause," he spat. "You haven't taken responsibility for your actions at all. You still believe Abby was beneath you because she was human." He stared at her, realization dawning. "You still believe it's okay for the Blood Shadows to feed on humans, don't you?"

"You don't know what it was like," Lucia argued. "When your father closed the portals, the Kruorumbrae cannibalized *us*. The people of the Light. He upset the balance. But with the humans, there is a natural order—"

"No," David growled. "There is *nothing* natural about what the Shadows do. You should know that better than anyone. And tell me this—if you are so worried about our own people being 'cannibalized,' why are you okay with our people being courtesans?"

"I'm not," Lucia insisted. "That was a temporary solution and not of my doing."

"So what then?" David asked, throwing up his hands in frustration. "Your plan was to reopen the portals and declare open season on mankind?"

Lucia glared at him. Then she turned and calmly walked over to her bed. She sat down, her back straight like a proper lady's. "Tell me, boy, have you ever made tea?"

"What?" He stared at her, bewildered.

"Tea. Have you ever, in the life of privilege afforded to you, boiled water?" she asked. As she spoke, she arranged the folds of her skirt as though she were holding court, not residing in a prison cell.

"Yes. I have, actually," he snapped, his jaw clenched. "Believe it or not, in my privileged life I actually managed to do a few things for myself. What's your point?"

"What would happen if you put a stopper in the tea kettle and let the steam build up? Just let it build and build?"

"You'd have a bomb," he answered.

"Exactly. That is what happened when your father closed the portals. My plan was to defuse that bomb by letting a little steam escape. That's all."

David narrowed his eyes. "A few lowly humans sacrificed for the greater good, then. Is that it?"

Her black eyes were hard. "You can save your sarcasm. It was us or them."

"It doesn't have to be," David argued. "Not if I exterminate the Shadows. Then they won't prey on anyone."

"Genocide, is it?" Lucia asked in a nonchalant tone. "Well then, answer me this. How does that make you any better than the Kruorumbrae? They have existed in this world for a very long time. In spite of past efforts to exterminate them, they've maintained a foothold in Cai Terenmare. And you, my darling boy, are going to have to figure out how to be Solas Beir for *all* of us—not just those who side with the Light."

"I don't think so," David replied, shaking his head. "The Blood Shadows are predators." He thought about it. "No, actually, 'predator' is not the right word. A predator hunts for food. But the Shadows don't just hunt to survive, they take pleasure in killing. They are evil. And I have a solution for dealing with evil."

Lucia laughed derisively. "I guess you've got it all figured out. But by your definition, aren't some humans evil too? Don't some of them take pleasure in killing?"

"That's different," David insisted. "And only a few humans fit that description."

"And how do you know that all the Kruorumbrae do? Have you met them all? Did you conduct a survey?"

David glared at her and crossed his arms. "I've met enough."

"A handful, at most." Lucia brushed a smudge of dirt from her skirt. Her defiant eyes burned into his. "Did you ever stop to ask *why* they do what they do? Whether or not they had a *choice* in becoming what they are? And did you ever think for one second about how they are entirely excluded from your kingdom? From your council? They have no voice except for what Tierney has given them."

David stared at her for a moment and then narrowed his eyes. "I think we're done here."

"Oh yes, I quite agree," Lucia nodded. "We're done."

"I won't come back down here," David warned, stepping away from the bars. "The next time we see each other, it will be at the trial."

Lucia smiled, but there was no humor in it. "I'll be there. Think about what I said."

Ardal looked up at the glaring sun. It had not moved from its position. In the Wasteland, it was always high noon. He looked back at the girl, at his reflection and hers on the surface of the water. Her eyes had cleared, like she had awakened from a dream. It was time. She was remembering whom she had been. Now he would tell her whom she needed to be.

"There was a man," the girl murmured. "He was very important to me. Is he...?"

"Yes," Ardal said, putting his hand on her shoulder. "My Artan and your David are one and the same. And now the time for talking is done. Now, Abigail, you must go to him and stop him from making a terrible mistake. Lucia will soon stand trial for her misdeeds, and David will put her to death. You must help him understand why she must live. There is a plague coming, and David will need Lucia if he is to stop the Sower. If David executes Lucia, he too will die, and all of Cai Terenmare will be lost to the Darkness."

Abigail Brown looked around at the endless sand surrounding her. "But how can I go to him? I don't know where I am. I don't know which way to go." She sounded small, her voice that of a lost child.

"Follow the raven. He knows the way home."

Abby blinked. The man was gone, and only her own reflection remained. She turned to see the raven a little way off, hopping impatiently again. She followed him, breaking into a run. The raven took to the air, gliding low and flying slowly enough for Abby to keep pace. When she turned midstride to glance behind her, the sapphire pool had vanished. All she could see was the sand stretching to the horizon.

Ahead the raven stopped. He was waiting for her. She doubled her pace, panting in the unrelenting heat as she hurried to catch up. Just as she reached him, he rocketed up into the sky.

"Wait," she called. Taking a breath, she traced his flight upward with her eyes. There was something up there, something suspended high above her in the middle of the sky. It was small and glinted metallically in the bright sunlight. Abby watched as the raven snatched it out of the air and brought it back down to the sand below. She knelt as he hopped over to her and placed the object in her hands.

All of her memories came rushing back. "The silver hand mirror," she mused. Then it caught on the sticky blood on her fingers and she fumbled it. The mirror fell to the sand. The latch clicked, and the engraved lid of the case popped open. On the glass, Abby could see the reflection of a sky, but it wasn't the cobalt one above her. The sun within the mirror was just rising.

Suddenly she felt very small. She looked down at her fingers, her hands, but they were gone. In their place were white wings. She was the white raven once again.

The black raven cocked his head toward her and then dove through the glass of the mirror. Abby followed.

She found herself flying through a pitch-black tunnel and then out of the darkness into a sunrise tinted coral and pink. She was soaring high above a different desert, under a different sky. She circled back to take in the gaping mouth of a cave at the top of a rock spire. The Eye of the Needle, it was called. And the raven was named Brarn.

Brarn carried the silver hand mirror in his talons. They flew west, away from the rising sun.

TRIALS AND TRIBULATIONS

David surveyed the Great Hall as the last members of his court council filed in and took their places. The cavernous room was swarming with spectators. It was possibly even more full than it had been on the day of his coronation. The news that Lucia would be held accountable had spread like wildfire through the towns nestled in the forests surrounding the castle and across the villages of the Great Plains.

She was standing in front of him now in yet another cage. This one was smaller, positioned in front of the dais where he sat on the throne. Obelia stood beside him on his right, and Eulalia sat on a second, more delicately carved throne on his left. The other council members stood in a semicircle flanking either side of the dais. Around them, crammed into every square inch of the room, stood the throng who had come to watch Lucia die. *People are pretty much the same in all worlds,* David reflected. *They want to see a show.*

In all of Cai Terenmare's history, had there ever been a criminal as notorious as Lucia? There had been other wrongdoers, surely, creatures spawned of darkness who had committed unspeakable acts. But the only person who rivaled Lucia's infamy was Tynan Tierney.

He hadn't had a trial. He had been deposited directly into

the Wasteland. *Why was that?* David wondered. Tierney hadn't assassinated a king, but his crimes against the people of Cai Terenmare had surely merited execution, not banishment. Maybe it was because losing your mind in the Wasteland was considered a fate worse than death.

Lucia's wheeled cell had been specially constructed for her trial. It was only wide enough for her to stand in. Immediately after leading her out of the dungeon, her guards had thrust her into this iron rectangle and rolled her into the Great Hall. At first glance, Lucia's cell resembled a classic English phone booth, except that instead of being painted the cheerful, iconic red, it was the dirty gray color of impenetrable steel, and it had open panes rather than glass windows.

Upon closer inspection, David could see that the edges of the panes had been sharpened like razors, and at various points along the cell's framework, barbaric-looking spikes jutted inward. A small, glovelike metal box stuck out from either side of the cell, and they might have appeared comically out of place on a red phone booth. On the rolling cell, however, they looked sinister, as though they were part of a torture device.

Made from the same enchanted iron used in the dungeon to keep prisoners from using magic, these rude gauntlets bound Lucia's hands. Presumably, this was because of the widespread fear that if she had access to her hands, she might torch her way out of the cell and escape. Or toast a few of the spectators attending her trial.

David had a feeling that this extra precaution was little more than useless in keeping Lucia caged, but kept this thought to himself. If the tiny cell put their audience at ease, so be it. With the crowd teeming as it was, overflowing through the hall doors and past the castle's foyer into the town square, the last thing he wanted was to incite a riot by stirring panic. Even so, he had seen Lucia's formidable powers in action and doubted such a prison could contain her if she really wanted to escape.

She had been surprisingly compliant about her imprisonment however, submissive even. That worried him. It made him wonder what she knew that he didn't. Had she really resigned herself to being executed? He couldn't imagine the defiant woman standing before him raising a white flag. In one form or another, he had known her his entire life, and he could not recall a single instance in which she had backed down from a fight. And then there was the moment she had actually stepped into the box and allowed the guards to cuff her hands within those iron mitts. As her dark eyes burned into his from across the room, he could see nothing in her expression that spoke of defeat. If anything, she had looked amused; a sly smile sat on her lips. She had a plan. Of that he was certain. But if her plan wasn't to escape, what was it?

David realized the crowd had fallen silent and was watching with rapt attention as the head of the court council stepped forward to begin the trial. Obelia retrieved a scroll from the ceremonial table beside the dais. Unrolling the piece of parchment, she read the charges against the accused. Her strong, authoritative voice carried across the hall: "Lucia of Caislucis, you have been charged with high treason. You are accused of assassinating the former Solas Beir, Ardal; kidnapping Artan, heir to the throne; and cursing Artan's mother, the dowager queen, when she tried to rescue her child. Upon Artan's return as Solas Beir, you engaged in an assault on the Solas Beir and four of his advisors. Lastly, you are accused of conspiracy to overthrow the Solas Beir, acting as accomplice to the Kruor um Beir, known enemy of the realm. Those bearing witness against you are His Majesty, the Solas Beir; Her Majesty, the dowager queen; Cael of Caislucis and Marisol Cassidy of Newcastle Beach, advisors to the Solas Beir; and the court council. Have you a statement of defense regarding these charges?"

A tangible tension hung in the air as the audience waited

to see how Lucia would respond. She stared straight ahead as though everyone around her were beneath her notice. "No," Lucia said quietly. "I am guilty."

David could hear the collective gasp of the crowd. No one had expected Lucia to admit her guilt. Most people faced with the prospect of execution would have pleaded not guilty, or, in the presence of overwhelming evidence of guilt, would at least present some statement detailing the reasons why they should be spared. Again he wondered if Lucia wanted to die, if she was trying to sabotage herself.

Obelia herself seemed surprised. She studied the prisoner, seeming to gather her thoughts. "Very well then...I shall open for debate your sentencing. The charges against you are grave and, according to the laws of the realm, merit execution. Are there any on the Solas Beir's council who support the sentence of death?"

There was a moment of silence as the council members stared at each other. Tentatively, Gorman, the Caislucis historian, raised his hand.

Obelia acknowledged the small, indigo man. "Gorman? You wish to address the court?"

Gorman looked around at the other council members and then at the crowd. He turned to address Obelia. "Aye, Councilwoman. The accused has admitted her guilt in crimes against the kingdom. Crimes that are serious indeed, depriving us of an honorable leader and threatening the safety of the royal family and, by extension, all of Cai Terenmare." He turned and bowed formally to David. "Your Majesty, though it pains me to recommend execution, I see no alternative, considering the accused's actions."

Eoin, the tall, gaunt council member standing next to Gorman, nodded. "An example must be made." Around him other council members murmured in agreement.

Rising from his throne, David approached Lucia's cell,

evaluating the woman standing inside. Lucia met his gaze, her eyes steady. He turned to address the spectators. "It is true that an example must be made. But is there no alternative to execution? Must she die?" He could hear whispering among the throng. He stared out into the crowd.

Some of those attending the trial seemed to object to the idea that the prisoner might live. David saw anger in many faces and fear in others. Those closest to Lucia's cage seemed to shrink back, pressing up against people in the rows behind them.

Erela, her wings folded behind her, spoke next. "Solas Beir, we must consider the risks of keeping the prisoner alive. If she were to live, she would have the potential to cause further harm."

More harm than she has already caused, David thought, frowning. He turned to the council. "A show of hands then. Who thinks the accused deserves death?"

Immediately, Eoin raised his hand and nodded. "Death," he said, his deep voice booming into the silence of the hall.

Around him the other council members slowly raised their hands. Cael and Marisol exchanged a look, and hesitantly raised their hands. Everyone's hands were raised except for the queen's.

David turned to her. "Mother? What do you think?"

Eulalia looked pale. She clutched the arms of her throne, a strained expression on her face as she looked from Lucia to David. "I cannot..." she began, and then shook her head, unable to finish. She tried again. "She is my sister." Her eyes were wide, pleading with him.

"Nevertheless," Obelia said quietly, placing her hand on Eulalia's. Her tone was firm, but not unkind. "You serve the kingdom, Your Majesty. You must speak your truth."

Eulalia nodded and looked into Lucia's eyes. Lucia's gaze was steadfast, unyielding. She drew herself up to her full height, not out of defiance, David thought, but to hold herself with as much dignity as she could muster under the circumstances. In spite of everything, David admired her strength.

"Death," Eulalia whispered, and then looked away.

Lucia didn't flinch. The expression on her face was fixed like stone. David could see she had anticipated this. But while Lucia seemed unaffected by her death sentence, Eulalia looked as though she might weep.

Obelia continued, looking at each council member as she spoke. "The council has recommended execution. Are there any who have grounds for reprieve?"

No one on the council responded.

Obelia turned to address the audience. David could hear murmuring among the throng. "Are there any who will speak for the accused?"

A hush fell over the crowd—the silence in the Great Hall was heavy, suffocating.

I will speak for her.

Abby? David looked up. That was her voice, no mistake. She was here somewhere—he could sense her. His heart began to beat wildly. *Where is she?* He looked frantically around the room, trying to find her among the spectators, and then, when he didn't see her, he spun around, studying the council members to see if they too had heard her voice.

Several council members were shifting uncomfortably as the silence dragged on, but they seemed unaware that something had changed.

But I heard her, he thought. *That wasn't my imagination.* He could feel her. *She's somewhere close.*

David looked at Lucia. Her dark eyes glittered as she turned her face toward one of the arched windows, its stained glass tilted fully open to the courtyard to let in the sea breeze.

There was the sound of feathers rustling, and then a large black raven flew into the room, carrying something shiny.

Brarn, David thought. He watched as the bird landed on the ceremonial table beside the dais. The silver hand mirror clattered across the polished wood, spinning to a stop. Council members and audience members alike gasped, taking in the raven with wide eyes.

David stepped down from the dais and picked up the mirror. *Where did Brarn get this?* He thought, puzzled. *From Lucia?* As far as David knew, the mirror had last been in her possession. After Malden stole it from Nysa and gave it to his mistress, Lucia used it to free Tierney from the Wasteland.

David looked from the mirror to the raven. Brarn blinked his large, gold-rimmed eyes and cocked his head toward the open window.

Suddenly the window grew bright with blinding light, and those closest to it drew back. There was a second rustling of wings, and a white raven emerged in a beam of sunlight.

As the bird soared into the Great Hall, it began to stretch and change. Feathers shimmered like the facets of a diamond as they fell away from the form of a young woman, her arms outstretched like wings as she descended the shaft of light. She landed lightly on the stone floor of the hall. Her skin glowed in the sunlight, and her light brown hair gleamed golden. She was arrayed in a long dress of silk so white, it seemed to glow as well. As she lowered her arms and raised her head, the last of her feathers wafted away like vapor.

"I will speak for Lucia," Abby proclaimed, meeting David's unbelieving stare.

"Abby," David breathed, his heart caught in his throat. Suddenly, the raw, persistent ache that had plagued his soul since he lost her was gone, replaced by a feeling of exhilaration. In two long strides, he crossed the distance between them and was enveloping her in his arms, his face buried in her hair as he crushed her to him. "Abby," he murmured.

After a moment, Abby disentangled herself from his arms.

"David," she said, smiling up at him. She caressed his cheek, holding his gaze, and he felt himself getting lost in her sparkling blue eyes. In that moment, everyone else in the Great Hall ceased to exist.

"I thought I would never see you again," he whispered, cupping her chin. "I thought you were dead." He pressed her to him again and kissed her.

She kissed him back, but then took a step backward, looking up at him with regret. "I'm sorry. I was trapped in the Wasteland. Brarn found me and brought me back."

"The Wasteland?" He stared at her, bewildered. "How did you end up in the Wasteland?"

She shook her head. "Long story. I promise, I'll tell you everything." She gripped his hands in hers. "David, listen. You can't execute Lucia. If you do, all of Cai Terenmare will be lost."

"What do you mean, lost?"

"Destroyed. We need Lucia to help us stop the Sower." Abby looked around the room, her eyes widening at the sight of so many people, as if she had only then realized they had an audience.

David followed her gaze. Everyone was staring at them. He could hear whispers from the crowd, and many among the throng had forgotten how to shut their mouths. Even a few of the council members' mouths gaped open in surprise. He chuckled. "Leave it to you to make a mind-blowing entrance."

Abby laughed and grinned up at him. "I do like to make an impression."

"Um-hmm." He kissed her forehead, breathing her in, savoring her closeness before returning his attention to duty. "All right, let's dismiss this crowd so we can sort this out," he said, turning toward the dais. From the corner of his eye, David could see that Marisol was beaming at them and Eulalia had started weeping, but with tears of joy. Abby's family and Jon's mother had returned to their old world to wait for news about

Abby and Jon—they would be so relieved to know Abby was safe.

David looked at Lucia. She had a strange look on her face. He wasn't sure if that was because she was surprised that Abby was alive, or shocked that Abby was willing to speak on her behalf.

David led Abby up the steps of the dais. Keeping her hand locked securely in his, he turned to address his people. "I apologize for the *slight* interruption." Around him laughter erupted. He smiled. "But I am sure you share my joy that Abby, our c'aislingaer and my betrothed, has returned!" He grinned at Abby and held up her hand.

At this, the crowd burst into applause and excited chatter. The people of Caislucis had grown to adore Abby and had mourned the loss of their dreamwalker and future queen when they thought she had been killed by the Daughters of Mercy. David waited patiently, letting the applause die down before continuing. He eyed the spectators seriously.

"I know you came here today to see justice served, and I appreciate the concern each of you has shown for the safety of our kingdom and my family. There have been new developments regarding the accused, and I need to take some time to understand how this will affect the council's recommendations for sentencing. For now, I grant the prisoner a stay of execution."

At this, the crowd grew agitated. David heard several loud objections. He raised his hand and the audience quieted.

"I understand this may anger some of you, and I know you have good reasons for your anger. Please rest assured that I will be thorough in my examination of these new developments, and justice will be served." He glanced over at the royal guard. "Guards, please escort the prisoner back to the dungeon."

Half a dozen armed men surrounded Lucia's cage and began to wheel her through the middle of the Great Hall. People stepped back, giving the prisoner and her escorts a wide berth. Lucia said nothing, but she shifted in her cell and kept her eyes on David and Abby until she was out of sight.

When she was gone, David turned his attention back to the crowd. "Thank you for coming today. We will send word to each village when we have reached a decision regarding the prisoner's fate." With that, he nodded to Obelia and stepped down from the dais, leading Abby out of the hall. As he entered the corridor leading to his chambers, he could hear Obelia dismissing the crowd.

"Some people aren't very happy with us," Abby whispered, glancing back into the Great Hall. She had picked up on the tension in the air when David halted the trial, and she could still see people lingering in the hall, looking outraged. Even some of the council members seemed angry about the stay of execution. The tall man standing next to Gorman in particular.

David squeezed Abby's hand. "It'll be okay. I'm just so happy to have you back. Lucia can wait." He slipped his arm around her waist and pulled her close to his side as they walked. She felt her skin prickle at his touch. She had forgotten how warm he was. "I've missed you so much, Abby," he said. "I need to hear about everything that happened."

"I missed you too." How could she have forgotten the love of her life when she was trapped in the Wasteland? Abby felt robbed of time she could have spent with him. "There's so much to tell. So much that affects Lucia too, and your decision about what should happen to her. I'm glad you didn't kill her."

David sighed and offered a weak smile. "Me too. I didn't want to be an executioner."

She nodded. "I know."

He held the door of his chamber open for Abby. "Now that

you're here, I'm in no state to play judge either. You've completely derailed my ability to think straight." He shoved the door firmly closed with his foot and pulled her to him.

"Well, I'm sorry for messing with your head." Abby brushed his hair from his forehead affectionately, studying him. Tiny details from her memories were coming back now. His hair was longer than she remembered, like he'd stopped cutting it. Apart from that, though, it was as if they had never been apart. It was funny how easy it was to be with him again. She grinned and threw her arms around his neck. "Not too sorry, though."

He laughed and scooped her up into his arms, kissing her hard before finally setting her back on her feet. "I hope you don't mind being my prisoner, but I am seriously not letting you out of my sight. Ever."

She smiled. "Sounds like a vast improvement over the prison I was in."

He settled down in a comfortable chair, pulling her onto his lap so he could keep her wrapped up in his arms. "The Wasteland..." he mused. "That explains why I couldn't sense you." He looked at her. "The connection between us, the warmth I feel when you're close to me—that was severed. I really thought you were gone. I was dying without you."

Abby placed her hand over his heart. She too could feel the tug of an invisible thread connecting their souls. "I'm so sorry. I would have come back sooner if I could have."

"I know." He pressed his forehead against hers. "How did you end up in the Wasteland?"

She frowned, remembering. "It was the silver mirror. The Daughters of Mercy chased me into the Eye of the Needle, and in the pitch black of the cave, I thought I saw sunlight streaming through the wall. It looked like a hole I could fly into where they couldn't reach me. But it wasn't. I flew through the mirror into the Wasteland, and then I was powerless. I couldn't stay in my raven form anymore. I fell, and everything went black. The next thing I knew, Brarn was there, pecking at me, trying to get me to stop counting."

David stroked her cheek. "But you were gone for so long. You were in a counting trance all this time?"

Abby shrugged. "I guess so. It felt like I was waking from a dream, but I didn't know who I was or where I was. There was just this urge to keep counting. But the pull to follow Brarn was stronger than the compulsion to keep counting, so I got up and followed him. He led me to a pool of water, and then I met your father."

David's eyes widened. "What?"

"Well, not your father exactly...your father's spirit. Ardal told me he had made a terrible deal with the Western Oracle."

"Wait," David interrupted, squinting like he was trying to remember something. "Lucia told me something similar, that my father made a deal that resulted in the Sower being born." He grimaced. "So it's true then. The Sower is my brother. Er, half-brother, I mean." He looked ill.

"Are you okay?" Abby asked, putting her hand on his arm.

David swallowed and nodded slowly, meeting her concerned gaze. "Yeah. I'm fine. I'm just trying to, uh, digest this information without losing my lunch. The thought of my father with that bloated sea monster..." He cringed.

Abby groaned. "Oh, well when you put it like *that*..." She shuddered. "So gross. I might toss my cookies too. Or gouge out my eyes."

David laughed. "Oh, how I've missed you. I know, I already said that."

Abby smiled. "You can keep saying it."

"I will. So what else did my father say?"

"There was a woman, a human woman, who he loved before he married your mother." Abby studied his face, gauging his reaction before continuing, but David didn't seem surprised by the news that Eulalia wasn't his father's first love. Maybe

Lucia had told him that part as well.

"The girl he loved was attacked by the Kruorumbrae. That's why he was so adamant about closing the portals to protect humans," Abby continued. "He also told me that when he married Eulalia, Lucia felt jilted and turned to Tierney. Lucia assassinated Ardal because she disagreed with his stance on the Blood Shadows. Then, after the coup failed and Tierney was thrown into the Wasteland, his followers wanted to kill you, so she tried to hide you in my world. Oh, and Ardal also told me she is the key to stopping Tierney and the Sower, and that you can't kill her or Tierney. If you kill Lucia, the Sower will win, and if you kill Tierney, you'll die."

"So far this matches Lucia's version of the story. Maybe she really was telling me the truth." His eyes widened. "Maybe *everything* she said was true."

Abby opened her mouth to reply, and then shut it when she heard a loud knock at David's door.

"David?" she heard Eulalia call.

Suddenly self-conscious, Abby slid off his lap and moved over to the chair beside his.

David looked at Abby and then toward the door. "Yes," he answered. "We're here. You can come in."

Eulalia entered the room, her hand in Cael's. Marisol, Erela, and Obelia followed.

"Is everything all right?" Eulalia asked.

"Yes," David nodded. "I'm sorry for ending the trial like that, but I needed a moment with Abby. I was being selfish."

Eulalia shook her head. "No, that is perfectly understandable. Abby, we are so happy you have returned."

Abby smiled. She rose from her chair and pulled both Eulalia and Cael into an embrace. "Thank you. I can't tell you how good it is to be back." She saw Marisol hanging back almost shyly. "Marisol." She reached over to squeeze her friend's hand and then hugged her.

"I missed you, Abby," Marisol said, holding Abby tight. "Things haven't been the same without you."

"I missed you too." Abby looked around and then frowned. "Where's Jon?" Marisol's hand flew to her mouth. Abby was shocked to see her choking back a sob. Abby felt her heart catch in her chest, and she turned to David. "David, where's Jon?"

"He was captured at the Eye," David said solemnly. Abby felt her breath rush out as if she had been punched in the gut. She sank back into her chair, gripping the armrests for support.

"It was Malden," Marisol explained. "He grabbed me, and Jon offered himself to Lucia as a hostage to take my place. They took him back to the city."

Abby's eyes widened in alarm. "But he's okay, right?" She reached over and clutched David's hand. "Tell me he's okay."

"We don't know, Abby," David said.

"We have been trying to get a message to Hedeon," Cael said. "But the knight seems to have disappeared, and communication with the Eastern Oracle has ceased."

"What about the other oracles?" Abby questioned. "Have they heard anything? Surely the Southern Oracle..."

Cael shook his head. "*All* communication with the Eastern Oracle has ceased. Even for the other oracles."

"Lucia seemed to think Jon is okay," Marisol said quietly. "Because he's friends with David, she thinks Tierney will see the value of keeping him alive."

"We *will* rescue him, Abby," David assured her. "We've been working on a plan. It's just that after I healed Lucia, I was out of commission for a while. I only woke up a few days ago."

"You were in a coma?" Abby asked.

David nodded. "Pretty much."

An image flashed in Abby's mind as she remembered all Ardal had revealed to her: Lucia falling, then sinking to lie battered on the bottom of the Eastern Sea. She cupped David's face, looking him up and down, inspecting him for any sign of the injuries he must have absorbed when Lucia's shattered bones and internal wounds were transferred to him. "Why didn't you tell me you'd been hurt?"

David gently pulled her hands away and held them in his. "I'm fine. Totally recovered."

Cael crossed his arms. "He has been pushing himself much too hard. He took my wound at the Eye of the Needle after a Blood Shadow sliced me open, and then, not much later, took Lucia's injuries. Healing two people that close to death was dangerous."

Marisol nodded, mirroring Cael by crossing her arms too. They almost looked like father and daughter. "And completely reckless. He's had a death wish without you."

David glowered at Marisol and Cael. "Tattletales." Abby narrowed her eyes at him, and he shrugged sheepishly. "Yeah, so, I guess I have a lot to tell you too."

Abby punched his arm. "I guess you do."

David scowled at her and rubbed his arm. "Ow. Honestly, woman. I think I've been damaged enough lately. Do *you* have to injure me too?"

She shot him a smug look. "If that's what it takes to make you stop acting like an idiot."

"Fine." He laughed and held up his hands in surrender. "Message received."

Eulalia smiled, looking from David to Abby. "It is good you returned when you did, Abby. Someone needs to make sure he behaves himself."

Abby eyed David. "I agree."

"What happened to you, Abby?" Marisol asked.

Abby gestured for everyone to sit down and then quickly told her story a second time. When she got to the part where Ardal was unfaithful to Eulalia, she treaded carefully, worried she would offend the queen. Surprisingly, that wasn't the part Eulalia objected to.

"This spirit you spoke to claimed to be Ardal?" Eulalia asked.

"Yes," Abby said, "and everything he said seems to corroborate with what Lucia told David."

"I see," Eulalia replied. Her hands had been nestled primly in her lap as she listened to Abby's story. Now she raised them and began to rub her temples as though her head ached. "Yet there is something about this that rings untrue."

Wings unfurled over the low back of her chair, Erela studied the queen and then turned to Abby. "I agree. You cannot believe anything Lucia says, c'aislingaer. She has proved herself untrustworthy time and again."

"But the two stories match," David insisted. "If they didn't, I would agree that Lucia is lying."

Eulalia turned to David, looking doubtful. "I understand why you think that, but it is not just Lucia I am concerned about. There is a very old saying: No prophet comes from the Wasteland."

"What does that mean?" Abby asked. It had not crossed her mind that Eulalia might not believe her.

Eulalia returned her hands to her lap and met Abby's alarmed gaze. "It means the Wasteland is a treacherous place, and you cannot trust your senses there. People see all kinds of strange things in the Wasteland. Maybe you did have a vision, but perhaps you were seeing things that were not there. No one could blame you for being confused," Eulalia explained. Abby started to object, but Eulalia held up her hand. "Or, it could be that you did speak with someone, but it was not Ardal. It could have been a trickster spirit. That is not unheard of either. There is simply no way to know what you saw or who you were really speaking to. And there is no way to know if Lucia is speaking the truth."

Cael had been quiet, but now spoke. "I agree with Eulalia and Erela. Lucia has a history of deceit. And Erela is a Daughter of Mercy. She has the uncanny ability to sense when people are lying, and to influence people to tell her the truth. During the time in which she has served on the council, I have seen a number of people suddenly turn to her and confess their guilt, from a kitchen servant who was stealing food to a guard who was sleeping while on duty."

"In that case, can't Erela use her abilities on Lucia so we know the truth?" David asked.

Cael's smile was grim. "I am afraid Erela's powers work best on those who are weak of will. As you well know, Lucia is anything but weak."

"That's true," David agreed. "She's one of the most headstrong people I've ever known." He sighed, and then laughed, throwing his hands up in exasperation. "This is hopeless."

"Well, there's one other thing we can try. I haven't talked to her yet," Abby suggested. "I could see if the details of her story change, and maybe I'll be able to sense whether or not she's lying. I don't have Erela's abilities, but I *am* an empath. Maybe I can push her somehow. It worked with the Southern Oracle."

"True," David said, taking her hand, "but then again, it didn't work at all with the Daughters of Mercy."

"You tried to influence my sisters?" Erela asked.

Abby frowned, remembering her encounter at the Eye of the Needle. "I tried. And failed miserably."

"That is not surprising," Erela replied.

"Uh, thanks," Abby said, shocked by Erela's bluntness.

Erela held up her hand. "No, you misunderstand me, c'aislingaer. Daughters of Mercy are not ruled by emotion. A cai aislingstraid has the ability to influence the emotions of others, but is also vulnerable to being influenced. An empath's emotions are fluid. Daughters of Mercy do not bend so easily. That is why you could not push them."

Cael nodded. "That is also why Erela was asked to serve on the council. We valued her judicious perspective. She was considered a bold choice though. There has never been anyone like Erela in all of Cai Terenmare. Daughters of Mercy are conformist by nature. A dissenter was unheard of. But the other council members have come to appreciate her wisdom."

"Thank you, Cael," Erela said. "C'aislingaer, you said the silver hand mirror was housed within the Eye of the Needle?"

"Yes," Abby replied, guarded. "Why do you ask?"

"I have a theory about how it got there," Erela explained. "I believe the mirror was Tierney's gift to my sisters to win their loyalty to his cause."

"Why would that make them side with him?" David asked.

"The mirror would allow them to hunt without limitations," Erela said. "In all worlds."

Abby felt her stomach turn as she realized the implications of this. She shuddered. "That would mean Tierney is not just interested in ruling Cai Terenmare. Or Earth. He wants unfettered access to everything."

"It is possible," Erela agreed.

"*All* worlds..." Abby muttered to herself. "That reminds me. When I was talking to Ardal—or whoever the spirit was," she added, glancing at Eulalia, "he mentioned that his father had been called by the Light to the higher realms. At first I thought that meant he had died, but is it possible he went to a different world?"

"Possibly," Eulalia replied. "When someone speaks of the higher realms, they might be referring to another world. More likely this refers to joining the Light. In essence, abandoning the physical form to become light itself, continuing one's existence on a spiritual plane. It is not death, but a beginning."

"Oh." Somehow that still sounded like a kind of death to Abby's ears. "So Ardal's father gave him the throne and then joined the Light?"

"Such is our belief," Eulalia nodded.

"Ah. Well, I was just curious," Abby said, feeling awkward. "So, thanks."

Eulalia smiled warmly and patted her hand. "I am always happy to answer your questions, Abby."

"Thank you." Abby returned Eulalia's smile, even though she wasn't sure how she felt about the queen doubting her account of speaking with the former Solas Beir in the Wasteland. It wasn't the first time she and her mentor hadn't seen eye-to-eye.

Abby's mind returned to the conversation she'd had with Eulalia before visiting the Southern Oracle. At the time, Abby had been plagued with dreams of Tierney as he attempted to seduce her to join his cause. Eulalia had asked Abby to visit the Blood Altar in the Southern Oracle's rainforest so she would understand Tierney's true nature and the danger she faced.

Now Abby realized the queen had been right about Tierney, but still, it had been an uncomfortable conversation. She had hated the feeling of arguing with a mentor she admired, and the thought of betraying David had gnawed at her insides. She had felt frustrated with Eulalia and disgusted with herself. But the pain of confessing to David about her dreams of Tierney had been much worse. Abby felt those old emotions rising to the surface and forced them back down, trying to focus on the present. It didn't work. Her stomach began to ache.

She looked up to see David watching her and prayed what she was feeling wasn't written on her face. He gave her a long look, and then turned to address the others. "Well, it has been an exciting day. I'd like to check in with Lucia, so maybe we can continue this conversation later. I need time to think about all this before making a decision about her."

To Abby's relief, no one else seemed to notice her internal turmoil, not even Eulalia.

"Of course, my dear. I imagine you would also like more

time with your betrothed." The queen winked at David and Abby and took Cael's hand, smiling. Together they rose and left David's chambers. Obelia and Erela followed.

Marisol stayed behind a moment. "It's good to have you back, Abby." She glanced at the chamber's open door, seeming to wait until the others were out of earshot.

Abby could hear footfalls echoing against the stone floor and walls of the corridor, already fading as the others reached the end of the hallway.

Marisol looked back at Abby meaningfully. "For the record, I *do* believe you."

There was nothing forced about Abby's smile now. She stood and hugged Marisol tightly. "Thanks, Sol. That means a lot to me."

Marisol smiled back, but her face was pinched. The void Jon had left in her life was tangible. Abby could almost reach out and touch the fear and sadness radiating from her friend.

"Don't worry about Jon," Abby urged. "I'm sure he's okay. I'd feel it if he wasn't. We *will* get him back."

"We have to," Marisol replied. Her eyes were filling up with tears again. "I *love* him, Abby. I didn't tell him until they were about to take him away. I was waiting until he said it first, but I should have said it sooner. I just never dreamed I'd lose him like that..."

"He's probably kicking himself for not telling you sooner too," Abby said. "He wanted to, even back when we were on our way to see the Southern Oracle. I think he's felt that way about you for a long time."

"Really?" Marisol asked, swiping at her eyes.

"Yes. He has." Abby squeezed Marisol's shoulder. "He's okay," she repeated. "Everything is going to be okay, and before you know it, he'll be back with you again."

"I hope so. He means the world to me."

Abby smiled. "Me too. If I get anything else out of Lucia,

you'll be the first to know."

Marisol managed another bittersweet smile. "Thanks." She turned to leave. "See you soon." Abby nodded, and Marisol closed the door behind her.

Abby turned back to David and sighed. He held open his arms and she gratefully collapsed in his embrace. He enveloped her, his strong arms wrapped tightly around her. His lips brushed against her forehead.

"For the record, I believe you too," he murmured.

"Thanks." She rested her head against his chest, relieved to feel her anxiety slipping away at his touch.

"I have an idea," he said, running his fingers through her hair. "How about we get this talk with Lucia out of the way, and then grab some food and hide out in here?"

Abby's stomach rumbled, surprising her, since a few minutes prior she had felt ill and food was the last thing on her mind. "Oh my goodness, yes. I'm starving."

"I'll bet," he said. "You've been in the Wasteland for weeks."

She tried to remember when she'd last eaten. He was right. Her last meal had been the lunch they'd shared in the City of the Eastern Oracle, right before she'd gotten trapped in the Wasteland. In that strange dimension where time itself was frozen, her physical body must have been in a state of suspension, somehow separated from the need for sustenance. She glanced down at herself. Annoyed, she put her hands on her hips. "You know what? All that time without food and I don't think I lost a single pound."

He laughed. "Um, I think that's a good thing, actually. You'd be wasted away to nothing but skin and bones." She cocked her head at him, doubtful. He gave her a peck on the cheek. "Oh, stop. You're perfect, Abby. You know I like a girl who eats. Now come on." He grabbed her hand and dragged her out the door good-naturedly.

She let him, feeling all her worries about Jon, Eulalia, and the Wasteland fade for the moment.

Unfortunately, her feeling of peace was short-lived. Halfway to the dungeon, the tall man from the trial intercepted them in the Great Hall.

"Solas Beir," he called. "A word, if I may."

"Of course, Eoin," David answered, looking guarded. "If it's about Lucia though, you should know I'm still conducting my investigation, so the stay of execution stands."

Eoin hesitated, studying his king. "No, Sire. It is not about the traitor."

Abby saw a dour look cross David's face, but he did not respond to the councilman's use of the term 'traitor.' Instead, he smiled diplomatically. "All right then. What can I do for you, Eoin?"

"I bring grave news," Eoin replied. "There is trouble in the north."

"What kind of trouble?" Abby asked.

The man eyed Abby suspiciously. She couldn't help but feel like she had overstepped a boundary somehow. Maybe Eoin was a traditionalist like the Eastern Oracle, and wasn't too keen on women having a voice. "Murder, my lady. A shepherd was found dead and drained on the Highlands, north of Nuren."

David's eyes widened in alarm. "Was there a bite mark?"

Eoin nodded. "Yes, Your Majesty. His corpse bore a fearsome resemblance to your description of the man in the Barren."

"What?" Abby asked, looking from Eoin to David. "What man?"

David's face fell. "Daudi. On our way back to Caislucis, we found his body. He had been bitten by something and then completely drained. All that was left of his body was a dried-out husk."

Abby covered her mouth with her hand, trying to contain

her shock. "Oh! Poor Yola...her brother..."

"Yes," David said, nodding solemnly. He slipped his arm around Abby's shoulders. "I'm afraid the village of Nuren suffered many losses from the Daughters of Mercy. And we still haven't rescued the girl."

"Aziza," Abby sighed, remembering the little girl she'd tried to save from the clutches of the Kruorumbrae. "So you're saying a Daughter killed Daudi?"

David and Eoin exchanged a look. "No," David replied. "It wasn't a Daughter. We believe it was the Sower."

Abby sucked in a breath, feeling dread creep into her veins.

"There was a third attack, the remains identical to the other two bodies. The perpetrator seems to prey on those working in isolation," Eoin reported. "That victim was a fisherman. He was found in his boat, which was severely damaged and had been wedged between the rock monoliths just off the shore of Yakez."

"Yakez?" David asked. "Where is that? I've not heard of it."

Eoin narrowed his eyes. "That is not a surprise. The village is not far from Caislucis, a few hours ride north along the coast, but it seems to be beneath the notice of royalty."

David raised his eyebrows but didn't respond. Eoin seemed unaware of his antagonistic tone. Or maybe he didn't care if he made David angry.

"Yakez is a very small village. It is also where I was born," he finished in a huff, crossing his arms over his chest.

"I see," David nodded slowly. "Well, I will speak to Cael about coordinating a trip up north. I'll speak with the people of Yakez personally, as well as with both victims' families. I'll also provide the families with additional food and resources to ease their losses."

Eoin uncrossed his arms. He seemed satisfied with David's answer. "Thank you, Solas Beir."

"It's the least I can do," David said. "I can't bring back their loved ones, and for that I am sorry. We'll leave at first light tomorrow. Will you join us, Eoin?"

"I would be honored."

"Good," David replied. "Then I'll make arrangements with Cael as soon as I speak with Lucia. If you'll excuse us...."

"Of course, Solas Beir, of course." Eoin bowed and stepped aside. "You have much to do."

David smiled and took Abby's arm, escorting her down the corridor that led to the dungeon. Just outside the dungeon's iron doors, Abby stopped him.

"What's with that guy?" she whispered. "Seems like he's got a grudge against you."

David frowned. "Eoin can be a little intense, but he's okay. Erela trusts him."

Abby scoffed, crossing her arms. "Yeah, well, my creep-o-meter says otherwise."

David raised an eyebrow. "Creep-o-meter? That a technical term?"

Abby shrugged. "Working title."

"Hmm. I'll keep an eye on him," David said, looking over his shoulder down the long corridor.

Abby followed his gaze. Eoin had remained in the Great Hall and was engaged in a conversation with a fellow council member.

"I think he's harmless though," added David. "He's one of the newer council members, and his philosophy can be rigid, but he's been outspoken about disparities between the rich and poor. I can understand why, especially now that I know where he's from. Things in Cai Terenmare are changing, Abby. I hope for the better."

"How so?"

"Even in my father's day, the Solas Beir's word was law. He was a radical leader in closing the portals and granting sanctuary to outcasts like Erela, but still, people didn't really have a say in things," David explained.

"What about the court council? He consulted with them."

"The council's power was limited, and it tended to represent the elite. Less wealthy, isolated villages experienced more than their share of raids from the Kruorumbrae and had fewer resources for survival. If Yakez fits that description, I can understand why Eoin might have a problem with the royal family. But things started to change in the absence of a Solas Beir. The council's power grew, and poorer regions finally found a voice. Some people aren't all that eager to embrace a new monarch. They fear losing the ground they've gained. But Cai Terenmare is not a democracy. There will always be a Solas Beir, just as there will always be oracles." David smiled conspiratorially. "But *I* happen to think more representation from the people is a good thing. Maybe we can finally balance things out so resources are distributed equally."

Abby stared at him. "Huh. I'm gone a few weeks and then…" she murmured, cupping his face in her hands, "just look at you."

David seemed puzzled. "What?"

She grinned. "You've become a *real* leader, kid. I'm proud of you." She leaned forward, standing on her tip-toes, and kissed his cheek.

He reached up and rubbed his cheek. "Thanks…*kid*." His grin was lopsided, goofy. "You do remember I'm older than you, don't you?"

She shrugged. "Have it your way, geezer."

He chuckled. "Whippersnapper." He tugged open the dungeon door. "Shall we?"

"What are you doing over there?" Hedeon asked Jon in the

darkness of their cell. He sounded annoyed.

Jon hadn't realized he'd been making noise, but lying on his stomach on the cold, stone floor, catching his breath, he guessed he *had* been breathing heavily. And possibly grunting a bit. "Push-ups," he answered. Then, realizing the word would be unfamiliar to someone from Cai Terenmare, and Hedeon wouldn't catch his meaning, he clarified: "It's a kind of exercise. I've been in this cramped cell for a long time, and I don't want my muscles to atrophy. I'm trying to keep myself strong. Plus, it passes the time."

"Ah," he heard Hedeon reply.

"What are *you* doing?" Jon rolled over and sat up, stretching out his legs. He hadn't heard much movement from the other side of the cell.

Hedeon laughed hoarsely. "Lying here. Healing. Trying to move as little as possible."

"Any thoughts on how we can get out of here?"

"Sadly, no. The best idea I have is to change into my spirit animal when the guards next bring food and threaten them into releasing us."

"Will that work?"

"Probably not," Hedeon replied dryly. "I have also considered ripping the door from its hinges."

Jon thought about it. Exactly what kind of animal did Hedeon change into? He tried to imagine David or Cael having the strength to destroy an iron door. Cael's wolf wouldn't be capable of it, but David could do it if he used his mind rather than his lion's muscles. And if this guy was all about brute strength, did he really want to share a cell with him when he turned? Maybe, if it meant escaping without getting mauled. "So, uh, what's your spirit animal?"

"A rather large and frightening bear." From the sound of Hedeon's voice, Jon suspected he was smiling, and Jon couldn't help but grin in return.

"That's handy. How about you change now and try destroying the cell door?" He felt a glimmer of hope.

It took Hedeon a moment to respond. "I cannot." It didn't sound like he was smiling now.

Jon felt a sinking feeling in the pit of his stomach. "Why not?"

"I am not strong enough yet," Hedeon admitted. "Changing takes energy, energy I do not possess. I have not healed enough. It would help if we could get a decent meal instead of that thin broth they have been bringing us." He coughed, and Jon could hear him shift his body and clear his throat. "Less and less frequently, I might add."

Jon frowned. "Not exactly a five-star prison."

"Had I known I would someday be on this side of the bars, I might have made it easier to escape," Hedeon replied, his voice echoing off the stone walls.

"So we wait until you're healed enough to try breaking out."

"Yes," Hedeon agreed. "But I do not think it will work. The builders of this dungeon knew they needed to reinforce the cells for those of us with powerful spirit animals. For once in my sorry life, I wish I could turn into a mouse and crawl through those bars."

"Or a rabbit," Jon murmured, "like someone else I know."

"Really? Who is that?"

"My friend, Abby." The thought of his best friend brought on a pang of homesickness for Caislucis, and Jon wrapped his arms around his knees. Jon missed her and his mom and Marisol so much he could feel his heart thump with an ache that enveloped his entire chest. David and Cael too. What he would give to see his mother and friends again...to hold Marisol once more. Thinking about that last kiss at the Eye of the Needle threatened to crush the air from his lungs.

"Abby can transform? Interesting," Hedeon mused. He was

silent a moment before asking, "What are the chances of her and the Solas Beir coming to save us?"

Jon swallowed, forcing back a wave of sadness. "I don't know," he managed. His voice didn't sound as choked up or desperate as he felt. "I don't even know if they made it home okay. I think we're on our own."

Lucia sat up on her bed and swung her legs over the side when she heard steps on the stone stairs. *David.* He rounded the corner, the c'aislingaer's hand in his. Lucia stood, but remained veiled in the shadows at the back of her cell. *Let him make the first move,* she thought defiantly.

David and the girl stopped just in front of her cell, where there was a sliver of light on the floor. "Step forward, Lucia," he said. "We need to talk."

She did, but kept her tongue as she studied him. David looked different. The sadness in his eyes had vanished. That was good. Seeing him grieving had pained her. He had been reunited with the girl, but Lucia could live with that. She might even get to live a bit longer because of Abby's return.

She was grateful, but that didn't mean she liked the girl any more than she had before. Still, something about Abby had changed since their last encounter. The girl seemed more sure of herself. And then there was the fact that she could take the forms of not just one, but two animals. With rare exceptions involving the power of a Solas Beir, that was unheard of in Cai Terenmare. *Rabbit* and *raven. And both of them white. Intriguing.* "You're alive," Lucia said to Abby.

"I'm hard to kill." The expression on the girl's face was guarded but smug. Her arms were crossed, her gaze fearless. "As are you."

Lucia was surprised to catch herself laughing at the girl's

sauciness. This was not the meek child who had fled from a ballroom confrontation once upon a time. Then again, much had happened since their argument over David at the Autumn Ball in Newcastle Beach. "It appears so."

"Was this your plan all along?" David asked, eyeing Lucia suspiciously. "That Abby would return to save your neck?"

The smile on Lucia's face froze and she glowered at him. "No. I had hoped *you* would be the one to speak for me. *She's* supposed to be dead."

"Sorry to disappoint you," Abby replied. "I guess the Daughters had a different plan, one that involved me being detained in the Wasteland."

Lucia narrowed her eyes and turned away. "I had a feeling Tierney was keeping a secret from me," she muttered.

"Why didn't he just kill me?" Abby asked. "Why keep me prisoner?"

Lucia turned back to Abby and smiled cruelly. "Because, my dear, he wants you to take my place at his side. That's why he tried to kill *me*."

"He's wasting his time. I'll *never* join him," Abby vowed. Then she threw up her hands and sighed, the defiance in her voice fading into something else. Frustration? Yes. But the girl seemed resigned as well, the storm within her losing some of its bluster. "I don't even know why he's so interested. I'm just a human, after all."

Lucia raised her eyebrows. Was the girl flattered by Tierney's attention? Abby seemed awfully eager to discount his interest, almost as though she needed to convince herself of where she stood. She hoped for Abby's sake, and David's, that was not the case, but Lucia knew all too well what it was like to be courted by darkness. "Tierney seems to think you are something more. How long have you been able to change your form?"

Abby laughed, but there was no humor in it. "That's a

recent development. It seems to happen every time my life is in peril."

"Then why didn't you change your form when Calder attacked you?" Lucia asked.

Abby scowled. "Like I said, I'm just human. I can't control shape-shifting any more than I can control my dreams."

David stepped toward the bars. "She didn't have that ability then. She gained the power to change her form *after* she came to Cai Terenmare."

"And the wounds she received from her encounter with Calder? Did you heal her?" Lucia asked.

David frowned. "I couldn't. I wasn't Solas Beir yet. We lowered her into the waters of the healing pool."

Lucia nodded, satisfied she knew the answer. "That explains it. Her latent powers were magnified by the pool, and stress triggered the change."

Abby looked at David. "What about Jon? The pool healed him too. But he can't shape-shift. Not that I know of, anyway."

David thought about it and looked at Lucia. She nodded encouragingly. "Well," he said, staring at Abby as he worked it out. "Jon's injuries weren't as bad as yours. We just poured some of the water over him, and he healed."

"He was never submerged," Lucia concluded.

"Right," David replied. "And you were always a cai aislingstraid, Abby, even though you didn't understand your empathic and dreaming abilities. So I think Lucia is correct in thinking your potential was magnified. I do think Jon has gotten stronger though, and it's likely he'll live longer because of his exposure to the healing pool and Cai Terenmare."

Abby bit her lip. "I sure hope you're right about that."

David slipped his arm around Abby's shoulders and gave Lucia a stony look. "He'll be okay. He'd better be."

Lucia held David's gaze but said nothing.

Seemingly unaware of David's threat to Lucia, Abby asked

another question. "If the water is that powerful for healing, why don't we carry it with us when we travel? That sure would have come in handy when Cael was bitten by the toothed toads." She turned to David. "It would keep you from overextending yourself when you heal people, too."

"Unfortunately," Lucia explained, "the water loses potency when you remove it from the pool. It is not the water that is special, but the pool itself. It is the reason Caislucis was built here. We are standing on sacred ground. Were you to bottle the pool's waters, you'd have a refreshing drink, but little else."

"Sacred ground that's now in jeopardy," David replied, "because of Tierney and his Sower."

Lucia nodded, grasping the bars in front of her. "The Sower is coming soon. I can feel it. You must stop him at all costs. If you don't, he'll destroy everything."

She had tried to warn Tierney about the dangers of using the Sower to seize the throne, and he became enraged that she had dared to question his judgment. Soon after that, he had thrown her off the balcony. Tierney was a fool. His arrogance in believing he could control that abomination would be the death of an entire world.

"But we don't even know what he looks like," Abby protested. "Unless, of course, he favors his monster of a mother," she muttered to herself.

"A leviathan like the former Western Oracle could hardly go unnoticed for long, even in Cai Terenmare's vast seas," Lucia agreed. "He has likely inherited his mother's intelligence and ability to camouflage himself, which is a terrifying prospect."

"I'm not sure he's in the sea at all," David said. "When we were crossing the Barren, we found evidence of a creature we'd never encountered before, something with the ability to change form. It had bitten a man and then sucked the juices from his body, leaving mummified corpse. But we didn't see the perpetrator. The only other clues about its identity were reptilian footprints leading to the body, and humanoid prints leading away."

"So you don't know for sure it was the Sower," Lucia surmised.

"No, not for sure, but what else could it be?" David asked. "There have been two more attacks since, and it sounds like the same creature was at fault. Tomorrow we leave Caislucis to see what's left of the victims and speak to any witnesses."

"I suspect you won't find any witnesses," Lucia said, gripping the bars more tightly, her knuckles turning white. "If it was the Sower, he will have been clever. He wouldn't leave witnesses alive. Nor would he waste the opportunity to feed, not if he is still in flux and needing energy to take his mature form. Once he does that, he will come to you."

"Yes, but the question is, will he be a man or a beast?" David asked.

"Ah, there's the rub," Lucia said, smiling bitterly. "All I know is what the prophecy says: The Sower comes to sow the seeds of strife. My interpretation is that the Sower's methods will be covert. He won't burst into Caislucis wreaking havoc. I suggest you be wary of strangers."

"Stranger danger. Well that clarifies things," David muttered. "Thank you."

Lucia didn't appreciate his tone. She narrowed her eyes at him. "I'm sorry. I wish I knew more, truly I do. But Tierney discovered my loyalty to *you* before I had the chance to ask for more details," she spat.

David glared at her, eyes blazing, jaw clenched. "You've had a funny way of showing that loyalty," he growled. "I hope I don't have to remind you that your reprieve of execution is conditional. If you betray me again, I *will* kill you."

"David!" Abby gasped, her hand flying to her mouth in shock.

David looked at Abby. Lucia saw a flicker of remorse cross

his face, but that was quickly overshadowed by steely determination. She felt a stab of pain that his rage was directed at her, and yet a sense of pride he had grown so strong. She hoped she'd had something to do with that in playing the role of a surrogate mother for so many years.

"Come on, Abby," David said, taking her hand. "It's time to go." Without another look at Lucia, he started leading Abby toward the dungeon stairs. The girl looked back over her shoulder at Lucia.

"Wait," Lucia called to her.

Abby looked up at David. From his angry stride, Lucia could tell he had no intention of continuing the conversation. The girl stepped in front of him and placed her hand on his chest.

"Wait," Abby pleaded.

He stiffened and stopped, but didn't turn around.

Abby peered around him at Lucia.

"Why did you do it?" Lucia asked Abby.

The girl looked perplexed. She blinked her eyes. "Do what?"

"Why did you help me?" Lucia asked. "You could have let him kill me."

Abby looked at David and then back at Lucia. "I didn't do it for you. I did it for him. I didn't want him to become something he's not."

Then the girl turned back toward the stairs, her hand firmly in David's, taking him away with her.

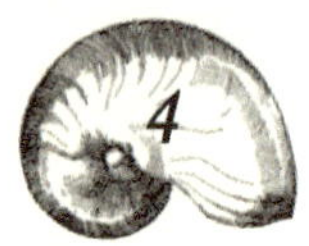

YAKEZ

"I'm sorry," Abby apologized, once the dungeon door was closed.

"For what?" David asked. He looked confused.

"For undermining your authority," she explained. "When you said you would kill Lucia if she betrayed you again, I shouldn't have chastised you. You're my boyfriend, but you're also Solas Beir. I should maintain a united front with you around other people."

"Don't apologize. What I said *was* a little harsh," David admitted.

"Did you mean it?" Abby asked, studying his face. "Would you really kill her?"

David frowned. "I don't want to. I don't want to kill anyone."

"But you would if you had to?"

David stroked her cheek. "I'd do almost anything if it meant protecting you. And the kingdom of course." He sighed. "All right. No more disagreeing in public. We can always disagree in private, I guess."

"We *could* do that." Abby grinned mischievously. "Or we could do other stuff."

David raised an eyebrow and looked her up and down. She

laughed and skipped teasingly out of reach.

He leapt forward, capturing her in his embrace. "What kind of stuff?" he murmured, leaning into her, his lips brushing against her neck.

Abby felt herself quivering as his touch radiated warmth across her skin. Then her stomach rumbled. Loudly.

He froze, and then burst out laughing.

She wriggled out of his arms, giggling. "Sorry. I'm ravenous."

"So I heard. Let's revisit this conversation after we've vanquished the beast living in your stomach," he grinned. "Race you to the kitchen."

On the way, they ran into Cael. David asked him to make arrangements to travel to the Highlands and Yakez.

"Of course, Solas Beir. Eoin spoke with me as well, and I guessed you would desire a visit with the victims' families," Cael reported. "Most of the tasks to prepare for the trip have already been completed. We shall leave in the morning."

David clapped him on the shoulder. "That's why you're the best, Cael," he said. "What would we do without you?"

Cael shrugged modestly and gave Abby a warm smile before returning to his work.

After loading a substantial amount of food onto a large tray, David and Abby had retreated to his chambers to share dinner.

David watched Abby contentedly licking her fingers. They'd managed to score an entire roast chicken, a loaf of bread, a bowl of strawberries, and a carafe of fresh milk.

Abby happily downed a glass of milk. "You have no idea how thirsty I was after I woke from my trance in the Wasteland," she explained, almost apologizing as she wiped her mouth with the back of her hand.

He didn't mind. Nor did he mind that she'd gobbled more than her fair share of the berries, half of the bread, and three-quarters of the chicken. She was starting to get some color back in her cheeks, and the dark circles under her eyes were fading.

David hadn't wanted to say anything, but even though she hadn't lost weight, there were other signs she had started to waste away in her desert prison. To his relief, the food was helping. She seemed much more like her old self.

Abby blotted her mouth with a napkin and tossed it on top of her plate. Then she sighed with contentment and leaned back in her chair, her hands draped lightly over her stomach. "Why is it that food tastes so much better when you're starving?"

David smiled. "The same reason distance makes the heart grow fonder. What we love becomes more precious with the risk of loss."

He stood up and walked over to his wardrobe, retrieving a small, carved box. He knelt on one knee beside her.

Abby sat up straight and stared at him, her eyes growing wide.

"I know you already said yes," he explained, "but it wasn't the most romantic proposal. When we returned from the rainforest, I got this for you, and I meant to give it to you after we got back from our visit with the Eastern Oracle. But then..." He heard his voice catch, and he cleared his throat. "Well, then I thought I'd lost you. Now that you're back, I don't ever want to be away from you again."

David opened the box. Inside was a ring with an oval-cut cerulean jewel.

Abby gasped. Her eyes glistened, threatening tears.

"You are the love of my life, Abigail Brown. Would you do me the honor of becoming my wife?"

She cupped his face in her hands and kissed him. "Yes, I will. I love you, David."

He grinned and slipped the ring on her finger. She kissed him again, and he pulled her off the chair and onto his knee. She slipped her arms tighter around his neck, running her hands through his hair. He cupped the back of her neck, his other hand against the small of her back, crushing her against him as he kissed her.

When he let her go, Abby took a moment to admire the ring. "Is that a sapphire?"

He studied the stone, pleased with his choice. The ring was understated but elegant, a perfect fit for her long, slender fingers. "It's the Cai Terenmare equivalent. It's called naidyris stone, the jewel of the sea. It changes color as the light changes. It can go from a lighter blue to a deeper greenish-blue, just like the ocean." He looked up at her. "Just like your eyes."

She beamed at him, her beautiful eyes lighting up. She was radiant. He tried to memorize everything about her in that moment, so he would never forget a single detail.

"Stay with me tonight," he whispered, brushing her hair away from her forehead. "I swear I'll behave myself, but I don't want to be without you."

"All right," she said softly. Then she giggled and shot him a wicked grin. "Kinda needy though, aren't you?"

He gave her the best annoyed look he could muster while struggling to keep a straight face. "Hmph. Your diplomacy skills need some work, my queen."

The color drained from her face. "Oh, holy crap."

David's eyes widened in alarm. "What?"

She looked panicked. "The queen thing…I'm not responsible enough to be queen. I can't be trusted with an entire kingdom!"

He cocked his head at her and grinned. "Not backing out on me, are you?"

She punched his arm playfully, and he groaned in mock pain. "No, of course not. But seriously, what are you thinking? I don't know how to be queen."

He laughed. "Welcome to my world, love. I still don't know how to be king either. Guess we'll have to figure it out together."

Abby felt nervous settling into her mare's saddle. She had taken pains to select an outfit practical enough for the long ride to Yakez, but elegant enough to befit a queen. She'd been trying to channel Eulalia, if Eulalia ever wore pants, which, Abby realized, she didn't. Looking at her engagement ring, Abby wondered for the hundredth time since waking how she could *ever* step into Eulalia's shoes.

Becoming queen by virtue of marrying David wasn't a surprise, but the responsibility of leading a nation hadn't seemed real the first time he'd proposed. Being with him had been foremost in her mind, and she hadn't thought much about what would follow. Plus, they had been trekking through a rainforest, covered in filth, hungry, and exhausted, not to mention fighting off hordes of nasty, venomous toads and a witchy lamia who thought it a hoot to deprive people of sleep by screaming like a banshee.

Abby had not felt terribly queenly at the time. She had been more focused on survival and on the precious few moments of peace she'd gotten to share with David. In some ways, that had been easier than having to think about the rest of the kingdom.

Now, astride her mount, Abby realized the guards who would be joining them were her personal guards, since she was queen-to-be. She felt her stomach sink.

Surveying all of her subjects-to-be who had gathered at the Caislucis gates to wish them well on their expedition, she felt like a fraud whose shortcomings would be revealed at any moment. As she rode through the town square and out the gates, she glanced down at her ring again, rubbing the naidyris stone like a talisman, hoping she would conduct herself in a manner worthy of these people she'd grown to love.

After waking in David's arms, Abby had slipped away to her own room to change, and then she and David had visited the queen in her chambers to show her the ring before the three of them joined Cael and Marisol for breakfast. Abby's discomfort about eventually becoming queen deepened as she watched Eulalia's handmaidens fuss over her, helping the queen pin up her hair and don her jewelry. Abby tried to envision herself with an entourage of maids to help her dress and aides to assist in everything from correspondence to organizing a royal wedding. It was difficult to see herself in the role.

Although Abby welcomed help fulfilling her responsibilities as queen and didn't mind the idea of not having to do her own cooking and laundry, the concept of someone helping her get dressed seemed ridiculous. She was used to doing things for herself, and valued her privacy. The thought of having someone follow her around her room, serving her every need, was strange. She simply wasn't that kind of girl.

On the other hand, Abby liked the idea of helping people. Even though she was riding to Yakez because something terrible had happened, she was glad to have access to resources that could help the people there. She thought back about visiting Nuren after the Daughters of Mercy had raided the village. It had felt good to be able to help the people there after a tragedy. It was better than sitting idly on the sidelines, wringing her hands. Taking action was the part of being queen she looked forward to.

She was pulled from her reverie by Brarn lighting on her saddle horn. Startled, she almost shooed the raven away, ordering him to fly back home where he'd be safe. Then she thought better of it. Brarn could take care of himself just fine, and had an uncanny knack for sensing things others could not.

By observing his behavior, Abby might uncover some new clue about the Sower.

"I suspected he might be joining us," David said, his horse matching pace with Abby's. "He seems more reluctant than ever to leave your side."

Abby smiled. "I don't mind. If it wasn't for him, I'd still be in a trance, counting sand." She looked around. They were traveling down the main road leading from Caislucis and had almost reached the forest where they would turn north to Yakez. She'd been so deep in thought, she hadn't heard the cheers of farewell from the crowd when they set off or noticed that they were well past the city gates.

Cael was leading the riders, and Fergal was perched on his stallion's regal neck. The tiny green faery looked valiant in his trim waistcoat with a sword the size of a needle at his side. He gripped a few strands of the horse's mane to keep from falling off. Eoin rode after Cael. Abby and David were a few horses behind, in the middle of the group, surrounded by guards.

Directly behind them was a cart laden with supplies for the shepherd's family and the people of Yakez. Eulalia had remained at Caislucis since she and Cael would be taking their vows in a few days, and there was still much to do before the ceremony.

Abby turned her attention to the front of the party. She would have thought Marisol would be riding next to Cael, but her friend was absent. "Where's Sol? I thought she was coming."

David's brow furrowed. "She changed her mind at the last minute. She offered to help Eulalia with the wedding."

"Huh," Abby muttered. "That's odd. I figured she'd want to be in the thick of things. It's not like her to miss out on a chance to explore new territory."

"Normally she *would* be game for an adventure," David agreed. "She and Eulalia have grown close though, and Sol's been a big help to her these last few weeks while I was out cold.

Without Sol, I don't think my mother would have left my bedside, and she had to at some point. She couldn't neglect her duties to constantly watch over me. But I think staying busy also helped Sol keep from obsessing about Jon." He lowered his voice. "And I think after finding Daudi's body in the Barren, Marisol's seen enough death for a good long while."

"Sounds like it was pretty disturbing to see him like that," Abby whispered. She felt a chill run down her spine, and she cringed at the thought of what lay waiting in Yakez.

David nodded. "It was. I'm not looking forward to inspecting the remains of the other victims, but I need to see how they compare to Daudi. You, however, don't have to look."

Abby pushed her dread aside. "I think I probably need to though, to see what we're up against."

David frowned. "I wish you wouldn't. I'm not forbidding you from looking, but I don't want you to see that."

"You don't have to protect me, David."

"I know," he replied, his eyes intense. "But don't you know I want to?"

She smiled. "I know you do."

They crossed under the bower of trees marking the entrance to the North Forest, and the bright morning sunlight dimmed. Brarn launched himself from his perch and flew ahead, just under the twisting canopy of branches. Abby stared after him.

"Where's he going?" David asked.

Abby shrugged. "I have no idea. But he'll come back when he's ready."

Suddenly Abby's mare whinnied, rearing up on her hind legs. Abby gasped in surprise, dropping the reins. She clutched the saddle horn, tightening her thighs against the horse's sides to steady herself. David reached out and grasped the loose reins.

Abby focused her emotions, projecting a sense of calm. The mare settled on all fours, quiet but not quite relaxed. Her ears were flattened and her nostrils flared as though she smelled something foul.

Abby stroked her mare's neck gently. "What is it, Rana?"

She heard an agitated snort to her right and realized David's horse was having a similar reaction to whatever was in the forest.

David studied his uneasy steed for a moment and then handed the reins back to Abby. He drew his sword. Around him, Cael and the guards did the same, staring wild-eyed out into the shadowed trees lining either side of the narrow dirt road.

"Kruorumbrae?" Abby whispered, resting her hand on the hilt of her sword.

David held up his hand. "Wait...listen..." Silently he shifted in his saddle, peering past the wall of trees.

Abby held her breath, waiting. She sensed a change in the air. It was getting heavier. She could feel it pressing down on her shoulders, smothering her. She could even feel it throbbing within her skull; the pressure forced its way into her sinuses and ear canals, making her ears ring. She massaged her ears and worked her jaw, trying to stop the ringing and ease the swollen feeling.

There was something else. An electric tension, the kind of stillness preceding a bolt of lightning. But then the ringing faded and there was no sound—no leaves turning on a breeze, no twittering of birds in the trees, no jabbering squirrels scurrying up the branches, no crack of twigs as unseen animals moved in the underbrush.

There was no sound at all.

Abby rubbed her ears again and felt the pressure dissipate. But she couldn't hear a thing. Panicked, she grabbed David's arm.

He swiveled toward her and, seeing the fear on her face, widened his eyes in alarm. "What's wrong?"

She stared at him and then let out a long breath, relieved.

She shook her head. "For a moment, I couldn't—"

She was cut off by a low rumble, building to a thunderous crescendo. The trees began to tremble and then violently shake.

Behind them was an ear-splitting crack as one of the trees fell across the road, narrowly missing the supply cart. The terrified horses skittered and pranced in a tight group, bumping against one another as they huddled in the middle of the road away from the trees, afraid to continue forward. Abby tried again to project a sense of calm into her mare and the other horses.

A gaping sinkhole opened beside the road. Abby let out a scream, her concentration shattered in an instant as the ground fell away. She couldn't see the bottom—just dirt and pebbles plummeting into darkness.

"Cael!" David shouted. "We've got to get out of here!"

Jerking the reins of his horse, Cael goaded his stallion forward, keeping to the far side of the narrow road to avoid falling into the hole. The other riders followed, single-file, and the cart driver forced his donkeys onward.

As one wheel of the cart skirted the edge of the sinkhole, Abby cringed, waiting for the cart to tip. All around them, she could hear other trees falling.

Cael led the group into a clearing. Here, the trees still trembled slightly, but the ground had stopped shaking. The bright sunlight streaming onto the tall grass was a welcome sight, and Abby felt a sense of relief as it warmed her skin.

Cael took a quick count. "All accounted for, Solas Beir."

David thanked him and looked around. "Is everyone all right?"

Abby, Eoin, and the guards nodded, and the cart driver leapt down to check on his load. "The supplies are secure, Your Majesty," he reported.

"Good. Thank you," David said. He turned back to Cael. "Earthquake?"

Cael, for once, seemed surprised. "I do not know, Solas Beir. I have never experienced anything like that before."

Now David was surprised. "Oh. Well, I have. We had a few of those in Newcastle Beach."

"Yes," Abby chimed in, nodding her head vigorously. "I remember waking up to one in Santa Linda. Stuff fell off the bookshelf in my room. But I've never felt one that strong."

"Nope," David agreed. "Nothing quite like that. Although, supposedly, there was one that bad the night Lucia destroyed the portal at the mansion." He took Abby's hand. "What were you going to say, Abby?"

"What?" Abby stared at him, puzzled.

"Before the shaking started," David explained. "You were about to say something."

"Oh…yeah," she nodded, remembering. "There was this moment, before the shaking, when I couldn't hear anything. I felt pressure in my head and ringing in my ears, and then everything went silent. I thought I'd lost my hearing. Did you experience that?"

David shook his head. "No. I mean, things got quiet—I couldn't hear the usual sounds you hear in the forest—but I didn't feel any pressure or experience any ringing." He looked around. "Did anyone else feel what Abby felt?"

"No, I felt nothing like that," Eoin answered.

The other riders shook their heads.

Abby frowned, scanning the sky. "I wonder if Brarn knew what was coming and that's why he took off. The horses certainly seemed to sense something was wrong."

"Yes," Cael agreed. "I believe all the animals have fled this part of the forest."

"The faeries too," Fergal observed. "I can sense when my kin are near, and I can tell you, they are nowhere near here."

"What do you think happened to them?" David asked.

"Nothing good, I am certain," Fergal grimaced.

Abby's eyes widened in alarm. "Do you think the Blood Shadows took them?"

Fergal furrowed his brow, considering. "Faeryfolk share a strong bond. I would have sensed if they had been attacked. But there is nothing. They have simply vanished. But we faeries also have a strong connection to animals. If the forest animals sensed danger and fled, the faeryfolk around here would take that as a cue to follow. Whatever it was that caused the ground to shake must have frightened them off."

"So what *was* that then?" Abby asked. "If it wasn't an earthquake?"

"I don't know," David replied, "but I say we don't stick around to find out. Let's get to Yakez."

The village of Yakez was even smaller than David thought it would be. There was a smattering of stone huts with thatched roofs and colorful shutters to guard against winter storms. The people themselves were dressed less colorfully, the men in simple grey pants and tunics, the women in long, plain dresses. Fishing boats lined the dock at the tiny marina. A few boats drifted out beyond the rock monoliths offshore, but most of the people seemed occupied in mending nets.

Eoin acted as spokesperson, introducing David to the men and women at the dock. Yakez was governed by an elected council of tradespeople, and all but the youngest members of the village voted on political matters. The people seemed to lack many of the material possessions taken for granted at Caislucis, but Yakez was clearly a close-knit, hardworking community.

Eoin introduced David to the victim's eldest daughter, Aine.

"I am sorry about your father," David said.

The young woman nodded her head slightly in

acknowledgement, but didn't make eye contact. Instead, she stared vacantly off into the distance, as though her grief had overtaken her mind. Abby put her arm around the girl.

Eoin measured the young woman with a knowing look. "This has been exceedingly difficult for Aine, not just because she lost her father, but because now she must provide for herself and her younger sister and brother," he explained.

"I lost my parents too," David said to the girl. "If it's all right with you, Aine, I'd like to pay my respects to your father. I've also brought supplies to help care for you and your family. I'm sorry I can't do more."

The girl looked up briefly to meet his gaze, her hands nervously bunching the fabric of her long dress. "Thank you, Solas Beir."

Eoin nodded his thanks to David, and then took Aine's arm, guiding her away to look at the supply cart.

David felt a sense of helplessness as he watched them walk away, haunted by the nagging feeling that he had failed yet another person. *No,* he thought angrily, pushing away the guilt gnawing at his insides. *This is Tierney's doing. He's the one who unleashed the Sower on these people.* Strengthening his resolve, he turned and entered the hut to view the body. Abby and Cael followed.

The remains looked strikingly similar to those of the courtesan he and Cael had found in the Barren: a mummified corpse, drained of its bodily fluids. On the man's forearm, David could make out a semi-circle of red dots where the victim had been bitten.

The difference was that instead of being left to bake under a desert sun, this body had been found on the coast. The moist sea air had hastened the decomposition of the body, sprouting a fine growth of mold in the crevices of the man's leathered skin and adding yet another layer to the stench of death.

Abby retched and covered her nose and mouth.

David placed his hand on the small of her back. "You okay?"

She nodded and swallowed, keeping her nose covered and breathing shallowly through her mouth. "Is this what Daudi looked like when you found him?"

"Pretty much." David exchanged a grim look with Cael. "It's the same as before."

"Whatever is doing this may now be in the sea. It will be hard to find," Cael said.

"If it is the Sower, and his mother was the old Western Oracle, it makes sense he'd be at home in the water," Abby reasoned. "Maybe Nerine can help us."

"I can help you."

The three investigators turned to see Eoin standing in the doorway, a grim, determined look on his face as he stared at the corpse.

"How?" asked David.

"I have been talking with the fishermen. They seem to be having trouble catching fish of late," Eoin replied.

David raised his eyebrows. "You don't think..."

Eoin nodded. "I do. I think the fish have vanished. Just like the faeries and the forest animals."

Abby's mouth dropped open. "So what do we do?"

Eoin looked at her. "One of us is going to have to get in the water to see if my suspicions are valid."

"I'll go," David said, moving toward the door.

Placing his hand on David's arm, Eoin stopped him. "No, Solas Beir. This is my village. I need to know what is happening to it." He smiled weakly. "And I think you will find I am better suited to the water than you are."

David looked at Eoin questioningly. "What if you encounter the Sower down there? He could kill you."

"The life force of Yakez is fishing. If I do not find out what is happening, my people will suffer," Eoin explained. "Is my life worth more than theirs?"

The Sower watched the Solas Beir and his friends conversing. He was so close, and yet none of them sensed his presence, not even the c'aislingaer. He smiled to himself. He was tempted, just for a moment, to leave his hiding place and move closer, to see if he could get within striking distance of the young king, to fill him with his venom. To watch his friends scurry as they tried in vain to save him. But he dared not. He couldn't risk discovery just yet. Not until he was finished sowing.

Abby stood anxiously on the wooden dock with Fergal perched on her shoulder. After walking to the marina, Eoin had transformed into his spirit animal. As a lean, muscular sea lion, he effortlessly slipped off the dock, vanishing beneath the surface of the dark green water in the bay.

He'd been down there a long time. *Too long,* Abby thought.

"Do not fret, my lady," Fergal said, picking up on her nervous energy. "Eoin will be fine. Yakez is his home, after all."

Abby forced a smile, her face pinched. "I know, Fergal. I just wish I could see what's happening down there."

She wasn't the only one waiting anxiously. David had taken to pacing back and forth along the dock, staring intently at the murky liquid. Visibility was limited to the first few feet—after that, there was only blackness.

Abby started at the sound of something breaking the surface and whipped her head to look down the length of the dock. Near the pilings, she saw a shadowy form bobbing. Then it disappeared beneath the sea again.

David and Cael had seen it too and hurried down the dock, swords drawn.

A figure shot up from the dark water, landing with a thump on the deck in front of them.

"Eoin?" David asked, hesitantly.

The sea lion shuddered, his brown fur dissolving into the shape of a man. Eoin clambered to his feet, shaking himself off. He eyed David and Cael. "Startled you, did I?"

David sheathed his sword sheepishly. "Sorry."

"My fault," Eoin panted. "I had to dive deep to get enough speed to make it onto the dock. It is higher than it looks from up here."

"What did you find?" David asked.

"Absolutely nothing," Eoin spat. "No sign of the Sower and no clue as to where the fish have gone. I circled the entire bay. It is void of life."

Cael put his hand on Eoin's shoulder. "You need not worry about the people of Yakez going hungry, my friend. I am sure the supplies we brought will hold them for a while."

Eoin nodded, looking toward the village. "I should advise them to ration."

"We'll provide more food," David assured him, "and we'll figure out what's going on. I'll send word to Nerine when we return to Caislucis."

"Thank you, Solas Beir," Eoin replied. "Perhaps the answers we seek lie in the Highlands with the second victim."

But they didn't. Another day of riding only led to the confirmation that the shepherd had died of the same causes as the fisherman from Yakez. And to more frustration. Abby could feel it coming in waves off of David and the others—those same feelings of bewilderment and helplessness she felt from having no answers and much too little in the way of consolation for the victims' families.

There were no witnesses to the Highlands attack, although

some of the shepherds reported restlessness among their domestic animals during the night before the victim was discovered at first morning's light. David vowed to find the culprit and send supplies. Other than that, not much could be done, and the party rode mostly in silence during the long journey home.

On the upside, Abby noted that Eoin seemed to have newfound respect for his king. She looked at Eoin, who was riding alongside David while discussing the situation. The disdain she'd seen on Eoin's face the day she'd returned from the Wasteland had disappeared.

David sighed. "I just wish I could do more to help them. I can't return those men to their families." His shoulders were bunched as though he were carrying a heavy load. Abby understood. She felt the same load on her shoulders, the same desperation to find answers.

"What you did is more than past Solas Beirs would have done," Eoin replied. "Thank you."

Upon returning to Caislucis, David sent word to Nerine as promised, and then Abby noticed that the somber mood surrounding the topic of the Sower was temporarily lifted as the focus shifted to the royal wedding.

The small town surrounding the castle surged with visitors. Wedding guests converged from the North and South Forests, the Highlands, and the Great Plains. With the festivities, Abby might have forgotten about the Sower entirely were it not for the absence of faeries and animals in the woods around Caislucis.

Brarn, at least, had returned, but he wasn't the same. When he was in her room, the raven restlessly flitted back and forth from his iron perch to the wooden chair next to her bed.

Thinking he needed more room to fly, she kept the door to her balcony wide open, but Brarn stayed close to home, never soaring beyond the castle walls. After a few days, he even stopped his short flights over the enclosed courtyard below her room, refusing to venture beyond the confines of her marble balcony.

Abby stared down at the courtyard, where servants were busy setting up chairs and draping flower garlands for the wedding. She visually traced the curves of the nautilus outlined by silver tiles nestled among the pavers of the courtyard, taking comfort in the familiar, spiraled shape of the Sign of the Throne.

Brarn was perched beside her, looking rather morose for a bird. She reached over to stroke his feathers, and he gave her a halfhearted nod before turning his attention to her chamber door.

Abby heard a soft knocking, and left the raven to answer the door. She opened her door to find the corridor empty. Well, almost empty. She heard someone clear their throat.

"Down here, my lady," Fergal called.

She glanced down. "Oh! I'm sorry, Fergal. Please, come in."

"I beg your pardon, lady," Fergal said, stepping over the threshold, "but I thought perhaps, since you are a c'aislingaer..." He looked up at her, shifting his weight uncomfortably.

Abby knelt down and held out her palm. "What is it, Fergal?"

The green faery hesitantly stepped onto her palm, and she lifted him up to eye level.

"This is a difficult thing for me to admit," he replied, "seeing as how I pride myself on my valor."

Abby tilted her head to one side, studying him. "You are one of the bravest people I know."

Fergal smiled. "Thank you for saying so. I must confess, however, that since our journey to Yakez, I have been quite afraid."

Abby studied his face. "Of the Sower?"

"Of that. Of...well, of everything. I have, these past nights, been plagued by nightmares, and I find myself easily startled. It is as if some unnamed fear has settled over me. I have not been myself. I thought perhaps you, being a cai aislingstraid, might understand. Have you ever been afraid?"

Abby barked out a laugh.

Fergal eyed her, clearly taken aback.

"I'm sorry, Fergal. I'm not laughing at you, I promise," Abby explained. "Your question struck me as funny because I'm afraid *most* of the time. Now more than ever."

"What frightens you?"

Abby sighed. "The real question is, what doesn't frighten me? I have nightmares too, but I'm also freaked out about the Sower and scared about the war with Tierney. Not to mention, I'm terrified that when I become queen, I'll make horrible mistakes that end up getting people killed." She let out a breath, feeling a sense of relief at being able to voice her fears.

Fergal looked puzzled. "But you always seem fearless to me."

Abby laughed again. "It's an act, believe me." She smiled. "But we were talking about you. What do you think triggered your nightmares?"

Fergal was silent a moment, considering her question. "The earth shaking, I think. Ever since that moment, I have felt unsettled. It is not outright terror, but a subtle, more insidious fear. I feel almost ill from fright."

Abby looked over at Brarn, who was watching them with ebony, gold-ringed eyes. "You know, Brarn has not been himself either since that trip. I wondered if he was sick. Maybe he's afraid too."

Fergal studied Brarn and nodded. "Perhaps."

"The two of you share a bond," Abby said. "Maybe you and Brarn are picking up on something the rest of us can't feel. You did say that the forest animals and faeryfolk could sense danger, and that's why they left."

Fergal turned back to her. "Indeed I did. Perhaps," he said softly, "we should consider leaving as well."

Abby shook her head. "David would never abandon Caislucis. There are too many people relying on him. And then there's the wedding—Eulalia and Cael have waited so long to be together..."

"Of course. Apologies, my dear lady." Fergal hung his head in shame. "I spoke out of cowardice. But I cannot help but feel that the Solas Beir is in terrible danger."

"It's all right, Fergal," Abby replied, lifting his chin with her finger. "There's no need to apologize. I don't disagree with you, and I'm sorry if what I said sounded harsh. I think you're right. David *is* in danger. I can feel it too." She sat in a chair and placed her hand on the low table in front of her so Fergal could step down from her palm and stand on the table. "I think maybe we need a plan B."

Fergal looked up at her. "I beg your pardon?"

"The wedding is tomorrow. There's no way David would consider leaving with all the festivities," Abby explained, rubbing her temples. Her head had started to throb. "Cael has taken extra precautions with the guards for the safety of the guests—but what if that's not enough? I think we need to be ready for anything."

Fergal nodded. "I quite agree. What do you suggest we do?"

Abby thought about it. "We prepare for the unexpected. If something terrible happens, our first responsibility is to get the Solas Beir to safety."

"I could hide a cache of weapons from the armory," Fergal suggested. "Just in case we need to defend ourselves or make a quick escape."

Abby nodded. "That's a good idea. I don't want to alarm

David or create more stress for Cael and Eulalia on their big day, but I think having a few extra people watching for trouble is a smart idea. I'll talk to Marisol and Erela." She smiled. "The four of us will make a formidable team."

Fergal grinned, and drew his tiny sword with a flourish. "That we shall. Woe to the enemy who crosses our path."

Abby chuckled. "Woe indeed."

Fergal sheathed his sword and bowed gracefully. "Thank you, my lady."

"You are quite welcome," Abby grinned.

Fergal hopped down from the table to head for the door and then stopped, looking up at her. "You need not fear ruling Cai Terenmare. From what I have witnessed, you will make wise decisions. I, for one, shall be honored to call you queen."

Abby had to choke back a wave of emotion before she could respond. "Thank you, Fergal. That means the world to me."

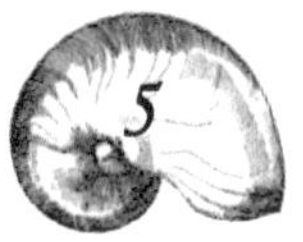

STRIFE

Jon's stomach growled. It was difficult to keep track of time in the unending blackness of his cell. He was fairly certain it had been two days since his last meal—more broth and a measly heel of bread that he and Hedeon had split. The guards had been visiting the dungeon less and less often. Twice a day, once a day, and then, finally, not at all.

Jon felt faint from hunger and sick at the thought that he and Hedeon would likely starve down here, abandoned. He was thirsty too, but he'd managed to catch a little moisture on his tongue from a persistent drip filtering through a crack in the ceiling. The water tasted foul, leaking from who knew where, but he was desperate. He hoped it wasn't sewage. He prayed it wouldn't kill him. His intestines twisted in his abdomen when he remembered stories he'd heard about bacteria in bad water and people getting diarrhea. He breathed out and tried to relax. Slowly, the cramp in his side eased. Now was not the time to become a hypochondriac.

When he'd first found himself locked in the dark, Jon had been sure the sound of dripping water echoing off the stone walls would drive him mad. Now he found the noise reassuring and dreaded the moment it would stop.

All other sound had ceased. No longer could he hear

footsteps from the floors above or voices filtering through the heavy wooden door to the dungeon. The silence was terrifying.

Something had happened in the City of the Eastern Oracle, something significant enough to draw the guards from their posts. At first, Jon had hoped that meant David had brought the fight to the city, that he'd soon see the faces of his friends when they came to rescue him. But if the battle had begun, Jon would have heard noise.

The armory was just outside the dungeon. He'd gotten an eyeful of the city's weapons before he'd been half escorted, half dragged into this dank hole. Jon had visited the armory at Caislucis many times. War would mean the metallic clang of weapons being carried, the whirring of a grindstone honing the edges of swords, and the restless talk of soldiers preparing to shed blood. But there was nothing, no sound except for *drip, drip, drip*.

Jon had tried to keep his sanity by maintaining a semblance of a daily routine: walking around the cell, stretching, doing push-ups and sit-ups to break up the long periods of sitting and waiting. Now he was so hungry, it seemed wise to conserve his energy since he didn't know when—or if—he would get to eat again.

Hedeon spent most of his time sleeping, trying to heal. Jon had no idea how quickly Hedeon's bruises were fading, but the man assured Jon he was getting better each day, and hoped he would soon be strong enough to take on his animal form. Jon hoped that happened before they both starved.

Jon had just dozed off when he was awakened by light pouring into the long corridor between the cells of the dungeon. He shielded his eyes against the harshness of it. After being in the dark for so long, he found that the brightness of the torchlight made his eyes sting and water.

He could hear someone entering the prison, cautiously navigating the steps. Hope rose in his chest. Which of his friends had finally found him? *David? Abby? Cael? Maybe Marisol?* He missed her most. It had almost killed him to leave her on the edge of the Barren, to watch tears streak down her face after the last kiss they shared. If it was her, he'd scoop her up in his arms and shatter the record for world's longest kiss, just to make up for the last one.

He leapt to his feet and crossed over to the cell door, craning his neck to catch a sideways glimpse at who was coming to rescue him.

A wave of nausea washed over him when he recognized who it was. The footsteps echoing in the corridor didn't belong to a friend coming to break him out of jail. They belonged to a monster, coming to break *him*.

Abby watched the queen's handmaidens place her delicate silver tiara on her head and then weave brightly colored jewels into her hair. Eulalia was arrayed in a wedding gown with all the colors of a Joseph's coat rose: bright red and fuchsia tones tapering to shades of coral and golden yellow. The full skirt blossomed outward like shimmering, silky petals. The overall effect was cheerful, like the promise of warm spring days after a hard winter.

After hearing about Fergal's fears, Abby had been feeling as though a weight had settled on her shoulders. She found herself on edge, anxious about the monster who had killed the men in Yakez and the Highlands, wishing she could foresee where he would strike next. But her dreams betrayed no clues as to the creature's plans or whereabouts.

Seeing Eulalia so happy in her brightly colored gown, however, was a welcome reprieve from Abby's worries, like a breath of the fresh sea air wafting in from the open window of the queen's bedchamber.

The wedding customs of Cai Terenmare were different from those Abby had grown up with in Santa Linda. Not only was the event to be more colorful, but it also included pastoral elements originating from the farming and shepherding communities that surrounded Caislucis.

The bride was preceded by an entourage of "sowers," a chosen few important to the bride and groom who readied the path she would walk by casting a mix of seeds and wildflower petals on the ground. This ritual represented the hopes of the community for the couple's joyous union and the continued prosperity of their family and friends. The irony that wedding attendants were called sowers was not lost on Abby, but she knew it was an honor that she was selected as one—and the seeds she was to sow were much less nefarious than those of the Sower's prophecy. Her basket of seeds and petals was sitting at her feet next to her chair in the queen's parlor.

Marisol was standing by the parlor's oriel window, gazing out at the Western Sea through the beveled diamonds of the glass. She and Abby were identically dressed, wearing long, flowing gowns in fuchsia, accented in orange and yellow. The colors complemented the queen's dress, but the gowns were not as elaborately decorated.

Abby and Marisol were to serve as attendants for Eulalia, and, as was customary, David would sow with them before joining Cael up front to serve as the Cai Terenmare equivalent of a best man. Originally, both David and Jon were going to stand up for Cael, but with Jon held captive, his place in the wedding was vacant.

Abby felt a dull ache in her chest. She wondered if Jon was okay and worried that she'd never see her best friend again. It was as if there were an ever-present hole in her heart.

She studied Marisol. In some ways, the loss had to be worse for her, with Jon finally admitting his love for her, only to be snatched away. Then there was Marisol's guilt. Marisol had confided to Abby that the reason Jon was imprisoned was because he'd wanted to save her, and she felt terrible about it. She was proud of him, but it didn't ease her guilt.

Abby saw a tear roll down Marisol's cheek and guessed she was thinking about Jon too. She stood and put her arm around her friend's shoulders.

Marisol brushed away her tears and let out a long breath. She turned to Abby and gave her a bittersweet smile. "I know this is supposed to be a happy day. But I miss him so much."

"I do too," Abby said, holding Marisol tighter.

Marisol leaned her head on Abby's shoulder. "It's just been so frustrating. We haven't even *tried* to rescue him. I know part of it was waiting for David to recover, and then there was the news about the Sower's new victims, but this *wedding*..." She looked over at Eulalia, surrounded by her handmaids, and lowered her voice. "I'm so happy for Eulalia and Cael, but celebrating while Jon's still out there somewhere feels wrong." She sighed.

"I know," Abby whispered. "It's been hard. There's a void in our lives without him."

Marisol nodded. "It's terrible to say—but I can't help feeling like if he were one of *them,* they'd be making more of an effort. But he's just a human, so...you know, not a big loss."

"I don't think Cael feels that way," Abby countered. "He and Jon grew close. He cares about him the way he does about all of us."

"I know." Marisol looked out the window. "Eulalia has been good to me too, including me in everything. I'm being unfair. But still, it's how I feel."

"I still feel like an outsider sometimes too," Abby admitted.

Marisol turned to stare at her, shocked. "But you're *so* not. I mean—you're going to be queen someday."

Abby shrugged. "I'm still human."

"Not quite," Marisol argued. "You're a c'aislingaer, like

Eulalia, and you can shape-shift. Jon and I—we're just regular human beings. We don't have any superpowers. And that's exactly my point. Why would these people try to rescue a regular human? What value does Jon hold for them?"

"He has value to *me*," Abby assured her. "We'll get him back. I promise."

Marisol nodded solemnly and then turned to stare out the window again. "Look," she said, pointing at the ocean.

A large wave was rolling onto shore, its white crest sparkling with light. As it began to break and touch the sand, a woman with long white hair appeared, stepping out from the curl of the wave. She wore a sweeping silver gown that was completely dry.

"Nerine," Abby murmured, smiling. She'd never witnessed the mermaid come ashore. It was a mesmerizing sight.

The new Western Oracle turned back to the wave, which stood as still as if it were frozen in time. She reached into the curve of the water to grasp someone's hand. A striking man emerged, his hair the same color as Nerine's, his aqua-colored tunic and pants dry as her dress. She favored him with a smile, and he leaned down to kiss her cheek. Then he raised his head, looking up to the window as if aware of Abby's gaze. His stare was so piercing, she found she couldn't look away.

"Who is *that*?" Marisol breathed, her eyes wide.

"I have no idea," Abby murmured.

Breaking eye contact, the man escorted Nerine up the beach toward the carved stone stairs leading to the castle. All along the beach, more waves rolled in, revealing merpeople coming ashore as they broke.

Abby heard a knock at the door behind her and turned to see David peeking hesitantly through the narrow opening. "Okay if I come in?"

"Yes, everybody's decent," she replied with a sly smile.

"Whew." He wiped his brow dramatically. "Didn't know

what I was walking into." He peered into the queen's chamber and cringed at the hive of activity. He turned back to Abby and Marisol. "You two look beautiful."

Marisol smiled. "Thanks."

Abby kissed David's cheek and then took a step back to take in his wedding attire. He looked handsome wearing his diadem, the Sign of the Throne, and a traditional long-sleeved Cai Terenmare tunic made of scarlet silk and embellished with embroidery in colors that complemented the girls' gowns. His black pants and boots were more subdued.

Abby grinned. "You don't look too shabby yourself."

David laughed. "Thanks, I think. So, is my mother almost ready? The guests have all arrived."

"I think her maids are just about finished with her," Abby replied. "Apparently getting ready for a Cai Terenmare wedding is a long and complicated process."

David brushed his fingers against Abby's cheek. "Hmm...I'll have to keep that in mind when it's our turn. But if you take this long getting ready, I'll worry you changed your mind."

Abby leaned into his touch. "Never. I'll be there."

David smiled. "I'll hold you to that. I'd better get back to the courtyard. I'm sure Cael's getting antsy."

Abby giggled. "Cael, nervous? I don't believe it. The man has slain how many terrifying monsters?"

"True, but the dude's never gotten married before. That's an entirely different kind of terrifying." David's eyes were wide with mock horror.

Marisol covered her mouth with her hand to hold in her laughter. Abby didn't even try—she burst out laughing. David grinned and headed toward the door.

"Wait," Abby called. "Don't forget your basket." She retrieved a basket sitting next to hers and Marisol's.

David stopped, eyeing the delicately woven basket with real horror. "*Awesome*. Speaking of terrifying..." He sighed and took the basket from Abby. "Well, I guess if I have to be a flower girl, I'm at least in good company."

Abby and Marisol giggled, and then Abby shoved him toward the door. "Get out of here. See you downstairs."

Malden's twisted grin stretched sickeningly wide across his ruined face, and his glowing red eyes were full of malice. In his goblin form, he stealthily descended the dungeon stairs.

Silently, Jon knelt down and shook Hedeon awake. The former captain of the guard opened his eyes just as Malden reached the cell door.

Startled, Hedeon rolled onto his knees, away from the bars. In the torchlight, Jon could see that Hedeon looked much better than he had the last time Jon saw him, when the knight was thrown into their shared cage after days of torture. His facial features were actually distinguishable, no longer the swollen, mangled mass of pain they were before. Jon only hoped Hedeon was strong enough to help him fight Malden. They had no weapons.

Jon thought back to his very first confrontation with this monster at the Buchans' house in Newcastle Beach. What he wouldn't give now for a simple cylinder of table salt to pour over the beast's head. Or even a silver-plated butter knife.

Malden chuckled as he held up a set of keys, jingling them in triumph. Jon stepped backward into the cell and slipped his arms around Hedeon, tugging the knight to his feet.

"You knew it would come to this eventually, boy," Malden purred.

"Where's Lucia?" Jon asked, cursing to himself when he heard his dry voice crack from hunger, thirst, and terror. He couldn't afford to show weakness. Not now.

Malden's sadistic grin stretched wider, impossible as that

seemed. Jon imagined Malden's skull connected to his jaw by a hinge, flipping backward to open wide like a great white shark's, revealing rows of needlelike teeth, right before they sank into his flesh. *All the better to eat you, my precious little boy,* Jon thought.

"Ding-a-lingy-dong, that witch is dead," Malden sang gleefully. "*Everyone* is dead or long, long gone. There's no one left to hear you scream."

"Where are the guards?" Hedeon demanded, his voice surprisingly strong and imbued with a tone of authority.

Malden's mad eyes shifted from Jon to Hedeon. He fixed his gaze on the knight. Smiling, he inserted the key in the lock.

"What do you mean, everyone's dead or gone?" Jon asked, hoping he could keep the imp talking until he could think of a way to subdue him. "What happened out there?"

Malden returned his gaze to Jon and then turned the key. The cell door swung open, groaning on rusty hinges. "The Sower happened. My master unleashed a plague upon the world, and now all of Cai Terenmare will burn, baby, burn." He giggled to himself and sniffed the air. "But the City of the Eastern Oracle will burn *first*."

Jon looked toward the door of the dungeon. Smoke was wafting down the steps and into the corridor. *Fantastic.* There were just no good options for dying here. He'd been worried about starving to death. Now he was either going to be mauled and eaten, or burned alive. Neither fate was terribly enticing.

Malden took a step inside the cell, taking his sweet time, obviously savoring his victory. He was going to make good on his promise to punish Jon for the loss of Marisol, his *dulce*. Jon didn't regret keeping Marisol away from this monstrous thing, but he couldn't help but wince at being on the receiving end of his wrath.

The goblin boy winked at Jon and then, twitching, hunched forward, bracing his hands on his knees. The transformation was horrifying. Malden's skin began to stretch, his spine protruding as his flesh and bones twisted into a different shape. The Kruorumbrae lifted his head, his scarlet eyes glaring with hate as his face lengthened, developing into a feline muzzle that was somehow still humanoid. His long, yellow fingernails grew into talons. Spikes of thick, black hair began to sprout from his skin in oily clumps, leaving grotesque bald patches that filled in more slowly. The monster arched his back and stretched his muscles with a catlike yowl of pleasure and pain.

Jon trembled. He couldn't help it. He wanted so badly to be brave, but he couldn't stop the tremors shaking his body. He hated himself for it because he knew Malden was deliberately dragging out his transformation, forcing Jon to witness every grisly detail of the change.

The wretch could have shifted his form in an instant, simply gotten it over with, and taken Jon's head off with one swipe of those nasty claws. But no. That wasn't Malden's style. He fed on fear, and he was going to milk Jon of every ounce of terror, lapping up Jon's fright like sweet cream before finally ending him. This display of dominance would only be the beginning of the horrors to come.

Jon felt his knees shaking and feared they would buckle beneath him. He did not want to be on the ground, vulnerable, in front of this beast. He reached over, placing his hand on Hedeon's arm for support. To his surprise, the knight was trembling too—but not with fear, Jon realized.

Hedeon's brows were knit together in concentration, his eyes closed. He too was changing. Jon removed his hand from Hedeon's arm and took another step toward the back wall of the cell. If Hedeon was successful, this small cage was about to get really cramped, really fast.

Abby and Marisol waited with David just inside the banquet hall, peeking out at the rounded courtyard. At the end of a path lined with flowers was a raised platform encircled with more flowers. Cael and Obelia were already waiting at the top. Cael did look a little nervous, although Abby could tell he was trying not to show it. He was dressed in an outfit similar to David's, but his tunic mirrored the queen's colors and was more embellished.

Guests sat in a circle around the dais. Dignitaries like the new Western Oracle and the court council members sat in the innermost circle. Abby could see the white-haired man from the beach sitting next to the mermaid princess, and behind them were other guests from Nerine's undersea kingdom.

Nerine was the only oracle present, but Abby wasn't surprised. Although the Northern and Southern Oracles had been invited, travel to Caislucis wasn't easy, and they were on high alert because of the Sower. Their time was better spent preparing for war than attending a social event, even if it was the wedding of the dowager queen to a friend they respected. As for the Eastern Oracle, after his confrontation with David and refusal to become an ally, it came as no shock that he wasn't invited.

Unlike David's coronation, where everyone wore white, the wedding guests were arrayed in a riot of color. Even Erela, who always wore white, had traded her usual Grecian-type gown for a fitted, scarlet dress that was a stark contrast to her billowing wings.

Abby surveyed the guests, looking for familiar faces. Some of them, like Gorman and Fergal, Abby knew well. Other guests she had never met, and that worried her. She hoped Cael's soldiers had been thorough in ensuring the safety of the royal family and their visitors.

It also alarmed her that there was not a faery in sight, other than Fergal. She'd hoped the wedding festivities would entice them out of hiding, providing a sense of normalcy. The faeryfolk always turned out in droves for celebrations. It felt like a bad omen not to have them present.

Abby glanced across the courtyard to her balcony, expecting to see Brarn perched there, but he too was hiding. He'd looked morose again that morning, moping about, refusing to eat.

As the music started, Abby pushed her morbid thoughts aside. She looked up to see David watching her with concern in his eyes. She forced a smile, and he reached down to brush a stray curl off her forehead.

David stroked her cheek, and then he turned to Eulalia. "Ready?"

Jon bit back a shout of relief as he saw Hedeon's fingers curl into paws, long bear claws erupting from them. A growl thundered from deep within the knight's chest, and then he exploded into a mass of dark brown fur.

Malden scowled and swiped at Jon, but the grizzly bear knocked him back, shoving him into the iron bars of the cell across the corridor. Jon heard Malden's skull ricochet off them with a satisfying clang.

Shaking off the blow, Malden leapt through the air, raked his claws across Hedeon's chest, and sank his teeth into the bear's shoulder. The bear grimaced and then lowered his shoulder to drive his attacker into the bars again.

When Malden's head bounced against the bars a second time, his jaws went slack, and Hedeon used his weight and momentum to spin and toss Malden into the open cell, frighteningly close to Jon, who shut his gaping mouth and leapt to the side.

Jon pressed himself against the wall and then slipped

around the unconscious beast and out the cell door. In the corridor, the bear was hunched forward, blood dripping from his shoulder. He was breathing hard.

Jon took the opportunity to slam the cell door shut, locking Malden inside using the key he'd left dangling in the lock before shoving the key ring into his pocket. "That'll hold him, won't it?"

"I hope so," Hedeon growled. He dissolved into a more human-looking shape, but the wounds on his chest and shoulder remained.

"What now?" Jon asked, lifting his shirt to cover his nose and mouth, a thin barrier against the thickening smoke.

"Now we get out of here before the whole palace burns." Hedeon glanced back into the cell. "May he burn with it."

The smoke was worse in the armory. Above him, Jon could hear the creak of wooden ceiling beams crackling with flames. He pressed his shirt tighter over the lower half of his face, holding it in place with one hand while rubbing his eyes with the other. The smoke stung, making them tear up.

Hedeon grabbed a leather sack and threw it to Jon. "Quick as you can—fill that with whatever weapons you can find." He snatched a sword propped near the dungeon door and shoved it in his own bag before hiking up his own shirt to shield his face from the smoke.

Jon stifled a cough and looked around. There weren't many weapons left. Several swords, a mace, two bows with a quiver of arrows each, and a handful of daggers. Clearly the place had been ransacked before whatever it was that had led the guards to vacate the palace.

"I think that's it," Jon started. Then he noticed Hedeon standing silently over a body collapsed in the corner of the room. Hesitantly, he stepped closer for a better look.

"Garvan," Hedeon murmured. The dead man's eyes were still open, the look frozen on his decomposing face one of surprise. He had been run through with a sword. Reverently,

Hedeon reached over and closed the man's eyelids.

Behind them, one of the ceiling beams gave way, crashing to the floor.

Jon turned to see sparks drifting lazily up into the haze of smoke. "We have to go."

Hedeon nodded. "Come. There is nothing we can do for him now." He turned and charged up the spiraling stone staircase leading to freedom.

Eulalia was beaming. "Yes, I am ready."

Her handmaids fluffed out her train one last time, and she nodded for David to begin the procession.

Abby and Marisol flanked David as they walked the path to the dais, tossing seeds and petals. Abby found herself smiling, her heart lifted by the music and the warm smiles of the wedding guests.

The multitude of faces became a blur—until her gaze fell on the white-haired man sitting next to Nerine. As before, his eyes bored through her, and his expression was unreadable. He kept eye contact as she approached him. Then he blinked and turned with everyone else to see the bride.

Eulalia looked radiant floating down the aisle, and Cael looked happier than Abby had ever seen him. Gone was the stoic mask he wore as a soldier. He was simply a man gazing upon the love of his life, his heart open and unguarded. As his bride stepped up onto the dais, he took her hands in his.

Obelia led the ceremony. "Today we bear witness to the joining of two souls, forever bound by their love: Cael, first knight of Caislucis, and Eulalia, dowager queen of Cai Terenmare. Cael, will you speak your vows?"

"I will," Cael smiled. "Eulalia, I have loved you since we were children. Our lives took different paths, but you were ever in my thoughts, and you always will be. You are my breath, my heart, my life. I promise you that I will always love you, this day and all my days, in this world and in the worlds beyond." With that, he slipped a delicate silver ring onto her finger.

Obelia nodded and smiled, her eyes bright with approval. "And Eulalia? Will you speak your vows?"

Eulalia gave Cael a beautiful smile. "I will. Cael, my dear heart, you are my steadfast star, constant, faithful. Your love unfailingly guides me back to you. You fill my heart with love and light. I promise you that I will always love you, this day and all my days, in this world and in the worlds beyond." She took his hand and slipped a silver band on his finger.

Cael and Eulalia turned to Obelia, who recited, "With vows spoken, you are bound in the Light, husband and wife. Cael, you may kiss your bride."

Cael kissed Eulalia tenderly as their friends cheered. When they turned to face their guests, Obelia presented them, and the audience applauded.

It struck Abby as funny that, after months of preparation, the ceremony was over that quickly. It was the first wedding Abby had actively been a part of—she had never been a bridesmaid back home in Santa Linda—so she had little to compare it to. And she barely remembered her mom's younger cousin's wedding that she attended when she was eight. Abby wondered what her own ceremony would be like.

She looked up to find David holding out his arm to her, and she took it. Marisol stood on his other side. They followed Cael and Eulalia back up the aisle and into the banquet hall. This, Abby could see, was why it had taken so long to plan the wedding.

The décor was exquisite. Colorful silken tablecloths were spread over the tables, with candles and flowers covering every spare inch not taken up by food and place settings. Silken banners and flowers hung between arches and coiled around stone columns. It was a feast for the senses: bright colors, festive music, and the mouth-watering smell of food.

But before they could eat, the traditional Cai Terenmare greetings had to be observed, similar to a receiving line at a human wedding, except that instead of shaking hands, each guest wished the bride and groom well and kissed their hands before moving down the line to kiss the hands of the attendants.

It felt odd being touched by so many people, but not entirely unpleasant. Most of the guests expressed congratulations to David for his mother's marriage, saying the union had been long in coming, and Eulalia and Cael's happiness was well deserved. When David introduced Abby as his betrothed, she was showered with praise and good wishes.

Every trace of the dread she'd felt before the wedding faded—until Abby saw the white-haired man who had come with Nerine. She found herself sneaking glimpses of him as he greeted Cael and Eulalia. He seemed to adore the Western Oracle, doting on her with a smile on his handsome face. But his grey eyes were cold.

In between greeting guests, Abby studied the bride and groom, trying to detect if either of them sensed that something was amiss. Surely Eulalia, as an empath, could see there was something off about this man, the way the expression on his face didn't match his eyes. And what about Cael? During her hand-to-hand combat training with him, he had taught her to study an adversary's eyes to read intentions. But both of them just stood there, seemingly charmed.

Abby waited to see how David would react. He was watching her as though he sensed something was wrong, the same way he'd studied her before the ceremony had begun.

Nerine took Eulalia's face in her hands and gave her a kiss on each cheek. Abby looked quizzically at David, her eyebrows raised.

"Mermaid tradition," he whispered. "It's considered good

luck for a mermaid to kiss the bride and bless the marriage." He shrugged. "It's a Cai Terenmare thing."

"Oh. I had no idea Cai Terenmare weddings involved so much kissing by people other than the bride and groom," Abby whispered back.

David chuckled softly then cleared his throat as Nerine approached to kiss his hands.

"Congratulations to you, Solas Beir, both on the queen's marriage and on your own betrothal. Eulalia says you intend to marry the c'aislingaer?" she asked, with a smile and a wink at Abby.

"Thank you," David replied. He placed his hand on the small of Abby's back. "Yes, Abby and I will be getting married soon."

"How delightful! I too am now engaged." Nerine turned to the white-haired man. "This is my betrothed, Sholto. He is a noble from my father's court."

Abby was surprised. None of the other oracles were married, and she'd assumed the practice was forbidden. She thought back to her studies with Gorman on the history of Cai Terenmare.

Now that she thought about it, she could not recall any rule prohibiting oracles from marrying. Maybe the other three had simply chosen not to take vows other than the ones taken when they became seers.

"How do you do?" the man asked, taking David's hands and kissing them.

"Very well, thank you." David looked from Sholto to Nerine. "Congratulations to the two of you. I'm very happy for you, Nerine."

Nerine had just finished kissing Abby's hands. "Thank you, Solas Beir."

"How long have you been engaged?" Abby asked her.

Nerine laughed, her voice musical. "Oh, not long. But

Sholto and I have known each other for many years. My father was so pleased to hear our news."

She released Abby's hands, and Sholto moved over to take them in his. Abby found herself staring into his eyes.

"Greetings, c'aislingaer," he said, kissing each of her hands.

"Hello," she replied.

A wave of dizziness passed over Abby, and Sholto's eyes widened as she stumbled forward, her knees threatening to buckle beneath her. Sholto tightened his grip on her hands to steady her, and David grabbed her waist.

"Are you okay?" David asked.

Abby opened her mouth to reply and could only nod. Her thoughts were running every which way, and she couldn't form a coherent sentence.

"Are you certain?" Sholto asked, still holding her hands. "You are trembling."

David looked from Abby to Sholto. "I'm sure she's fine. She just needs some air—she's not used to meeting so many people all at once."

Sholto released her hands and David guided her away, out into the courtyard.

Looking over her shoulder, Abby could see that Nerine and Sholto had moved on to speak with Marisol.

David walked Abby to a chair and knelt beside her as she sat down. "What's wrong, sweetheart?"

He thought about how worried she'd looked before the wedding and the way she had seemed distracted walking up to the altar. Surely all the pomp and circumstance of the wedding hadn't freaked her out that much, had it? Maybe she was getting sick. He felt her forehead. No fever.

"That man," she managed, her voice shaky.

David glanced back into the banquet hall. "Who? Sholto?"

"Yes," Abby replied, her voice stronger. "There's something wrong with him." She looked down at her hands in her lap, and then held them up in front of her eyes, inspecting them.

David followed her gaze. He couldn't figure out what she was looking at.

She grabbed his hands and studied them, and then she looked at him. "Couldn't you feel it?"

"Feel what?"

"I don't know, exactly. Something bad." She frowned. "I feel... *dirty*."

He raised his eyebrows. "Dirty?"

She shook her head. "No, that's not the right word." She thought about it a moment. "Unclean." She stood up. "I'm going to wash my hands. You should too."

He rose. "Did the greeting ceremony gross you out?" He smiled, trying to make a joke. "I know there was a whole lot of kissing and hand holding involved."

She didn't laugh. "I just want to wash my hands, okay?"

David nodded and they walked silently to his quarters.

Toweling off her hands, Abby looked at David. He was following her example dutifully, washing his hands at the basin without question. She felt bad for snapping at him.

Abby placed her towel on the table beside the basin and moved out of the way, standing behind David so he'd have more room. "I'm sorry I grouched at you," she said, looking at him in the mirror.

He returned her gaze. "It's okay. You're not yourself today."

She slipped her arms around him. "I'm worried about the

Sower. It's got me on edge, I guess."

He dried his hands, put down the towel, and turned around, pulling her against his chest. "The Sower has all of us on edge. But it's more than that. I can tell."

"Yes," she admitted. "It's that man. There's something about him I don't trust. I don't even know why. It's just a feeling." She looked at her feet and took a moment to reassess their interaction. "He seemed perfectly nice...I'm being paranoid."

He slipped his fingers under her chin, lifting her head to look at him. "Don't start doubting yourself, c'aislingaer. If your gut is telling you something, I believe you." He kissed her and then smiled. "What do you say we go back downstairs and check him out? See if he's up to no good."

Abby and David had missed the beginning of the feast, and people had already started dancing. Cael and Eulalia were in the center of the room, happily swaying in each other's arms.

"Are you hungry?" David asked.

"I ate a little before the wedding, and now my stomach feels uneasy. How about you?"

"I'm a bit hungry, but I had a snack earlier, so I'll survive." He eyed the couples surrounding his mother and Cael. "Is your stomach too queasy to dance?"

Abby smiled. "Slow dancing, maybe."

He grinned. "That's the best kind." He led her out near the center of the room and took her in his arms. "And from here," he whispered, holding her close, "we can see everything that's going on without arousing suspicion."

She laughed. "Wow, you're really into this reconnaissance thing, aren't you?"

He chuckled. "Well, I wasn't into the flower girl thing. I'm much better at catching bad guys than I am at chucking flower petals."

"No argument there." She scanned the room. "Hello. What's this?"

He leaned in close. "What?"

"Nerine. She's sitting all alone."

The Western Oracle was seated at the feast table by herself, not eating, looking around like she'd misplaced something. Or someone. "Where's her fiancé?"

David circled them around, surveying the room. "No idea."

"You should ask her to dance."

David looked at Abby like a deer caught in someone's high beams. "What?"

"Come on, spy boy. Ask the girl to dance. See what she knows," Abby suggested, prodding him toward the table.

David raised an eyebrow. "*Spy boy?* My goodness, woman, there are more flattering names you could call me."

Abby grinned and put her hands on her hips. "You stallin', Corbin?"

He huffed. "No. I am *not* stalling. It's just...spy boy?" He scowled at her and Abby laughed. "Fine. I'll ask her." He took Abby's hand and led her over to where Nerine was sitting.

Nerine looked up with hope in her eyes as if she had been expecting Sholto, and then her face fell when she saw it was someone else.

Abby felt terrible for her. She elbowed David. He shot her a dirty look, and then turned back to the Western Oracle with a warm smile on his face.

"Hello, Nerine. I was wondering if you'd honor me with a dance."

Nerine looked around the room and then nodded. "That would be lovely."

Abby gave David a conspiratorial smile and mouthed, *See?*

Pointedly ignoring her, David gallantly held out his arm to

the mermaid. Nerine took it, and David led her onto the dance floor.

Abby laughed and strolled over to grab a drink. Her stomach was feeling better. She still didn't know why she had reacted to Sholto the way she did, but it felt good to be doing something. She wondered what, if anything, David would learn from Nerine.

Then, across the room, she spied Marisol heading out to the courtyard. Remembering how Marisol had manipulated the shopkeeper in the City of the Eastern Oracle, Abby realized her friend would make a much better spy than her betrothed.

David was just playing a game to humor her; Marisol would find answers. It would be so much better if Marisol talked to Sholto because she hadn't had a weird reaction like Abby's. Were Abby to ask questions, Sholto would know she was on to him.

Abby skirted the dance floor to follow her friend. It was fortunate she'd be able to talk to Marisol out there, with no one around to overhear them.

As she passed under the archway leading to the courtyard, Abby noticed that night had fallen. The banquet hall was brightly lit with candles and lanterns, and it took her eyes a moment to adjust to the dimly lit patio. She peered up at the sky; the stars were bright against the velvety darkness. The constellations were different than those of her world, but their beauty never ceased to amaze her.

Out of the corner of her eye, she saw someone moving in the shadows on the far side of the courtyard, beyond the dais where Cael and Eulalia had spoken their vows.

Marisol? She couldn't be sure without a closer look. Abby crept forward, trying to be silent, thankful she was wearing silken slippers with soft soles. The rustling fabric of her dress sounded overly loud in her ears.

Reaching the dais, she could make out the figure of a man.

Shocked, she looked away when she realized he had a woman pressed against the stone wall of the castle. She was intruding on some couple's intimate moment.

She was turning, determined to creep away unseen, when she had a disturbing thought. She thought about Nerine, sitting alone. *No. He wouldn't.*

Abby stared into the shadows, shielding her eyes against the light pouring out from the banquet room behind her. She gasped.

He would. Not only would Sholto cheat on his betrothed, he was doing it right now. Abby couldn't believe it. His back was turned to her, so she couldn't see his face, but she could see his white hair. There had been other white-haired merfolk at the wedding, but as far as she knew, Sholto was the only one wearing an aqua-colored tunic.

That's why she'd been so creeped out by him: because he was a lousy cheat. And the woman...Abby sucked in her breath. The woman was dressed just like she was.

Marisol! Abby felt heat rise to her cheeks. She was embarrassed to find her friend in a compromising situation and livid that, right before the wedding, Marisol had actually been *crying* over Jon.

Well, she wasn't crying now, was she? Jon was rotting away in prison, and Marisol was making out with some jerk she'd just met. *Talk about a master manipulator.* Abby had clearly been taken in by Marisol's supposed loyalty to Jon.

She stood frozen, debating whether she should march over to confront Marisol now, or sneak away and confront her later. Then there was a scream from the banquet hall.

Abby swiveled on her heels and ran into the hall to find David sprawled on his back, looking up in shock at Nerine.

The mermaid lunged at him, and he scooted away, crablike. Her eyes had turned white, and she seemed to be growling.

Around them, people stood in a loose circle and stared, unmoving. Even Cael seemed uncharacteristically frozen, watching Nerine in confusion.

Abby rushed over to David and helped him to his feet, avoiding a clumsy swipe from the Western Oracle. "What happened?"

David's eyes were wide with horror. "She...tried to *kiss* me," he stammered. "I thought she was drunk."

Abby eyed Nerine and took David's arm, making him back away to give the mermaid a wide berth. What was going on? Behind her, she could hear the Western Oracle panting.

Then, without warning, Nerine shrieked. Abby whirled around to see her charging across the dance floor toward them, her fingers hooked into claws.

There was a blur of red, and suddenly Nerine was on the floor, her neck cocked at an unnatural angle. Over her limp body stood Erela, her scarlet dress the color of blood.

"What have you done?" someone shouted.

Abby turned to see Sholto marching in from the courtyard, Marisol not far behind. "You killed her!"

At this, people seemed to come to their senses. "Now, just a minute," Cael interceded, his hand on the hilt of his sword. "She attacked the Solas Beir. Erela was only trying to protect him."

"Are you mad?" Sholto snapped, glaring at Cael. "Why would the Western Oracle attack your king? They were allies." He dropped to his knees, cradling Nerine's head as he rocked her in his arms. "My love, my *sweet* love..."

Abby felt like throwing up.

"You shall be avenged," Sholto murmured, closing Nerine's dead, staring eyes. He laid her on the floor and looked at David. "I demand justice. I demand you arrest the Daughter of Mercy!"

"Look," David replied, holding up his hands diplomatically, "I know it sounds crazy, but Nerine *did* try to kill me. I don't know why. She was fine one moment, and the next, she was acting really strange. Has she been ill?"

Sholto stared at David in disbelief before his face screwed up in rage. "Do *not* patronize me, Solas Beir. If you will not arrest a murderer when she is standing *right* there, within your reach..." His face grew red. "If you have no stomach for justice...what kind of king are you?" He stood up and brushed himself off. "No matter. I shall go to *my* king. I relish the thought of you trembling when the Sea King hears of this and breaches your shores, demanding his daughter's body." He turned on his heel and stormed out the door.

Behind him, the other merfolk spared a last glance at Nerine and then hurried after her fiancé. The silence that followed was heavy, as though no one dared to be the first to speak.

Finally Erela, looking terribly unsure of herself, hands clasped almost childlike in front of her, spoke softly. "I am sorry, Solas Beir. I should go."

"No, Erela, it's—" David began. But she was already gone.

Abby was certain he'd been about to say it was all right. But he was wrong. Nothing about this was right.

"What happened?" she asked again.

David looked at her, his expression still one of wide-eyed shock. "I wish I knew. We were dancing, and suddenly she was in my face, trying to kiss me. I told her no, but she wouldn't listen." His eyes were downcast. Abby put her hand on his arm. "I pushed her away. Not hard, I swear. I didn't mean to. I just reacted." He braved a look at Abby. "And now she's dead."

"It's okay, David," Abby assured him. "No one blames you."

He looked at her doubtfully, and Abby knew it didn't matter what she said. He blamed himself.

"Then what happened?" she prompted.

He swallowed. "Her face changed. Her eyes...well, you saw her eyes."

Abby nodded. "And then she tried to kill you?"

"Yes," he whispered. "She was so strong. She threw me on the ground."

There was a wet, choking sound, and Abby turned to see Nerine's body *moving*. The corpse shuddered with a spasm. Her back arched, her rib cage hitching up with a jerk. Nerine's eyes snapped open.

"She's still alive!" David cried, reaching for her body.

Abby grabbed his arm. "No, sweetie. She's not."

Nerine's head lolled to the side, and a milky fluid seeped from her lips. Cautiously, Abby inched closer, peering down for a better look. Behind her, David and Cael watched anxiously.

Everyone else was keeping their distance, which seemed perfectly sensible to Abby. But someone had to figure out what was going on. Listening to the dribbling noise coming from the corpse's lips, Abby was starting to regret volunteering for the job.

The white liquid dripped onto the stone floor and began to dissipate, flowing into the fine cracks of the porous stone tile. No, the word *flowing* didn't quite fit. This fluid was alive. It was wriggling with purpose, quite possibly with conscious thought.

As Abby bent down, she was horrified to see hundreds of translucent worms, their clawed limbs scrabbling in the liquid, squirming toward her slippered feet. She stood up quickly and backed away.

"They're worms," she said, holding her stomach, trying not to retch. "She's full of them."

Gorman snatched a glass decanter from one of the tables and poured out the water it held. Using a spoon, he scooped a sample of the liquid into the jar and then replaced the glass stopper. He held it up to the candlelight, studying it.

"What are they?" Abby asked.

"I am not sure," he answered. "But I suggest we burn the body as soon as possible."

"What about the Sea King?" David asked, looking distraught.

Abby nodded. Gorman's suggestion seemed callous. Nerine had been a friend and ally, and her father would be devastated by her death. They couldn't just dispose of her body like it was trash. Her attack on David had been out of character, and she still deserved the proper rites.

"If this is what I suspect," Gorman replied, "the Sea King may already be dead."

That was when Eulalia fainted.

PLAGUE

The wicked little wretch had been telling the truth about the state of the city, Hedeon observed. The normally bustling City of the Eastern Oracle was eerily quiet, a place for ghosts.

They'd encountered a few bodies during the sunset walk from the palace on the hill to the market at the city's gates, but not enough to indicate there'd been a battle. Not even enough for a proper rebellion, really. *What happened here?* Hedeon wondered as they searched the market.

The Sower. That's what Malden had said. Hedeon had heard rumors about a beast of legend, some abomination prophesied to be the ruin of Cai Terenmare, but he'd never entertained the thought that the fearsome creature might actually exist. He certainly never dreamed Tierney would be fool enough to release such a plague on his own world.

And the oracle? Clearly the Eastern Oracle had lost his mind to allow such madness to be unleashed.

As captain of the guard, Hedeon had suspicions about the breakdown in communication between the oracle and his court council, about the soldiers sent on strange missions throughout the city, and a fresh batch of courtesans delivered by the Daughters of Mercy—courtesans who were given uniforms but never taken to the inner sanctuary of the palace to serve. And the prisoner who'd escaped...Hedeon had been told she was a common thief, and yet the guards had been sent out to retrieve her, not by his command, but via a direct order from the oracle himself.

Given the number of soldiers the oracle dispatched, you'd think she was a murderer, he had reflected at the time.

Later, in the cell with Jon, he had learned the truth. The prisoner was not a thief or a murderer, but a child. A young girl taken from her home against her will, along with other kidnapped villagers, forced to serve as courtesans. But if the six who were kidnapped were never taken into the inner sanctuary, who was feeding on them? Or, maybe a better question: *what* was feeding on them?

During those last days at court, Hedeon had intuited that the oracle was hiding something. Now he believed he knew what that sinister secret was.

What if the villagers were an offering to the Sower, and through them, Tierney intended harm by returning them to their village, to their normal lives, unwillingly and unwittingly spreading the Sower's plague all the way to Caislucis?

But something had happened. The plan went awry somehow. Now the Sower had been unleashed, and the city was vacant. No oracle, no soldiers, no citizens, not even a single Kruorumbrae—except for Malden, of course. And Hedeon sincerely hoped he'd seen the last of that little leech.

"Who was Garvan?" Jon asked, interrupting Hedeon's thoughts.

After consolidating the few weapons they'd salvaged into one leather sack, they used the other to gather food from the abandoned carts at the market. The meat was spoiled and covered in flies, a sign that the city had been empty for days.

The bread they'd found had either hardened like stone or was covered in a fuzz of green mold. The fruit, however, was edible.

Hedeon finished off an apple before answering Jon's question. It wasn't a topic he wanted to discuss, but after all they'd been through, he supposed his former cellmate had a right to know. "Garvan was my second in command. I fear his death may be my fault."

Jon raised an eyebrow. "Wait—didn't you say it was your second in command who led the guards against you? That he betrayed your trust and took you to the torture chambers?"

Hedeon nodded. "Under Tierney's orders."

"Maybe he finally wised up. Maybe he realized you were right and rebelled against Tierney." Jon found a cart that sold leather casks and stuffed several into his bag.

Hedeon sighed. "I wish I could believe that were true. But I saw no signs of rebellion in the armory. I have not seen any in the city either." He picked up another apple and began munching on it, savoring the sweetness.

After days of not eating, even a meager amount of food seemed heavenly. He needed to get his strength up if he hoped to heal from the nasty gashes Malden had given him. He glanced up between bites to find Jon staring at him.

"What do you mean? We saw several corpses. Some of them had weapons. There had to have been some kind of fight."

"Perhaps a few stood against Tierney," Hedeon conceded. "But most people seem to have fled. And I do not believe Garvan expected to die. His sword was sheathed, and you saw the look on his face."

"He did seem shocked," Jon agreed, "but I don't get how that's your fault. Seems to me he had it coming, considering what he did to you. Those guards beat you to a pulp."

"When they were taking me away, I pleaded with Garvan for help. I said I had trusted him. Over everyone else, I trusted him. I should not have done that. I should have kept my mouth shut," Hedeon explained.

Jon looked puzzled. "Why?"

"Because I called him out in front of Tierney," Hedeon answered. "Knowing I had trusted Garvan, that we shared a bond, Tierney could not take the chance that Garvan would rebel and help me. Given how much his body has decayed, Tierney probably had him killed right after Garvan's soldiers dropped me in that cell. His corpse likely served as a warning to the others not to cross their new master."

A breeze picked up, whistling through the empty bazaar, making the loose canvas of a tent's doorway flap loudly in the twilight silence of the market. It was as though an ominous cloud had settled over the City of the Eastern Oracle, one that spoke of desolation and promised more destruction yet to come.

Jon shivered, and Hedeon found he could not blame him.

"Come. We cannot stay here," said the knight.

"Where will we go? West to Caislucis?"

Hedeon thought about it. "I doubt there are answers to be found crossing the Barren, and Caislucis may already be compromised."

Jon stared at him with growing horror.

Hedeon gave him a small smile, trying to reassure him. "I would rather find people. We need to figure out what happened here. Maybe there are survivors who would join us in our fight."

Jon swallowed as if trying to regain his composure.

Hedeon could only imagine the fears the boy must have regarding the fate of the Solas Beir and his other friends. But if the Sower had crossed the Barren, Caislucis was the last place he wanted to be.

"All right," Jon nodded slowly. "That leaves north and south, since we can't go west and the sea is east."

"North," Hedeon decided. "I have no wish to engage with the pirates and slave traders of Southport. There are villages to the north though, where we may find allies. From there, we can travel to the Northern Stronghold in search of more weapons and supplies. Perhaps, along the way, we will hear news of your

Solas Beir and how we might help him fight Tierney and the Sower."

Cael cradled Eulalia in his arms. She was alive, but unconscious. Her eyes fluttered open, and for a second, they looked white, like Nerine's had been.

Abby shuddered in revulsion and fear. She peered closer. No, Eulalia's eyes were blue. Unfocused, like she wasn't quite awake, but blue.

The queen moaned and closed her eyes again. Abby felt a sense of relief that she'd been mistaken. And yet, she couldn't shake a nagging sense of dread.

"Let's get her up to her room, Cael," David suggested.

Abby grabbed David's hand. "Be careful."

He looked from Eulalia's face to Abby's. "I will."

While Cael and David carried Eulalia up to her room, Obelia directed the royal guard to stand watch for the Sea King's arrival. Eoin helped several of the soldiers wrap Nerine's body and carry it out of the castle to be burned. One of the guards standing next to Abby squished the remaining worms with his boots.

"I suggest you burn those," Gorman said mildly. "Your boots too."

The guard scowled. "These are my best boots." He grabbed a goblet of wine from a nearby table, poured it over the pool of white liquid, and then dipped a cloth napkin in a candle flame until it caught. Dropping the flaming fabric into the puddle of wine, he marched off in search of his comrades.

Probably eager to burn the corpse, Abby thought, disgusted.

Gorman narrowed his eyes, staring after the insubordinate guard. "If anyone else falls ill because that fool tracked parasites through Caislucis on his boots, forget reporting him to his superior. I shall flog him myself."

"I'll help," Abby agreed. They were in trouble if the infestation could spread that easily. "But what about the worms that already crawled into the cracks? How do we know if we got them all?"

Gorman frowned. "We cannot know for certain."

Abby fought off another shudder. "We need to figure out what this is and how to stop it."

Gorman gave her a grim smile and held up the decanter. "Shall we go study our new pets?"

"Yes, let's."

In the Caislucis library, Gorman peered at the worms using a magnifying glass. "Interesting," he mused. "Take a look." He handed Abby the glass and disappeared into the library stacks.

The half-sphere didn't have a handle, and was heavy, like a paperweight. But it did the job. Magnified, Abby could see that the worms resembled maggots with feathery gills just behind their heads and stubby, clawed legs. She could almost see through their semi-transparent bodies, twisting with a sick, curling motion at the bottom of the decanter. On their tails, Abby could just make out the faint pattern of black and white bands.

Gorman returned and opened a dusty book, laying it out on the table beside the decanter. "Yes. Here it is, as I thought. Sea nymphs."

"Which are?"

"Mysterious creatures," Gorman replied. "Up until now, I assumed they were the stuff of legend. They are rumored to be a juvenile form of siren, but, seeing as how no one had ever lived long enough on the Island of the Western Oracle to witness the reproductive cycle of the sirens..."

Abby nodded, remembering Eulalia's story of the old Western Oracle, a monstrous anglerfish whose lovers were absorbed by her body and preserved, half-digested, but undead. And her daughters' lovers were promptly devoured after serving their purpose. "There's just one problem with your theory. The sirens are all dead. Unless you're thinking Nerine was infected decades ago."

Gorman shook his head. "No, I would venture to guess this is a recent infestation. You said Ardal made a pact with the Oracle? That the Sower was the result of that union?"

Abby nodded slowly with dawning horror. "The Sower comes to sow the seeds of strife," she said, reciting the prophecy. "A seed like a spore. Like a spore that will keep replicating itself until it becomes a plague!" She jumped up from her chair.

"Where are you going?"

"I have to talk to Lucia," she called, running out the door.

Lucia was sitting on her bench in the dungeon when Abby slid to a stop in front of her cell.

"C'aislingaer. How lovely to see you."

"I need your help," Abby panted, grasping the iron bars. "Did you hear what happened at the wedding?"

Lucia eyed her from where she sat, guarded. "Bits and pieces, yes, while eavesdropping on the soldiers down here. The Western Oracle?" She ran her finger across her throat in a pantomime of slitting it open.

"Dead," Abby confirmed.

"I see," Lucia said mildly. "By the Daughter of Mercy's hand?"

"Yes," Abby replied, her brows furrowed. She looked annoyed by Lucia's nonchalance. "Nerine was going after David like a rabid dog. We couldn't reason with her, so Erela had to kill her. Then she had to flee when Nerine's people demanded her arrest. But the Oracle's attack was totally out of character, almost like she was possessed. After she died, these worms crawled out of her mouth—sea nymphs, Gorman thinks."

"Did you kill them all?"

"We hope so," Abby answered. "Except for the ones Gorman took to study."

Lucia stood and crossed over to the iron bars. "You must be sure to kill them all. You mustn't let them spread. They will infect others."

The girl's eyes fell. "I'm afraid they already have. Your sister..."

Lucia stared hard at the c'aislingaer. The soldiers had said nothing about Eulalia. She struggled to keep her guard up, to keep her shock hidden from the girl.

"She's fallen ill," Abby explained. "I'm scared it could be the same thing Nerine had, but it's too soon to know for sure. She's unconscious."

Lucia stood silent. If Eulalia was infected, she was as good as dead—unless Lucia could think of a way to save her. She fought to keep her head clear. Emotion and panic would not help Eulalia.

Abby narrowed her eyes when Lucia did not answer right away. "If you know something about this, you *have* to tell me. Is it the Sower?"

"I'm not sure."

"Please, Lucia," Abby pleaded, gripping the iron bars of the cell. "This is not the time to hold back. David's in danger. I know you want to protect him. You wouldn't have risked Tierney's wrath if you didn't care about his safety."

That was true. She did want to protect David. But she wasn't holding back. Tierney had kept so many secrets from her—there wasn't much to tell. "These sea nymphs as you call them—they seem to take control of the person infested?"

"We think so. It's hard to tell since there's only been one

incident. But Nerine never would've hurt anyone. She saved you, remember?"

Lucia nodded. She didn't want to think about the debt she owed the mermaid. "So if these creatures infest a person, they cause aggressive behavior, in essence, creating strife, as foretold by the prophecy."

"I thought that too," Abby agreed. "But how do we get them *out* of people? We can't just kill Eulalia."

Lucia didn't want her sister to die, but the risk of infecting others was too high. "I fear if you don't, this may spread," she replied gravely. "There's no way to know if Nerine already infected others, or how many there could be. Eulalia may have already infected others too. I assume the infestation spreads through touch. Did Nerine touch anyone besides my sister?"

Abby stared at her, horrified. "Yes. *All of us.* There was the greeting line where Nerine kissed Eulalia's cheeks and our hands, and David danced with her. We could all be infected."

"How long was it before Eulalia showed signs of illness?"

"She collapsed soon after Nerine died. We thought it was from the shock of seeing Nerine killed, and then the confrontation with Sholto...I think violence affects Eulalia more acutely than other people because she's an empath," Abby explained.

As are you, Lucia thought, but held her tongue. How curious that the girl might have a greater ability to shield herself from intense emotions than her sister. Then again, perhaps it wasn't being an empath that had caused Eulalia to faint.

"My sister was always so sheltered, more fragile than others," Lucia replied. "But given that she developed symptoms so quickly, if others were affected, they too would be showing signs of infestation."

The color drained from Abby's face. "I have to get back to David then. He could still be in danger."

"Indeed. But perhaps Nerine and Eulalia are the only

ones—an isolated event. Perhaps we are not too late."

"What do we do now?" Abby asked.

"Keep her isolated," Lucia instructed. "Don't let anyone touch her. We must figure out how to get the nymphs out of her."

"Can David heal her?"

Lucia felt her stomach turn at the thought and she shook her head vehemently. "No, he mustn't try that. If he were successful, the result would be taking the infestation into himself, and I'm not sure he could purge them."

Abby cringed. "Like the time he took Nysa's injuries and had to vomit the venom?"

"Exactly like that," Lucia agreed. "Only I don't believe he would have the strength to purge the sea nymphs. If the Sower is involved, this may be exactly what Tierney wants to happen. Not to kill David, but to control him."

Abby had fear in her eyes and her knuckles were turning white as she gripped the iron bars. "That can't happen."

Lucia placed her hands over Abby's and felt the startled girl tighten her grip. Then, slowly, Abby let down her guard and relaxed her grip, keeping her eyes on Lucia's.

"It's up to you to make sure it doesn't," Lucia said firmly. "I can't protect him, now that I am detained."

"Understood." Abby looked as though she were considering something, and then asked, "What about the pool of healing? If we laid Eulalia in it—"

"No. You must not do that," Lucia interrupted. "That would corrupt the pool. My sister would rather die than introduce something so vile into that which we hold sacred."

"But we could take the water to her," Abby argued. "That wouldn't compromise the pool."

"You could try," Lucia said doubtfully. "If you did it quickly, before the water lost its potency..."

"But you don't think it will work?" the girl asked.

Lucia looked away. She had no doubt the sacred water would have some effect on the creatures inhabiting her sister's body. But she feared the result would not be healing. She thought the girl was about to get an education about just who it was she was dealing with. The ruthlessness of the Sower—and of Tierney. "I'm not certain what effect it might have."

"Well, we have to try something," Abby insisted. "I'll be back to tell you how it turns out."

"Perhaps you will," Lucia replied, keeping her dark thoughts to herself. The girl turned to leave, and Lucia reached through the bars and grabbed her wrist, stopping her. "Whatever happens, you must get David out. It doesn't matter what happens to *anyone* else—you have to be prepared to leave with him. Force him to leave if you must."

Abby nodded, and Lucia released her. As she watched the girl ascend the steps of the dungeon, she wondered, not for the first time, how things had gone so wrong. The boy she loved as her own son was once again in danger, and her sister was dying. She had been a fool to trust Tierney, to have fallen for him and his lies in the first place.

She gripped the bars of her cell and noticed how filthy her hands were. How many years had her hands been dirty while she blindly followed Tierney? How had a good girl from a noble family ended up branded as a traitor to the throne and locked away in a dungeon?

It had been her mother's fondest wish that one of her daughters would become queen. From the time Lucia was small, her mother had groomed her for the role, and Lucia flourished under her mother's praise. She worked hard to become an accomplished young woman, worthy of notice, distinguishing herself from her peers when she went to court.

When Ardal began to lavish attention on her, she was certain her mother's wish—and hers as well—would be fulfilled. She'd adored the Solas Beir, and she loved the idea of serving the Light by helping her people. She was a devoted follower of the Light, and had felt sure her faith would be rewarded.

When Ardal chose her younger sister to be his queen, it didn't just break her heart, it shook her faith. She'd felt as though everything she had known to be true had been yanked from beneath her feet. She questioned everything: her beliefs, herself, and the man she had thought she would marry.

It was no wonder she fell for Tierney. He found her at her weakest moment and gave her hope.

The first time she met him, she didn't even know who he was. He was simply a handsome stranger she met in the labyrinth outside Caislucis. She'd assumed he too was a wedding guest, and he hadn't corrected her.

As she came to know him, she wondered if he was her destiny, if the Light hadn't spared her a marriage based on politics for the gift of true love. By the time Tierney revealed his identity, it was too late. She was his. She had traded Light for Darkness, and there was no turning back.

David stood at the window in Eulalia's parlor, alternating between pacing and looking anxiously out the window, watching for signs of the Sea King's arrival. The ocean was calm, peaceful even, with rhythmic, rolling waves. There was nothing to suggest that this night was different than any other.

It was some time before he heard his mother stirring, calling for him. Hearing her voice, he felt a deep sense of dread. He found himself thinking about Margaret Corbin, the woman who had raised him. He couldn't stand the thought of losing Eulalia—not when he'd already lost his adoptive mother.

Forcing himself to put one foot in front of the other, David entered Eulalia's bedchamber. Cael was sitting next to her at her bedside, holding her hand.

The expression on her face was as peaceful as the sea outside. Her eyes were closed and she seemed to be resting comfortably. Maybe she *had* just fainted. It had been a stressful day. Maybe all she needed was rest.

David wanted to believe that. He sat down on the other side of Eulalia's bed and placed his hand on her forehead—it was hot with fever, erasing any hope that she wasn't sick after all.

He stole a look at Cael. The knight looked distraught, and rightly so.

It was rare for someone of the Light to fall ill. When it happened, it was seen as a bad omen, a sign that there was evil afoot. David was unsure if the Cai Terenmare superstition was grounded in truth, but he'd seen enough death lately to believe Eulalia's sudden illness was no accident.

Her dark hair was sticking to her sweaty forehead. Gently, David brushed it away. Eulalia opened her eyes. With relief, he noted they were blue and not white like Nerine's had been. He shivered, reliving the moment when Nerine changed after he pushed her away.

"David," Eulalia murmured, reaching up to stroke his cheek.

He hid his fear and smiled at her. "Hello, Mother. How do you feel?"

But she had turned away and was staring at Cael. "You," she said, her voice dropping an octave.

"My sweet wife," Cael murmured, smiling as he grasped her hand in both of his.

"You killed the Western Oracle," she accused.

"No, Mother. It was Erela who killed Nerine," David corrected her.

"Not the *mermaid*," Eulalia growled, narrowing her eyes at David as though he'd said something unimaginably stupid. "The *true* oracle."

"Who?" David stammered.

Eulalia tore her hand from Cael's grasp and slapped him hard across the face. Then, while Cael was still startled, she wrapped both hands around David's throat and began choking the life out of him.

Overcoming his shock, Cael grabbed her wrists, trying to release her hold on David's neck. But she was too strong. David could see dark spots blossoming in his vision. Behind him, he heard a door bang open. It sounded far away, surreal, as though he were dreaming, or falling down a very deep hole.

He was vaguely aware of Abby beside him. She placed her hand on Eulalia's forehead, wrenching it back, and the pressure around his throat eased. Someone was shrieking.

David staggered back, away from the bed, before collapsing on the floor. Then Abby was kneeling over him, calling his name. She helped him sit up and coaxed him into drinking something. Whatever it was burned his throat as it went down.

"Good!" Abby yelled close to his ear, over the commotion. "Your bruises are fading. You're going to be okay."

David looked up at her, puzzled.

She held up the glass of clear liquid. "Water from the pool of healing." She put the glass on a table and, for the second time that evening, helped him to his feet.

On the bed, Eulalia continued to shriek, bucking against the hands restraining her. Eulalia's handmaidens had come in and were holding her arms as Cael ripped a sheet into strips to secure her to the bed.

David could see it was going to take more than that to hold her, but Cael was clearly improvising with what he had on hand. Eulalia's eyes had faded to white, and on the pale skin of her forehead was a scarlet handprint.

Abby followed his gaze. "I had to do it to stop her from killing you."

He swallowed. His throat still ached. "What did you do?" he managed.

"I dipped my hand in the water and touched her forehead. I would have dumped the entire glass over her head, but I had to use it to heal you," Abby explained. "I think we're going to need a lot more water if we want to heal her."

"I *do* want to heal her," David replied.

Eulalia stopped screaming and thrashing. She looked at him curiously, muttering in an unnaturally low voice that was somewhere between gibberish and snarling. David stepped toward the bed and placed his hands over Eulalia's body, intending to heal her.

"No!" Abby pushed his hands away, forcing him to step back. "Stop! You can't heal her."

"Of course I can." He started to push past Abby, but she placed her hands flat against his chest, blocking his way.

"No. You *can't*. She's infected like Nerine was. If you take her illness, you won't be strong enough to purge the worms," Abby cautioned.

David gasped, realizing the implications. He thought about the strange worms that had been inside Nerine. If there were worms inside Eulalia, they would be in him too if he tried to heal her. He pictured his own eyes turning white, his hands winding around Abby's throat. He shuddered, trying to erase the image from him mind. "But we have to help her somehow—she's my mother. I can't lose her like I lost my other parents."

"I talked to Lucia about the pool of healing," Abby said. "We can't immerse Eulalia without corrupting the pool, but Lucia thought we could try pouring water over her. I don't know if it will heal her, but I think we should try it."

"And you trust Lucia?" Cael snapped. "Why should we listen to her? For all we know, she is still involved with Tierney. It would not be the first time she has tried to kill her sister."

David stared at the red mark on Eulalia's forehead. It was

fading slowly. "The water will hurt her."

"It could *kill* her," Cael warned. There was a helpless, tortured look in his eyes.

"We have to try *something*," Abby argued. "And David—you need to stay away. You seem to be triggering this aggression. It's the same as the attack with Nerine. Whatever this is, it's clear the intent is to destroy the Solas Beir."

"You said she has worms in her. Like Nerine," David repeated.

"Gorman thinks they are sea nymphs—parasitic spores from the Sower that are controlling her," Abby clarified. "If we pour the healing water on her, they might be forced out."

"But she could also die," David frowned. "I agree with Cael. We can't risk that."

"What we can't risk is her killing you. Or worse, this spreading to you," Abby said quietly.

David knew by the stubborn look in her eyes that she was done arguing. He hated to admit it, but she was right. The powers of the Solas Beir under the control of the Sower would mean the destruction of Cai Terenmare.

"Come on," Abby urged, taking his arm. "Let's go get more water."

David allowed himself to be guided out of Eulalia's room. In the hallway, Abby let go of his arm and closed the door behind them.

"I don't want to leave her, Abby." David fought the wave of emotion crashing over him. "She could die while we're gone getting water."

"I know. I'm so sorry." Abby took his hand. "But I want you with me. I can't watch over you if you stay here." She looked at the closed door. "Normally I would trust Cael to protect you, but his judgment is compromised when it comes to Eulalia."

"I'm supposed to be the one protecting people."

"Not this time," she replied.

Abby and David each carried a bucket of water back to Eulalia's chambers. "I think you should wait in the parlor," Abby advised. "It'll be better if she doesn't see you."

David nodded, and sank into a chair. Abby carried both buckets into the bedchamber and then closed the silken screen separating the two rooms.

The moment Eulalia saw Abby approach, carrying water from the healing pool, she began pulling at her restraints, arching her back. "Hold her down," Abby ordered.

Cael pinned Eulalia's wrists to the bed, and her two maids each secured a leg. Eulalia snarled, and Abby saw Cael blink back tears. Her heart ached for him. He'd waited so long to be with the love of his life, and now, infected with a terrible madness, she was behaving like a feral animal. Not how he had imagined spending his wedding night, Abby was sure.

Abby brought the first bucket over to the head of Eulalia's bed. "I'm sorry," Abby apologized, and poured it over the queen from head to toe.

Eulalia shrieked and thrashed, bucking violently against her restraints. Her skin was smoking, turning an angry red.

Abby picked up the second bucket and poured it out over Eulalia's body. Smoke rose up like steam.

When it cleared, the queen quieted. She blinked and, for a second, Abby could have sworn she saw Eulalia's blue eyes. *Maybe the water is working. Maybe she'll be healed.*

Then Eulalia's eyes were milky once again, and the queen let out a low growl, staring at Abby. Abby's heart sank. She pictured sea nymphs writhing just under Eulalia's skin and wondered if the queen would ever be okay again.

Abby eyed the makeshift restraints. Already they looked worn, stressed from the queen's struggles. *She would kill me,* Abby thought. *If she got loose, she'd kill me without a second thought. She'd kill all of us.* "We're going to need to bind her better," she told Cael.

"I know," he replied, his voice hitching. He avoided her gaze.

"Okay," Abby said. "I'll take care of it."

Cael didn't respond. He just sat on the edge of Eulalia's bed, holding her wrists, staring at nothing in particular.

Abby opened the screen leading to the parlor, stepped through, and quickly closed it behind her. She didn't want David to see Eulalia's red, scalded skin.

He was hunched over in the chair, his eyes scrunched tightly closed, his hands covering his ears. He looked like a little boy. She touched his shoulder and he opened his eyes.

Cautiously, he took his hands from his ears. "Did it help?"

Abby felt her stomach clench. She swallowed. "No change. She doesn't seem to be getting worse, but she's not getting better." She hoped she wasn't lying to him, that Eulalia wouldn't take a turn for the worse. She also hoped Eulalia's skin hadn't changed color permanently. The red mark on her forehead had faded fast, but that was from when Abby had applied only a few drops of the healing water, not buckets of it.

"I need to find some chains to secure her better," she told David. "Then I think we should find Gorman."

It was nearly midnight when Jon and Hedeon finally stopped. During the evening's travels north, to where the dry desert rose in elevation to become a series of plateaus along the edge of the Eastern Sea, Jon had managed to shoot a scrub hare with a bow and arrow he'd found in the armory. Thinking of Abby with a twinge of guilt, he cooked the skinned animal over a campfire.

Hedeon sat sharpening a sword, looking thoughtfully to

the north. Jon followed his gaze. He could just make out the black silhouettes of mountains in the starlight. He didn't know why, but the further north they traveled, the more he had a sense that they were going in the right direction. It wasn't a sense of peace exactly, but a feeling of certainty, like something was drawing him forward. He had never experienced anything quite like it.

They hadn't seen any survivors from the city yet, but Hedeon had assured Jon they would reach the closest village in the mountains within two days. They hadn't found any horses back when they were in the city, so Hedeon had travelled in his bear form, carrying Jon and their supplies. Jon worried about his wounds from the fight with Malden, but Hedeon shrugged off his concern. The food they'd found seemed to have given Hedeon new vitality.

Jon took another peek at Hedeon's injuries. The gash at his shoulder and across his chest looked a little better than they had hours before. Good thing the man seemed to be a fast healer. Thinking about that made Jon recall another fast healer he knew, and the conversation David had with Hedeon before the battle at the Eye of the Needle.

"You said you knew David's father?" Jon asked.

Hedeon ceased his work and turned to look at Jon. "Did I?"

Jon removed the cooked hare from the spit and handed Hedeon a leg of meat. "You did. Back when we were riding in the iron carriage together...before things fell apart. When you told David what was really going on with the Eastern Oracle."

Hedeon nodded. "I remember. Yes, I knew Ardal very well. We fought together at the Northern Stronghold in the wars against the Kruorumbrae. That was a long time ago."

"So how did you go from being Ardal's ally to working for the Eastern Oracle?"

Hedeon laughed bitterly. "That, my friend, is a tale of woe."

Jon sat silent, waiting for him to go on. He realized that, in spite of sharing a cell with Hedeon, he didn't really know the man at all.

Hedeon sighed, picking at his food. "Even now, so many years later, it is difficult for me to discuss. But I suppose since we have a long road ahead of us, you deserve to learn about your traveling companion's sordid past."

Jon gave Hedeon a small but encouraging smile, and the knight continued.

"After the war, I settled in the east. My wife and I had two children. There was still trouble with the Kruorumbrae, of course, but Ardal was on the throne and things seemed to be getting better. Better than they had been under his father's rule. But then things started getting bad again. I believe you are aware that Ardal had to remove Tierney from his post as Southern Oracle?"

"Yeah, I heard about that."

"Yes, well, not long after that, Tierney declared himself Kruor um Beir, leader of the Blood Shadows, and things went from bad to worse," Hedeon explained. "If we thought the Kruorumbrae were vicious before...suffice it to say that attacks both on our kind and your kind increased, and it was a despairing time for both our worlds. For some reason, Ardal seemed more concerned about protecting humans than those in the Light. He began closing portals to bar the Kruorumbrae's access to humanity."

Jon stiffened, and the knight studied him intently.

"Forgive me. You must think me biased against humans."

"Are you?" Jon asked, guarded.

"Not like you think," Hedeon answered softly. "It is just that he was *our* king. His duty was to protect *us*. That is the reason the Solas Beir exists. I believe Ardal meant well, but his decision cost me personally."

The knight looked away, but not before Jon saw the agony in his eyes.

"What happened?" Jon whispered. He reached out to place his hand on Hedeon's arm, but the knight gave him a bittersweet smile and shook him off.

"I lived in Tarmon, the village I hope to reach by tomorrow evening or the next morn. It is...was," he corrected himself, "a lovely, quiet little town, where nothing bad happened. That is why I chose it. I had seen too much of war, and I wanted a peaceful life for my family. However, there was a portal in the mountains near there, and when Ardal closed it, the Kruorumbrae retaliated."

Jon felt a growing sense of dismay roiling in his stomach, but didn't dare interrupt.

"They slaughtered half the villagers. My wife and daughters were among the slain," Hedeon finished, unable to meet Jon's gaze.

"I'm so sorry."

"As am I." Hedeon rose and added more wood to the fire. He stared into the flames, silent.

"So after that, you went to the City of the Eastern Oracle?" Jon prompted.

"Not quite."

Hedeon turned, and Jon could see a storm in his eyes. He smiled, but there was no humor in it.

"After that, I killed every Kruorumbrae I could get my hands on. But that did not bring my family back. It only fueled my desire for vengeance. My actions attracted the attention of the Eastern Oracle. He sent soldiers to capture me, and I found myself, quite unwillingly, at court."

Jon's mouth gaped—he would have never guessed that Hedeon had been a prisoner of the Eastern Oracle before he was promoted to captain of the guard.

"The oracle was more charismatic in those days, and much more sane. He convinced me that we were fighting for the same side, that he too had suffered losses at the hands of the

Kruorumbrae," Hedeon explained. "I knew he was a politician, but I was floundering in my search for vengeance, for a reason to continue breathing. The oracle told me of his vision for a peaceful Cai Terenmare, where the Kruorumbrae could be controlled so there would never be another massacre like in Tarmon. He gave me purpose. I wanted desperately to believe him, and so I bought into his vision."

"But eventually..."

Hedeon nodded. "Eventually, the oracle's master plan lost its luster. And in trying to aid the oracle, I committed crimes of which I shall always be ashamed. But it seems my efforts were for naught anyway. Things fell apart again, just as they always do. I fear we shall never see a peaceful Cai Terenmare. I cannot believe in such a thing anymore."

"So why are you going with me to the Northern Stronghold?" Jon asked.

Hedeon smiled. "Because I have always lived by the sword, and I am too old to change now."

Jon laughed. "That's not a good reason."

"No, my young friend, it is not," Hedeon agreed, chuckling. "The truth is, even though I think peace is impossible, I believe in your friend, the Solas Beir. And I have no doubt this world is better off in his hands than in Tierney's or the Sower's."

Abby was worried about David. He was acting like he'd already lost Eulalia and was grieving her.

After she found chains and helped Cael secure them to Eulalia's wrists and ankles, she had discovered David hunched over in a chair again. He made no argument when she took his arm and led him to his room so he could change out of his wedding attire into something more practical. He was just going through the motions, complying with whatever she asked—until it came to food.

She had tried to get him to eat something while she changed into a tunic and pants behind a screen in her room, but he wouldn't. He just sat listless, absently tracing the shape of the silver nautilus hanging around his neck. Abby wasn't sure if the Sign of the Throne would protect him—certainly Eulalia had been able to get her hands around his throat without too much trouble—but she felt better knowing he was wearing it. She watched him as she sat on her bed, pulling on her boots.

"David."

He looked up at her as if he'd forgotten she was there.

"Come on, sweetheart. I know you're worried about your mom, but you have to eat," she pleaded.

"Can't."

She pushed herself off her bed and knelt in front of him, taking his hands, forcing him to see her. "Please, David. I know you don't want to, but do it for me. I can't do this without you. I need you to be strong. Eulalia needs you to be strong."

He met her gaze and she saw the full weight of the grief in his eyes. She remembered what he'd said about losing his adoptive parents. Eulalia's illness was forcing him to face the memory of their deaths. He'd lost so much in such a short time. Abby wondered how much more he would lose before the war was over.

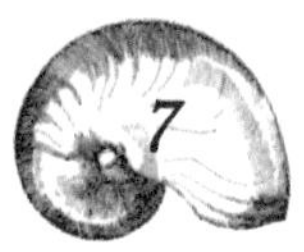

NUREN

Abby was right. David felt better after he'd eaten. Stronger. More focused—able to push aside the emotions threatening to cripple him. He couldn't allow his grief to take over. He'd be no use to anyone if he did.

They found Gorman waiting for them in the library, avalanched by books. There, David got his first close-up look at the sea nymphs. He picked up the decanter imprisoning the worms and held it up to a candle, slowly turning the jar in the light as he inspected them. Abby passed him a magnifying glass; he nodded his thanks and took a look.

The nymphs were nasty little creatures, scrabbling at the smooth sides of the glass decanter, trying to escape and wreak havoc. "So these are the things killing my mother?"

"Yes. We believe so," Gorman said gravely.

David set the jar and the magnifying glass back on the table. "How can something so small do so much damage?"

"I wish I knew, Sire," Gorman replied.

"What *do* you know?" David asked, irritated.

Gorman stared at him, shocked into silence.

Abby placed her hand on David's arm. She didn't say anything, but by the strained look on her face, he could see she was struggling not to admonish him in front of Gorman.

David placed his hand over hers. "I'm sorry," he apologized to Gorman. "My concern for the queen is getting the best of me. Please. Tell me what you've found out about these creatures."

"Not much, unfortunately," Gorman answered. "There isn't much written about them, or about the Sower, I'm afraid. But as I told Abby, I believe the nymphs are a juvenile form of siren. Based on what we've gleaned from the prophecy, I suspect the Sower is the offspring of the former Western Oracle. He injects his prey with the spore and can then control them."

David thought about what he'd witnessed with his mother, the way she acted as though she were possessed by something outside herself, saying things she would never say, trying to kill him. Gorman's theory made sense. "How do we get them out of someone who has been infected? Abby tried pouring healing water on the queen to force the nymphs out, but it didn't work."

Gorman shook his head. "No, I should think not. Anything you try directly on the victim will only hurt the person infected. The key, I think, lies with the Sower. If we can figure out how to sever his connection to the queen, perhaps we won't need to force the nymphs out. Perhaps her body will do the work for us, as if it were fighting an infection rather than an infestation."

"That's where we start looking then," David concluded.

"Yes, Sire." Gorman reached for a pile of books teetering on the edge of the table and handed several to David and Abby before retrieving a few for himself. "Perhaps one of these volumes will offer a solution."

David and Abby ended up spending the night in the library with Gorman, taking turns napping on the soft rug under the table as they desperately searched for a way to heal the queen.

Finally, several hours after the sun had risen, they decided to head downstairs to find breakfast and check on Eulalia. They had just entered the Great Hall when David heard a woman begging for an audience with him.

"Please! I must see the Solas Beir," the woman cried.

Guards were standing on either side of her, swords drawn. Obelia and Eoin were speaking with her.

"I am sorry," Obelia told the woman. "The Solas Beir is busy with matters of the realm right now."

"No one can be admitted to see him," Eoin said.

The woman was frantic. "I *must* speak with him. There is sickness in my village. It is spreading like wildfire."

David recognized the woman and crossed the room to intervene. "It's okay. I'll see her."

Yola turned and fell on her knees at David's feet. "Your Majesty," she breathed, prostrate on the floor.

David stared down at her, taken aback by the way she looked at him with such reverence, as though he were someone to be worshipped. But it wasn't just the idea of being worshipped that made him uncomfortable. The last time he'd seen this woman, he'd had the unpleasant task of telling her he had failed to save her brother and had come to deliver the man's corpse.

David grasped Yola's arms and guided her to her feet. "Yola, you really don't have to bow to me. Please—rise."

Yola seemed distraught and exhausted. Her eyes looked sunken with dark circles under them. But thankfully, they were brown, not white.

"Tell me what's troubling you," David said gently.

"A great evil has overtaken the village of Nuren," she explained in a rush. "Please—you must come and heal them."

David and Abby exchanged an apprehensive look. "What kind of illness, Yola?" Abby asked.

"People fainting, falling into a deathlike sleep. I tried everything to awaken them, but to no avail. It's like a spell has fallen over the village." Yola choked back a sob and grabbed David's hands, her eyes pleading. "My own daughter has succumbed to the sickness. Please, Solas Beir, I beg of you. I have seen your power. Only you can help us. Please." She looked like she was torn between falling to her knees in obeisance again and bursting into tears.

Abby looked at David. "Do you think it's the same thing affecting Eulalia?"

David frowned. "I hope not. This sleeping sickness sounds different than what my mother has. I mean, yes, she fainted, but then she woke up fairly quickly."

Yola's eyes widened. "The queen has fallen ill?"

"Sadly, yes," David said. "We've been trying to find a way to heal her. Were there any other symptoms with the sickness in Nuren?"

Yola shook her head. "No, Sire. One moment, all was well—people were going about their daily business—and the next, they were collapsing around me as I tended my goats. I was the only one unaffected. I tried everything I could think of to rouse my family, my neighbors, but they could not be awakened."

"Did the sickness affect your livestock too?" David asked.

"No—only the people of my village seem to have fallen under this spell," Yola confirmed.

"And how long has it been since they fell asleep?" Abby asked.

"The illness took hold of them at dawn," Yola explained. "After I realized I could not help them, I rode to Caislucis as fast as I could."

"You said that everything seemed normal in the village before people started fainting," Abby said. "Nothing unusual happened before that? Like someone visiting the village, a stranger?"

Yola shook her head. "No, not that I am aware of. I do not know why this is happening to us." She covered her face with her hands and began sobbing.

David put his arms around the weeping woman. "Don't worry, Yola. There must be something we can do to help." He looked at Obelia and Eoin. "Abby and I need to check on the queen. Could you take Yola to the banquet hall? We'll join you shortly and form a plan."

Obelia took Yola's arm. "Of course, Your Majesty. Come with me, my dear."

David and Abby found Cael sitting by the sleeping queen's side. Cael looked exhausted. David doubted he'd slept.

Worried he would trigger more aggression from Eulalia, David motioned for Cael to join him in the queen's parlor. Cael gave his sleeping wife a sad look and then left her side. Her arms and legs were bound to the bedposts with chains, and her skin had a pink tinge like she'd been sunburned.

"How is she?" David asked.

"The same," Cael frowned. "No more fits after you left, but her eyes remain white as milk."

"We've got more trouble," David informed him after glancing at Abby. "The village of Nuren has been hit with some kind of sickness. We don't know what it is, but it's possible it's related to what Eulalia has. Even if it's not, I have to try to help them. I need you to gather your best soldiers—we leave at once."

Cael hesitated, his face twisted in agony. "The queen...Solas Beir, I understand the gravity of this situation, but I am loath to leave with her so ill..."

David understood all too well the feeling of being torn between family and duty. He put his hand on Cael's shoulder. "I know—I feel the exact same way. But we found nothing that would help us in the library. What if the key to healing her is in Nuren? I'll ask Marisol to stay with her."

Abby stiffened at the mention of Marisol.

"What?" David asked her.

She shook her head. "Nothing. I'll tell you later."

"Okay," David said slowly, turning back to Cael. "We'll also post guards outside Eulalia's chamber door."

Cael nodded. "Thank you, Solas Beir."

Cael walked down with David and Abby to the banquet hall and then hurried away, shouting orders to ready the horses.

In the hall, Obelia and Eoin were sitting with Yola, eating fruit and flatbread. Eoin rose and stepped forward. "I am coming with you, Solas Beir. If this is happening in Nuren, it could be happening in the other villages. We must uncover the cause."

Obelia nodded. "I agree. I will come to help as well."

"I promised Lucia I'd give her an update on her sister," Abby said, gathering food onto a silver tray.

"Be quick," David urged.

Lucia's spirits lifted at the sight of Abby bearing a tray piled with food. The guards fed her regularly, but the rations they provided were of such poor quality, she found herself pushing them away more often than not.

She'd been tempted to raise the issue with David, but her pride stopped her. She didn't want pity for her squalid living conditions. She wanted freedom.

She thanked Abby for the food and then forced herself to eat slowly, hiding her ravenous hunger.

As Lucia ate, Abby told her about the trip to Nuren.

Lucia swallowed a piece of bread. "I don't like it."

"Neither do I," Abby agreed. "I have a terrible feeling about it. But we need answers." She looked down at her feet. "We tried pouring healing water on Eulalia."

Lucia froze, about to bite into a berry. "And?" She dreaded what the girl would say, but she had to know.

"It didn't help. She's still sick," Abby reported. "We've

spent hours trying to find a way to rid her of the nymphs. Maybe we'll find an answer in Nuren."

"Be careful, child," Lucia cautioned. "Keep David safe. Even if you must abandon everyone else."

When the girl left, Lucia looked down at her food. She had lost her appetite. She felt ill about David's vulnerability by leaving Caislucis and going to Nuren, and nauseated at the thought of the nymphs ravaging her sister's body.

And where was David? He should have come and told her about Eulalia's illness himself, rather than sending the girl. Did he hate her so much he couldn't stand the sight of her?

Screaming with frustration, she threw the tray at the bars of her cell. It bounced off with a loud clang and sent berries careening into the dungeon corridor.

Her act of defiance was met with a threat from the guard on duty. "Quiet down there!" he called from his station near the stairs. "Or I shall come and silence you myself. For good. I hardly think anyone would mind."

Seething, Lucia quietly retrieved the tray and sat down on her bench. She was angry with David and furious at Tierney for making the Sower an ally. Mostly though, she loathed herself for her part in Tierney's schemes.

David needed her help, whether he knew it or not. But she wouldn't beg for her freedom. She would find a way to free herself. Looking down at the tray in her lap, she conceived a plan.

The scene Abby encountered upon arriving at Nuren was shocking. The stark silence that had settled over the village felt wrong. Even the normally charming trickle of the stream and bleating of the goats sounded nightmarish, hollow and out of place against the lack of voices. And the sight of the people was almost more than she could bear. They were lying all over the village like they had dropped dead. A young man was sprawled next to a feed trough, his goats feeding around him, oblivious to his plight. A woman lay spread-eagle on her back in a chicken pen, her eyes closed, her face tilted to the sky. The woven bag of feed she had dropped was methodically being plucked apart by hens trying to free the seed within.

Near the granary David had rebuilt after it was destroyed by the Daughters of Mercy, the miller was draped over the grinding stone. A woman was slumped next to the pile of clothes she had been washing near the stream next to the mill.

The worst was Yola's daughter, crumpled near the doorway of her family's thatched-roof cottage, her face turned away. The tiny girl seemed a mere three years old.

Yola approached her daughter, looking as though she was afraid to find out whether or not the child still lived.

David nodded to Abby, and they stepped away to give the woman space to grieve if need be. He walked over to the miller and reached out to touch him.

Abby snatched his hand away. "Wait," she hissed, "something's wrong."

David looked around at the village. "I know. This is horrible."

Abby shook her head vehemently. "No. I mean, I know you want to help, but don't touch him. Don't touch anyone. We can't risk this spreading to you."

"But I promised I would help. We have to figure out what this is."

"No," Abby insisted. "Just wait a second...let me." She cautiously reached out, touching the man's neck, feeling for signs of life. She let out a breath she hadn't realized she'd been holding. "He's alive. His pulse is weak, but he's breathing. What *is* this?"

Her thought was interrupted by a strangled cry from Yola.

Abby looked over to see that Yola's daughter had opened her eyes—but there was something wrong. The expression on the girl's face was slack, and her eyes were trained on something above her, the sky perhaps. It was as though she wasn't seeing her mother at all. Yola was cradling the child, caressing her cheek, saying her name over and over, begging her for some sign of recognition.

Abby and David stepped closer, and then Abby saw that the girl's eyes had faded to white, like Nerine's had. Like Eulalia's had. The child wriggled from her mother's arms and stood slowly, facing Yola. The girl cocked her head to the side, studying Yola as if she were seeing her for the first time. Then she wrapped her tiny arms around her mother's neck, kissing Yola's lips. Yola's eyes widened, and her body went rigid.

"Yola?" David asked, taking a cautious step forward. "Are you all right?"

Yola's eyes fluttered closed and then snapped back open. She turned to David, and Abby gasped with horror as the woman's eyes faded from a rich, warm brown to a sickly white tinged with red.

"*Run*, Solas Beir," Yola whispered.

Around them, the other villagers opened their eyes and struggled to their feet. David stood wide-eyed and frozen as the people of Nuren shuffled toward him. Soon he and Abby would be surrounded. Cael barked orders to the guards, and the soldiers drew their swords, forming a circle around David and Abby.

This is what Lucia was worried about, Abby thought. She grabbed David's arm, surprised at her own strength, fueled by the adrenaline pounding through her veins. She dragged him toward his horse. "We have to get away from them."

He resisted, unable to wrench his gaze from the oncoming villagers. "But...there's got to be *something* we can do," he insisted.

Behind David, Obelia and Eoin looked on, terrified, waiting for him to take charge.

Abby reached up and turned his face toward hers. "David." He blinked, looking at her dazedly, as if he couldn't comprehend what was happening. "There's nothing we can do here. We *have* to go."

David looked back at the villagers and Abby followed his gaze. The crowd was growing more aggressive, clawing at the soldiers holding them back.

"Go!" Cael shouted to David before shoving the miller to the ground. Even as he fell, the man had his eyes on David and his hands were grasping like talons.

Reluctantly, David turned back to Abby. He nodded and pulled himself up into his saddle.

Abby breathed a sigh of relief—she hadn't been sure if he would comply. Quickly she leapt up and threw her leg over her own saddle, goading her mare forward. "Come on!"

David seemed to shake off his shock, and he kicked his stallion into a gallop. Eoin and Obelia weren't far behind.

They rode hard into the forest, trying to put distance between themselves and the village. Looking over her shoulder, Abby saw a lone rider coming up fast. She reined her horse to a trot. "Cael?" she called hesitantly, frightened of what she might see in his eyes.

Cael slowed, holding up his hand in greeting. His eyes were the same deep brown they'd always been.

"You escaped," David said, relief etched on his face.

Cael nodded. "Only just. The others..." His face fell. "They were overtaken."

Abby eyed Cael suspiciously, studying him for signs of illness. "Did any of them touch you?" She thought about him pushing the miller away, and how quickly Yola's eyes had changed when her daughter kissed her.

"I know what you are thinking, Abby, and you are right to

react with suspicion," Cael said, meeting her gaze. "But I swear on the queen's life I am not infected."

Abby swallowed. "Okay. I know you wouldn't say that lightly."

Cael shook his head. "No. I never would."

David looked from Abby to Cael. "Let's get back to Caislucis. We need to find out if this is happening in any of the other villages."

"Agreed," Abby said. "Let's go. I may have a theory about how this is spreading."

"How?" David asked.

"The kiss," Abby explained. "Yola's daughter kissed her, and she became infected. Nerine kissed Eulalia. And she tried to kiss you."

"But Nerine kissed Eulalia's cheeks—not her lips," David insisted.

"True," Abby replied. "And maybe that's why it took longer for Eulalia to show symptoms. Yola turned immediately."

David frowned. "That tells us how it spreads. It doesn't tell us how to stop it."

Abby reached over and squeezed David's hand. "We'll find a way. We just have to keep looking."

Entering the gates of Caislucis, they could see that all was well. In the town square, Abby could see merchants going about their daily business, and nothing looked amiss in the stables as she turned her mare over to her groomsman. "At least the illness seems to have been contained here. Maybe when we see Eulalia, she'll be lucid enough to give us some clue about how to cure her."

David sighed, walking toward the castle. "I hope so. To have to run from my own people and not be able to help them..."

He shook his head in frustration.

Obelia put her hand on his arm and nodded sympathetically. "I understand, Solas Beir. But you had no choice. If something happens to you—"

David frowned. "I know. I have to stay safe, and there are good reasons for keeping me from using my powers to heal people from whatever this is. But I feel useless." He pulled open the castle doors leading to the Great Hall.

Immediately, they were confronted by a dozen guards brandishing weapons. Phelan, the head of the guards, strode smugly to the entryway. The guards parted slightly to allow him though.

"Seize them!" Phelan commanded as the hall doors boomed shut. He was dressed in armor, as though ready for battle. The only thing missing was his helmet.

Eoin stepped forward to shield David, but he was overpowered. His arms were wrenched roughly behind him and bound, and the soldiers advanced to do the same to the others.

As a guard approached Obelia, she smacked his hands away. "How dare you? I serve as head of the Solas Beir's council." Her objections went unheeded as the soldier bound her.

Another guard grabbed Abby's arm. "Hey!" She attempted to draw her sword, but Phelan held the point of his weapon to her chest while the guard disarmed her.

"Phelan!" Cael growled, his hand on the hilt of his sword. "Lower your weapon and explain yourself."

Phelan looked genuinely surprised. He angled his sword down but didn't sheath it. "My apologies, Sir, but the Solas Beir himself ordered the arrest of your party." He held out his other hand. "Your weapon, Sir."

They were surrounded—there was no choice but to surrender. Cael unbuckled his belt, sliding the silver scabbard off the length of leather and handing his sheathed sword to

Phelan. Angrily, he secured his belt around his waist.

"What madness is this?" Eoin demanded, struggling against the iron grip of the soldier mashing his face against the wall. "*This* is the Solas Beir," he said as he directed his gaze toward David, who stood with his back against the closed doors, breathing heavily with outrage.

"Not anymore." The voice echoed through the hall, originating from the other side of the room.

The guards parted, and to her horror, Abby saw Sholto sitting on the throne, wearing David's diadem. Eulalia and Marisol knelt on either side of him, leaning their heads on his lap. Marisol's eyes were as white as the queen's.

Sholto shrugged the women off and stood. "I am Ardal's firstborn. *I* am the true Solas Beir."

"The Sower," Abby breathed. "I should have known."

"No!" David shouted as the guards seized him. "You're an abomination!"

Sholto smirked. "And you, little brother, are a fraud," he replied mildly. "All of Cai Terenmare is *mine*," he declared, his voice booming. His gaze fell on Cael. "Including these two." He gestured to Eulalia and Marisol and smiled. "Cael, my friend. How do you like my consorts? You killed my mother and my sisters, so I've taken hostage your wife and your protégé."

It was then that Abby noticed their shackled wrists and the iron collars around their necks. It occurred to her that Sholto might have forced Marisol to kiss him, and Abby wished she could take back all the horrible things she'd thought about her friend. No matter what Marisol had done or hadn't done, she deserved better than this.

Sholto laughed, running his fingers along the length of chain binding the women to the throne, causing it to jingle loudly. Eulalia and Marisol hissed, showing no sign of recognition for Cael. For any of them.

"No!" Cael cried out, his voice full of agony.

Cael tried to lunge past the guards, but David and Abby held him back as Phelan raised his sword to Cael's neck, awaiting his new master's next command.

Sholto grinned wickedly. "Bind them and throw them in the dungeon while I decide on a fitting method of execution."

Phelan kept his sword on Cael while the guards grabbed David and Abby.

"There are just so many delightful possibilities for ending you, *Lightbearer*," Sholto mused.

David scowled at his use of the word. Although the term "lightbearer" usually referred to a leader not yet crowned Solas Beir, in this instance Sholto was using it as a derogatory term, referring to a weak leader. A false Solas Beir. A fraud.

But the Sower wasn't done insulting David yet. He eyed Abby and chuckled. "Of course, perhaps I shall spare the girl and add her to my collection."

"Never," David growled. "Abby will never be yours, and neither will my kingdom! I am the Solas Beir, and you are an imposter." Escaping the guard's grasp, David shoved the other soldier away from Abby. He tried to draw heat into his palms to fight for her, but nothing happened. He studied his hands with disbelief. His powers had chosen the absolute worst time to fail him.

The guard who had seized David before grabbed him again from behind. Then there was a loud clang, and the guard crumpled to the floor. David turned to see Lucia holding the silver tray Abby had brought to her before their trip.

Sholto looked shocked to see her. "The traitor?" he spat. "You are supposed to be dead."

The guards froze, seemingly baffled that she had escaped the dungeon. David too wondered how she had managed that.

"Surprise," Lucia called mockingly. "If you think for one

second, Sower, that Tierney will let you keep that throne, you're delusional. You're just keeping it warm for him," she taunted.

Sholto scowled at her and then motioned to the guards, who stood waiting for his next command. "Well? What are you waiting for? Seize them all!"

"Go!" Lucia shouted, bashing another guard over the head.

Cael slipped from Phelan's grasp and fought him off. David retrieved his scabbard from the guard who had tried to bind him, now lying on the floor unconscious, thanks to Lucia. He drew his sword as the soldiers attacked, shielding Abby so she could grab her sword to cut Obelia and Eoin loose.

Together they beat back the guards and then fled the hall. David and Abby barred the guards from following them, holding the tall doors shut, while Cael wheeled a cart over and wedged it against the castle doors. It wasn't long before they heard the guards banging against them. They needed to run, to escape the city before the guards resumed their chase.

A shadow passed overhead. David looked up to see Abby's raven. "Brarn!" she cried, just as something grabbed David from behind and rocketed him up into the sky.

David twisted around to find himself in Erela's grasp.

"We must go, Solas Beir," she explained. "You cannot remain here."

"I can fly though," David protested. "We need to go back and help the others." He could see them far below, tiny dots against the cobblestone of the square.

Erela shook her head sadly. "No, I fear you cannot. I have been watching over you, Solas Beir, and I am afraid you no longer possess the power you once held."

"What?" *No,* he thought, *That can't be true.* "How is that possible?"

Erela ignored his question and descended, hovering over the others on the ground, her great wings flapping steadily. "I shall take him to the Northern Stronghold," she called. "Meet us there." Then she turned, spiriting him away from his home.

Looking back, David saw Brarn circle Abby's head. Abby watched the bird for a second, and then shivered as she changed into a white raven. She and Brarn joined him and Erela in the air.

Cael stared after Erela and then turned to Lucia. Obelia and Eoin were looking at the traitor with a mixture of relief and revulsion.

"How did you get out? Did you use your magic?" Cael questioned. If it was so easy to escape the dungeon, why hadn't she done it before?

Lucia shook her head. "No. I knocked out one of the guards and stole his keys." Then she gave him a wry smile. "And isn't it a good thing I did? You're welcome."

Cael huffed and crossed his arms, turning his attention to the town square. If only he hadn't surrendered his weapon. At least David and Abby had retrieved theirs—he wished he'd had the opportunity to do the same. He felt vulnerable without his sword by his side.

At least he could grab his horse. He marched over to the stable. The stable hand, who had taken his horse not minutes before, charged at him, wielding a pitchfork. Cael only had a second to avoid being impaled and register that the man's eyes had turned white before Lucia's round tray whizzed past him, hitting the man in the temple and knocking him out cold. Cael looked up to see her satisfied smile as she admired her handiwork. "Thanks," he said begrudgingly.

Lucia's smug smile widened as she put her hands on her hips. She was enjoying having him in her debt a little too much for his taste.

He heard rustling coming from the stable and saw the

other grooms gathering weapons from whatever was close at hand. Quickly, he pulled the stable doors shut and barred them with his attacker's pitchfork. The newly turned grooms slammed into the stable doors, trying to escape. "So no horses then," Cael muttered to himself.

From a side street, he heard a shout and turned to see Gorman running toward the square with Fergal perched on his indigo shoulder.

"Come friends!" Gorman called. "We must flee the city!"

"Where did you come from?" Obelia asked. She looked relieved to see that someone had escaped the Sower's cursed plague.

"We gathered what weapons we could," Fergal replied, pointing to the bag of swords slung across Gorman's back.

In spite of his anguish over seeing Eulalia and Marisol captured by the Sower, Cael felt hopeful as he relieved the Caislucis historian of his heavy load. He hid a smile and gave Fergal a stern look. "You stole them, you mean. From the blacksmith's shop."

Fergal frowned. "Yes, well, we could not access the armory or the cache of weapons I had hidden as a precaution. And the blacksmith is..." He paused, as if choosing his words carefully. "He is, you might say, no longer aligned with the throne. Better a sword in my hands than his." The faery put his hands on his hips, peering up at Cael. "I hardly think you can fault me for thievery at a time such as this."

Cael chuckled, quickly selecting a sword and testing its weight. "No, I cannot. Well done." He favored Fergal with a sly smile, soliciting a grin from the tiny knight.

"A wise move," Gorman agreed. "Only Fergal would have had the foresight to plan for a retreat." He looked up at Caislucis mournfully. "Never in all my years would I have thought we would be forced to flee our home."

"Actually," Fergal confessed, "it was Abby who counseled

me to prepare for the unexpected." He shifted his weight to balance on the indigo man's shoulder as Gorman took on his spirit animal form, an Asian elephant.

"Smart girl," Lucia murmured.

Obelia studied Lucia through guarded eyes. "I quite agree." She shivered slightly and changed into a cheetah. Arching her back and stretching her muscles, she readied her lean feline body for a long run.

Eoin studied the animal forms of his fellow council members. "I am afraid my ability to transform into a creature of the sea will be of little use today. I shall have to run alongside you."

"Or you can join me up here," Fergal called from his perch on Gorman's head. The elephant used his trunk to grasp Eoin around his waist and gently set him on his back.

Eoin patted Gorman's tough hide. "Thank you, my friend." The elephant nodded and he and the cheetah started off toward the city gates.

Lucia looked from the others to Cael. "Do you mind? I seem to have lost my ability to transform—along with my magic."

Cael narrowed his eyes, considering. "Fine," he said, annoyed, tapping his fingers on the hilt of his new sword. "Just this once. Do *not* make me regret trusting you."

She held up her hands non-threateningly. "I won't."

He shifted into his wolf form and allowed her to climb onto his back. Then he ran after the others.

Erela, Abby, and Brarn flew until the sun set. David could no longer see Cael, Lucia, and the others below, but he could see the tension in Erela's face, the frustration of having to fly slower than she was capable so the others could keep up.

It had taken some convincing to get her to slow down. Were it up to the last Daughter of Mercy, she would have already whisked David halfway across the world, far from the Sower's reach. She was not pleased when David suggested that they stop for the night.

"It is not safe, Solas Beir," she insisted. "The North Forest is too close to Caislucis, and the trees provide too much cover. We could be easily ambushed."

"I understand, Erela," David replied. "But we don't have a plan. We need to rest and regroup. And find food, if we can."

Reluctantly, Erela consented to setting David down in a clearing. She immediately took to the sky, circling the camp in search of enemies. David smiled to himself. Woe to any wandering Kruorumbrae she found. They would be toast.

Abby landed beside him and shifted back into her human form. She looked exhausted. David pulled her into an embrace and they stood there for a moment, just holding each other, relieved to have escaped the Sower's trap. David was furious about the Sower taking Eulalia and Marisol, as well as Caislucis, but he was grateful he still had Abby. He couldn't bear the thought of losing her again.

He pulled back and searched her face. "You okay?" he asked, running a thumb over her cheek.

She nodded, her eyes following Erela. "She makes a good point about being careful, but I won't argue about stopping for the night. We've been flying for hours, and boy, are my arms tired." She halfheartedly flapped her arms and smiled wearily.

In spite of the anger and grief he felt, David laughed. He kissed her and then captured one of her hands in his, leading her over to a soft patch of grass. She collapsed with a sigh and pulled him down to sit next to her.

Brarn landed beside them, and Abby stroked the feathers behind his head. In return, he gave her a beaky smile.

Within the hour, Gorman charged into the clearing and

stopped, kneeling to allow Eoin and Fergal to slide off his back before taking on his regular form. At his side, Obelia paced back and forth anxiously, peering into the forest with glowing, amber cheetah eyes. Satisfied there was no immediate danger, she transformed back into herself, turning when she heard Cael approach.

Lucia gave David a slight smile, her hands thrust into Cael's fur. David was certain she had never imagined the day would end with her hitching a ride on the back of someone she'd once tried to kill. He thought back to the battle at the Eye of the Needle. Cael had almost died at Lucia's command. Of course, Lucia had almost died soon after. They couldn't call things even, but maybe they could set their differences aside since Eulalia's life was in peril. More than that—the fate of Cai Terenmare was at stake.

David still hadn't made up his mind about Lucia. Could he trust her? He was sure she was no longer working for Tierney, but that didn't mean she didn't have feelings for him, that she wouldn't betray David in the heat of battle to save the man she might still love. She might not *want* to hurt David, but she might do it anyway. Love made people do crazy things—like betray their families and kidnap their nephews. She had proved that much already, no matter what she said about being loyal to David and not loving Tierney anymore.

Still, David couldn't help but smile, remembering Lucia beaning the guard with a metal tray during their escape from Caislucis. *That* was the Lucia he'd grown up with, even though she had gone by a different name back then. He hoped that was the woman she would be when they went to battle with Tierney and the Sower.

Lucia slid off Cael's back and he shook off his wolf form, changing back into himself. They didn't say anything to each other, but Cael nodded to her before leaving her standing at the edge of the camp. She seemed hesitant to approach the others, and instead busied herself by gathering firewood.

Cael rushed over to David and Abby. “Solas Beir.”

David rose, pulling Abby to her feet. “Thanks for carrying Lucia. I appreciate you taking care of her.”

“You are welcome,” Cael said. “I did it for you. And because that is what Eulalia would have wanted.” His eyes were full of despair.

Abby wrapped her arms around Cael’s waist. “I’m so sorry.”

Cael didn’t answer. His arms tightened around Abby’s shoulders, trembling as though it was all he could do to not fall apart.

David put his hand on Cael’s shoulder. “We’ll get her back. Marisol too.”

Cael let out a shaky breath, nodded, and then released Abby, showing his gratitude with a sad smile. He drew himself up, stowing away his grief as he watched Lucia fill her arms with dry branches.

“It might not be wise to have a fire tonight. The light would serve as a beacon, revealing our location.”

“True,” David agreed, “but we’ll need it for warmth and cooking. We’ll keep watch like we did in the rainforest.”

In his search for allies, David had led an expedition to the village of the Southern Oracle with Abby, Cael, Jon, and Marisol. It had been a harrowing trip, and they had encountered a number of vile creatures along the way. Of course, now they’d lost both Jon and Marisol. David wondered which of his traveling companions he would lose this time.

“Finding food will be difficult,” Cael replied with a frown. “I saw no sign of animals. They seem to have fled this part of the forest as well.”

“I think you’re right,” Abby said. “I can’t shake the feeling that something bad happened here.”

“It is the same sense of unease I felt swimming in the Bay

of Yakez," Eoin chimed in as he joined them. "Perhaps the Sower passed this way before he traveled to my village."

"It is possible," Cael mused. "I saw evidence of another earthquake. Several trees have fallen near the stream we crossed before we reached this clearing."

Eoin nodded. "I saw that too. One of the fallen trees has cut off part of the stream." He smiled to himself. "My abilities as a water creature may be of use yet." He turned and headed back the way they had come.

David and Cael exchanged a puzzled look and followed, Abby tagging along close behind. When they caught up to Eoin, he was studying a deep pool that had been separated from the stream by the downed tree.

"As I suspected." The councilman smiled and dove into the pool, transforming into a sea lion mid-plunge. When he surfaced, he held a fat, silvery fish in his teeth.

Delighted, Abby tugged the bottom of her shirt forward, forming a basket. Eoin tossed the fish into the air, and she caught it, giggling.

"Guess we'll have dinner after all," David laughed, holding out his shirt too.

Seven fish later, the sea lion broke the surface of the water and was replaced by a grinning Eoin. "I just took mine raw, but you may wish to cook yours," he suggested.

Abby scrunched up her nose, staring at the four fish wriggling in the pouch she'd made, their glassy eyes bulging. "Definitely. No sushi for me, thanks."

Eoin chuckled. "There will be more of the same for breakfast, so I hope you enjoy it."

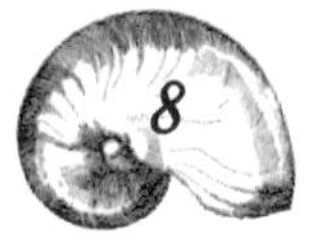

8

TIERNEY

After the guards announced his arrival, Tierney was escorted into the Great Hall for an audience with the Sower. It had been decades since he'd been welcomed into Caislucis.

Little had changed. He noted with amusement, however, that the large doors at the entrance of the castle had been damaged, and several of the guards boasted injuries, signs of a recent struggle. *The Lightbearer did not give up the throne easily,* he surmised.

The self-proclaimed Solas Beir had already made himself at home in the castle. Perched on the throne and dressed in fine clothing, the white-haired Sower was crowned with a silver diadem. Tierney suppressed a chuckle—he imagined Sholto plucking it from David Corbin's head before evicting the boy from his new home.

Sholto was speaking with Phelan. Hundreds of merfolk had been added to the ranks of the soldiers at Caislucis, and he was giving the knight instructions to merge the two factions into one army and prepare for the coming battle.

The dowager queen and one of the Corbin boy's young friends knelt, chained to the throne, and at Tierney's approach, the two women rose up and hissed at him, their milk-white eyes showing clearly that they were under the Sower's influence.

Tierney wondered which of them had been Sholto's first choice to add to his burgeoning collection.

Much to Tierney's annoyance, the Sower kept him waiting until he had finished conversing with the guard before acknowledging his arrival. *You'd think you might display more gratitude for the person who handed you the crown.* Tierney hid his irritation with a low bow, his arms held out, as was the custom in the eastern regions of Cai Terenmare. "Your Majesty," he purred. "You look well. I daresay that throne suits you."

Sholto gave Tierney a curt nod and raised his head proudly. For a moment, his form wavered, and Tierney could see the reptilian beast hidden just beneath the Sower's pale skin. Sholto's true form was that of a venomous monster, a creature that grew more powerful each time its spore infected another puppet. The man on the throne was just an illusion.

"I have what is rightfully mine. At long last."

"Your mother would be very proud," Tierney agreed.

The old Western Oracle had had her puppets too, he reflected. But while Sholto held his victims' minds captive, the Oracle had consumed the bodies and minds of her former lovers, absorbing them into her monstrous, bloated body. Yet, for all their differences, mother and son had one thing in common, besides being monsters, of course—a black-and-white banded tail.

Tierney could see no resemblance to the creature's father, but nevertheless, he *was* Ardal's firstborn. "I am certain your father would be proud as well to see his true heir seated on the throne."

The Sower frowned. "I never knew either of my parents. Only Meridoris, who kept me hidden until such a time as I could infiltrate the Sea King's court. But she is quite proud."

At this, Tierney heard a rustling sound. The sea hag emerged from a darkened room behind the throne, a room where the court council used to meet—but they would be meeting there no more.

As the snake woman entered the Great Hall, she towed a young girl tightly by the arm. Tierney recognized the child. She was a courtesan, one he'd given to the sea hag in the City of the Eastern Oracle as payment for her service of shadowing David Corbin during his journey to the Southern Oracle to gather information about the boy and his friends.

"Meridoris," Tierney smiled. "How lovely to see you again. And I see you've still got your gift with you."

"Greetings, my Lord," Meridoris crooned at him, settling into her place beside the dais. Her long, banded tail had a paddle at the end, like a sea krait's, and curved lazily behind her. "I have treasured my pet—thank you." She caressed the girl's head, running fat, stubby fingers over the child's dark curls.

The girl strained against the sea hag's iron grip, to no avail. Tierney winked at the courtesan, and she cowered. At least the child paid him due respect. But no worry. He would teach the Sower his place and take pleasure in watching him tremble.

Sholto eyed them, scowling at the interaction between Tierney and his serpentine nursemaid. "What news of the Eastern Oracle?" he interrupted.

Tierney ignored the Sower for a moment, making the new monarch wait while he tenderly grasped the lamia's hand, raised it to his lips, and kissed it with deliberate slowness. He could hear Sholto shift impatiently in his seat, but he held the sea hag's gaze, sensing her surprise and the increase of her pulse.

Flattering a creature like Meridoris was far too easy. "*Such* a pleasure," he murmured, relishing the look of adoration on her face before releasing her hand and turning to the Sower. "The Eastern Oracle has pledged his loyalty. I have sent him by way of Southport to find new recruits. They will join us on the battlefield."

"Good," Sholto replied, his grey eyes boring into Tierney.

"When do we march?"

"Soon," Tierney assured him. "And the Western Oracle? Is she," he chuckled to himself, "loyal?"

A bleak look crossed over the Sower's face. "Nerine is dead. At the hands of the last Daughter of Mercy."

"The outcast," Tierney muttered, narrowing his eyes. Erela had cost him much of late, coming to the Lightbearer's aid at the Eye of the Needle. When the time came, he vowed, she would pay for her defiance. Dearly. He hid his anger with a nonchalant smile. "No matter. We shall simply appoint a new oracle."

"Who?" Sholto asked, a suspicious look on his face.

Tierney could tell the Sower expected him to nominate himself as a candidate, and that Sholto wasn't keen on the Kruor um Beir gaining more power. But Tierney wasn't interested in becoming the oracle, especially since the position seemed cursed.

Those who served as Western Oracle tended to die violently. Besides, he had his sights set on a more ambitious role.

But who indeed? Tierney considered the available options. The dowager queen or the Cassidy girl were tempting choices, certain to be a slap in the Lightbearer's face. But the Sower seemed possessive of them, and they were too far under his spell to be capable of rational thought.

He looked over at Phelan, the knight who had served directly under Cael, now head of the royal guard. He was still capable of following orders, but he too was infested. No good. Tierney needed someone who hadn't been turned, someone the Sower cared about, who might serve as collateral should the plan go awry. Someone expendable.

His gaze fell on the lamia. *Why not?* She was like a mother to Sholto, and eager to please. As a bonus, choosing her would annoy the Eastern Oracle, who thought himself above a bottom-dweller like the sea hag. Normally, the man could be a tiresome bore, but when riled, the Eastern Oracle was nothing short of entertaining.

Tierney grinned and seized the lamia's hand, drawing her forward. "How about Meridoris?" he suggested.

Her mouth gaped open in astonishment.

"She has proved her worth time and again, and loyalty is a quality that should be valued above all others," Tierney explained, watching the sea hag's face light up with delight at his praise. He favored her with a brilliant smile. "I think it's time we elevated Meridoris to a place of honor, don't you?"

Sholto smiled, surprised and pleased with Tierney's choice. "I agree." He rose from his seat. "Step forward, dear Mother."

The snake woman gestured to a merman guard to hold the courtesan, and then slithered toward the throne, beaming at her surrogate son. She bowed slightly and lowered her head, her black-and-white striped tail coiled primly behind her.

Sholto stepped to the edge of the dais and placed his hands on her shoulders. "I, Solas Beir of Cai Terenmare, appoint you, Meridoris of the Deep, as the Western Oracle. I grant you power as a seer and authority over the sea, from the shores of Caislucis to the Eastern Cliffs. Do you pledge your loyalty and accept this charge?"

"I do," the sea hag replied, looking up at him, serpent's eyes set deep into her toadlike face.

"Then it is so," Sholto declared, leaning down to trace the shape of a spiral on the lamia's warty, mottled forehead. The shape glowed golden and faded. Meridoris bowed again and returned to her place beside the dais.

The Sower turned and settled into his throne, tenting his hands as he studied Tierney. "Now. We have two oracles who have sworn loyalty, and all the towns and villages in the west are under my control. What else must be done before we march?"

Tierney held up a hand. "First, tell me what happened with the Lightbearer—unless he is currently awaiting his fate in the dungeon?" Given the damage to the castle doors and the injuries of the guards, Tierney doubted it.

Sholto hissed and glared at Tierney, tightly gripping the armrests of the throne, as if that were the only thing barring him from releasing his rage. "The imposter resisted arrest, insisting he was the true Solas Beir," he spat.

Tierney nodded, unconcerned. He had suspected as much—disappointing, but no matter. Fortune would favor him, not David Corbin. Sooner or later the boy would be in his grasp.

"Of course, if he had been the true Solas Beir," the Sower smirked, "he would have proved his claim through a show of power. Instead he proved himself a coward and a weakling, relying not on his own strength to save him, but on a woman."

Tierney raised his eyebrows. "The c'aislingaer?" How had she escaped the Wasteland? Abigail Brown was full of surprises. It was a thought that both enraged and delighted him.

Sholto shook his head. "Not the c'aislingaer. Although she too was here." He smiled bitterly. "No, it was Lucia. The traitor *you* failed to kill."

Impossible. Tierney silently cursed, and then quickly covered his shock with a neutral expression. It would not do to show weakness. "How did she survive?"

Sholto scowled. "Does it matter? She is very much alive, and found her way back to the Lightbearer. Now they have fled the city together."

"In which direction?" Tierney questioned.

"North," Meridoris rasped.

Tierney turned to the sea hag, who looked frozen, her long tail rigid and perfectly still. Her voice had deepened, and her eyes were glazed over, staring straight ahead at something Tierney could not see. She was having a vision.

"The Solas Beir flies north with the cai aislingstraid and

the last Daughter of Mercy."

Before being appointed oracle, Meridoris had claimed to be a seer, but Tierney had been skeptical about the extent of her power, viewing it as merely a ploy to gain favor.

He had no doubt now. He recognized the power of an oracle when he saw it. He had been one once, after all. "Where are they going?" he asked, grasping her hands, trying to meld his power as Kruor um Beir with hers.

"To the Northern Stronghold," Meridoris replied. "Lucia rides with the first knight of Caislucis."

How very cozy, Tierney thought. "She has made an alliance with Cael?"

"And I have what Cael values most in this world," Sholto announced, grabbing the chain on the collar around Eulalia's neck and yanking hard.

The queen stumbled and fell face-first on the floor next to the throne. When she raised her head, dazed, her nose and lips were bloodied.

"He will not dare defy me," the Sower boasted. "But I grow weary of waiting to avenge my mother. Tell me when we march."

"Call your followers and tell them to come to Caislucis," Tierney said. "We will arm them, and take the battle north."

"And then?" Sholto asked impatiently. "Then will I *finally* have the pleasure of killing my brother?"

"Of course," Tierney nodded, bowing. "Your Majesty."

Sholto leaned forward, eyeing Tierney suspiciously. "And you will not rob me of this honor?"

Tierney smiled. "I wouldn't dream of it."

Abby was dreaming. She knew it was a dream because instead of being surrounded by the dark trees of the North

Forest, she was running through an emerald field of waist-high grass. The sun was encircled by a rainbow nimbus, and she could see crystalline drops of morning dew magnified on each slender blade of grass, rendered in the vivid detail of a c'aislingaer's dream.

Her slippered feet only skimmed the ground with each long stride, sending her sailing over the meadow as though she were leaping like a doe. The long white sleeves and skirt of her gown billowed around her as she ran.

He wasn't far behind. She didn't look back, but she could hear him in the crackle of wet grass as he bounded after her. He'd given up being subtle in favor of a full-on chase. She felt warm breath on her skin and laughed, skipping teasingly out of his reach.

The meadow gave way to mounds of small grey boulders, and ahead, the edge of a cliff. Another leap sent her twisting away from his eager grasp, and then she slowed to a walk, collapsing in a heap of happy exhaustion on the ground near the cliff's edge. She stared out at the waves below as she caught her breath.

He padded up from behind her, settling on his haunches next to her. From the corner of her eye, she could see his massive white paws. Eyes on the azure horizon, she reached up to scratch behind his ears, enveloping her fingers in silky fur.

He leaned his head into her familiar touch, purring. She smiled and turned to him, and to her surprise found herself face-to-face not with her white lion, but with a white tiger with clear blue eyes and long canines like sabers. He nuzzled her hand affectionately and returned his gaze to the cerulean sea.

Abby opened her eyes to find Lucia watching her with the same distaste she might have for a sewer rat. Involuntarily, she shrank under the woman's penetrating gaze and looked away. Her cheeks flushed with heat, Abby felt annoyed with herself for acting like a criminal.

There was no reason for Lucia to be scrutinizing her like she was a virus under a microscope. Abby hadn't done anything wrong, and it wasn't like Lucia could know that she'd been dreaming about Tierney. As far as Abby knew, Lucia wasn't a mind-reader. If she was, Lucia would have known that Tierney planned to throw her off that balcony and done something to save herself. Abby had firsthand experience with Lucia's ability to manipulate people, but still, she wasn't a c'aislingaer, so she couldn't know what Abby had dreamed. Could she?

A disturbing thought occurred to her: What if Lucia suspected something because she knew Tierney intimately? What if Lucia knew why Tierney was haunting Abby and had chosen not to share her information? Or what if—Abby shuddered with horror—what if she'd said his name out loud in her sleep?

Abby felt her face grow even redder. Was it possible for a person to die of embarrassment? She remembered how mortified she'd felt when she'd first started dreaming of Tierney, and then the shame she'd felt when she had finally told David about it. She felt like she'd been cheating on him, even though it had all been in her head.

She had kept her dreams a secret because she didn't want to hurt David, but she'd ended up hurting him anyway, and she never wanted to do that again. Abby had hoped she was past all that—she hadn't dreamed of Tierney since she'd returned from the Wasteland. But now he was back.

Abby felt a surge of defiant anger. She appreciated Lucia's help escaping the Sower, but it wasn't any of her business what Abby dreamed about. It's not like Abby had chosen to be a cai aislingstraid or had invited Tierney to invade her dreams. Even so, she was irritated with herself for feeling guilty, and she couldn't risk Lucia being the one to tell David about her continuing link to Tierney.

She sighed, resigned. There was only one thing she could to do to make sure there were no secrets between her and David—to keep his trust. She was going to have to tell him about her dream.

Abby surveyed her surroundings. David was already awake, moving around the campsite, packing up supplies and weapons with Cael and Fergal. Gorman was cooking fish that Eoin must have caught that morning from the pool near the camp. Eoin and Obelia sat talking with the Caislucis historian turned cook, pointedly avoiding conversation with Lucia. They didn't believe she had changed alliances.

Abby didn't think she was still loyal to Tierney, but given Lucia's past, she couldn't blame the council members for their lack of trust.

As she worked up her courage to talk to David, Abby smoothed her hair and pulled it back into a braid. Finally, when she couldn't stall any longer, she stood up and walked over to him. He was sitting on a large stump, sharpening his sword.

He smiled as he looked up from his work. "Good morning." He sheathed the sword and set it aside. Then he reached out for her hands, pulling her close to perch on his lap. "We made it through the night without getting ambushed."

Abby swallowed, thinking about how she was about to ambush him with bad news. She put her arms around him and buried her face in the crook of his neck. She couldn't do this to him again. She just couldn't.

"What's wrong?" he asked. "Another nightmare?"

She felt a flash of guilt at the concern in his voice. He stroked her hair, trying to coax it out of her. "Not a nightmare," she mumbled, thinking about how happy she'd felt in the dream, up until the point she'd realized she was with Tierney instead of David. "But not a good dream, either."

He froze, his hand cradling her cheek. "What did you see?"

She looked up at him, feeling drained. "Tierney."

The expression on his face darkened, but he didn't say anything.

She stared at her feet, avoiding his eyes. "I saw him in his animal form." She choked out a laugh, but there wasn't any humor in it, just humiliation. "I actually thought it was you at first, running behind me, but then I got a better look, and I realized it wasn't you. It was him."

David gently lifted her chin to look in her eyes. "Did he hurt you?"

Abby wanted to curl up and die—she didn't deserve for him to look at her like that, with so much love and concern. "No," she answered, hating herself. "It wasn't like that at all. He had changed, somehow. He was still a tiger, but he was good. His fur had turned white."

David's eyes widened in surprise. "What do you think that means?"

Abby shook her head. "I wish I knew."

Someone, her mother probably, had once told Abby that confession was good for the soul. Soaring through the air beside David and Erela, she still felt self-conscious about her dream, but she no longer felt weighed down with secrets, which was good, because she doubted she could fly carrying a burden like that. Her white raven was on the small side, after all.

David still wasn't able to fly, transform into a lion, or generate fire. Abby worried that he'd lost his ability to heal as well. She had offered to use her sword to make a small cut on her hand so he could try, but he wouldn't let her.

Lucia had lost her powers as well. She'd been quiet for most of the journey, only talking when spoken to. That didn't matter, because no one except David had any interest in conversing with her. In spite of everything that Lucia had done to him, Abby could see David still cared about her. He seemed relieved that she hadn't been infected by the Sower and certain she had chosen him over Tierney. Abby wasn't convinced, but reserved judgment for David's sake.

Obelia, Eoin, and the others hadn't made an effort to hide their feelings about traveling with a traitor, but they too kept their tongues in front of David. He'd worked hard to earn everyone's respect since he'd become Solas Beir, and even if no one trusted Lucia, they trusted him. That was enough until they made it to the Northern Stronghold and figured out how to help David get his powers back so they could defeat the Sower.

Lucia thought she had lost her magic when she'd almost drowned in the Eastern Sea, after Tierney tried to kill her. She'd been so close to death, it had taken Nerine several tries to revive her, to get her to breathe. After Nerine had brought an unconscious Lucia to David, he'd healed her, taking her injuries into his own body. Lucia suspected David had paid a terrible price for saving her. She feared he might never get his powers back.

"Maybe you should have let me die," she'd told him.

"You know I couldn't do that," David had answered.

Lucia hadn't replied, but the look on her face had been response enough. She'd looked at David with such pride and love, Abby felt hopeful that Lucia might truly be on David's side.

She could see Lucia below, signaling to David that Cael wanted to stop for the night. Abby and Brarn followed Erela, circling down to land in a narrow ravine carved by a creek between two hills.

Abby took on her human form once again. She was tired—they'd been flying for hours into a strong breeze, and as the sun dropped to the Western horizon, the wind had picked up. A storm was coming.

They had finally made it out of the North Forest and crossed into the Highlands, skirting the Barren. But here, the trees were stunted and craggy, and the green hills were dominated by scrub and boulders, leaving little protection from the wind whipping across them.

Cael found them shelter under a precipice in the gully that offered some respite from the weather. At least their campfire would hold out against the wind.

Abby shivered in David's arms as a gust howled through the ravine. On the hills around their campsite, the bare branches of the trees scraped against one another, rattling like dry, brittle bones. The wind whistling through them almost sounded like a scream. She very much doubted she would be able to sleep.

In the middle of the night, something awakened Abby. She must have dozed off in spite of the disconcerting sound of the wind. She rolled onto her back and looked around, puzzled for a moment, trying to remember where she was. The sight of the overhanging rock brought back the memory of the flight from Caislucis with a shock. They were still on the run, but they were safe for now.

She'd been sleeping on her left side, and her legs felt stiff and achy from lying on a patch of dirt so densely compacted, it felt like stone. She rolled onto her other side to find David sleeping peacefully beside her, and then lifted her head to see whose turn it was to be on guard duty.

Cael was on watch, sitting by the fire. Beyond the circle of light from the flames, she could see the silhouette of a man leaning casually against a tall boulder. *Tierney.* He wasn't even trying to hide.

This was a dream.

She rose, stepping over David's sleeping form, and around

the others slumbering near the fire's edge. As she approached, the dark lord stepped away from the shadow of the boulder, into the light, a sly smile on his face.

"Tierney."

He nodded to her. "Hello, love. You don't look surprised to see me."

She narrowed her eyes. "Should I be? You've been stalking me for months now."

Tierney grinned. "Stalking you? Is that what we're calling it?"

Abby shrugged. "Call it whatever you want. Haunting, harassing, terrorizing..."

He frowned and crossed his arms. "Terrorizing? Really? Come now, Abby. I thought you and I were beyond all that." He studied her face, and then reached out to caress her cheek.

She turned her head, avoiding his touch. "You tried to kill me. Several times. I would call that terrorizing."

He raised his eyebrows in surprise. "Remind me. When exactly did I try to kill you? Because believe me, love, if I wanted you dead, you would be." He stepped closer to her and cradled her cheek, turning her face to his. "But I don't want that, Abby. I really don't."

She gulped. *It's just a dream,* she reminded herself. *Pull yourself together.* She squared her shoulders and glared at him. "When? How about the toads in the rainforest? Just for starters."

He scoffed. "That? That was nothing. You were perfectly safe with me."

"David didn't think so."

Tierney smirked. "*David* overreacted. I am the Kruor um Beir. Nothing in this world can harm you without my permission."

Maybe it was true, that he did wield the kind of power granting him authority to keep her out of harm's way. But that last part, the bit about his permission, irked her. Not only was it arrogant, but he had all but declared open season on her and her friends at the Eye of the Needle. She had the scars to prove it. She huffed, looking away, out into the cold night.

"The Daughters of Mercy certainly seemed to have your permission. They tore my back to shreds as they herded me into their death cave." She shuddered, remembering the terror of being chased by winged women whose faces had been twisted to look like hers.

"Sorry, love. Wrong again."

Abby looked up at him, surprised at the tenderness she heard in his voice. "What?"

Tierney gazed at her, smiling sadly. He ran his fingers along one of the faint lines on her shoulder where the Daughters' talons had sliced her skin. Her injuries from the incident had healed in the Wasteland, but the scars hadn't yet faded.

"The Daughters wouldn't have hurt you if you hadn't resisted. Their instructions were to put you in a secure place until all this unpleasantness with the Sower blows over."

Well, there's no place more secure than the Wasteland, is there? Abby thought.

He stepped closer to her, staring into her eyes. "I couldn't risk him turning you. I like you just as you are."

She placed her palms against his chest, holding him at arms' length. "I don't understand. You're letting him destroy Cai Terenmare. He's taken almost everyone. Why save me?"

To her surprise, there was no arrogance in Tierney's eyes. He looked at down at her hands splayed against his chest, and placed his hands over hers, keeping her close.

"My intention is not for the Sower to destroy Cai Terenmare. Just to clear a path for me. Have no fear—his role is only temporary. Once he has fulfilled his purpose, he'll be gone."

Abby bit back her anger, thinking about Eulalia and Marisol standing beside Sholto like psychotic marionettes. "So that's it? His purpose is just to get the throne for you?"

Tierney shook his head. "Not just for me, love. I was hoping you'd join me."

"But *why*?" Abby spat, exasperated. She yanked her hands from his grasp. "Why do you want me to join you? Why would you think I'd even want to?"

He grinned. "Haven't you ever wondered why your dreams about me are more vivid than your dreams about anyone else?" He looked pointedly over his shoulder at David and then back at her. "You and I are connected, Abby. Don't deny that you feel it too."

Abby stiffened and put her hands on her hips. "What I meant was, why do you want me to join your *cause*?"

Tierney's gaze darkened and he stepped toward her. "You're a smart girl. I'm sure you can see that what's been done in the past to keep the balance between the Dark and the Light hasn't worked."

She shook her head, confused. "You mean the courtesan system?"

Tierney barked out a harsh laugh.

Abby couldn't imagine what there was to laugh about. "What's so funny?"

"The courtesan system is a *joke*," he growled. "I mean *everything*—all the efforts to keep a balance. Closing the portals, the efforts to keep the Kruorumbrae segregated and stop them from feeding. It hasn't worked."

She couldn't disagree. None of those strategies had solved the problem. They'd only slapped a bandage on a gaping wound that wouldn't stop oozing blood.

"Okay. So what's *your* plan?" Abby demanded.

He held her gaze, but his usual haughty arrogance had left his eyes. "I want to cure them. Cure myself. You said you saw what I did at the Blood Altar. What you didn't see is who I was before I became Southern Oracle." He hesitated, as though he were trying to gather his thoughts. "I wasn't always like this. Something at the Altar got its hooks into me, made me into this..." He seemed distraught as he wrung his hands, unable to go on.

Tierney's unsettled demeanor was so out of character that Abby found herself shocked into feeling sympathetic. She put her hand on his arm. "This what?"

He turned back to look at her, pain in his eyes. "This monster. I've become exactly what I once fought against. I see that clearly now."

"You don't have to be a monster," she whispered, stepping closer to him without even thinking about it.

"That's why I want the throne," he explained. "If I were Solas Beir, I'd finally have to power to cure myself. To cure them all. To set things right." He cupped her chin. "*That's* why I need you, Abby. You are a cai aislingstraid. I've felt your gift—you are more powerful than you realize. I've been waiting for someone like you for a very long time. Together, we could change the world." He moved close to her, as if to pull her into an embrace.

Abby suddenly realized what he wanted from her, and mentally cursed herself for lowering her defenses. For a second there, she'd actually felt sorry for him. She held up her hands, holding him back, shaking her head. "No. What you want is for me to betray David, and I can't do that." Abby planted her feet, determined not to bend, not to show weakness. "I *won't* do that." She looked back at the campfire, at David sleeping peacefully, with no idea of the danger he was in. "If what you say is true, that there's a way to cure you and the Kruorumbrae, then David and I will find a way to do it. That's all I can promise you."

Abby returned her gaze to Tierney, dismayed to see that he wasn't the slightest bit deterred by her statement of loyalty. If he really had been vulnerable before, he wasn't now.

His dark eyes glittered in the firelight as he reached out and ran his fingers through a tendril of her hair before brushing it back over her shoulder. "You're very loyal, Abby. I've always admired that about you. And you're genuinely good. You've been kind to me, even when I didn't deserve kindness."

Abby opened her mouth to answer and shut it, unable to come up with a suitable response.

"I do appreciate your promise to find a cure," he continued, running his fingers down her arm before grasping her hand in his. "There's just one problem. Power always comes with a price. Magic that powerful requires a sacrifice."

Abby's eyes widened in shock, and she swallowed, struggling to keep her expression impassive. "What kind of sacrifice?" she ventured.

"Someone has to die," he answered. He lifted her captured hand, studying their entwined fingers as if distracted, before meeting her gaze. "I'd offer myself, of course, but unfortunately, it has to be someone pure of heart. And we both know my heart is..." he chuckled, "well, a bit soiled."

Abby looked over Tierney's shoulder at David again. "I'll do it."

Tierney gave her a questioning look.

"If," she clarified, "you promise to leave David alone. He *is* the true Solas Beir. If you promise you will never hurt him or take the throne from him, I'll offer myself as sacrifice."

Tierney studied her intently. "I'm impressed," he mused. "You didn't even hesitate."

She squared her shoulders. "Like you said. I'm loyal."

"Yes, you are." Tierney lifted her hand to his lips, kissing it. "But you see, for this kind of magic to work, you can't offer yourself."

Abby raised her eyebrows. "Are you saying I'm not pure of heart?" Doubt crept into her veins now that she'd said it out loud. Because the truth was, she wasn't pure of heart. There *was* darkness inside her. These dreams of Tierney were proof of that. But even so, she'd die for David. And not just for him—for all of them, to save the whole kingdom. Was this what it meant to be queen? To give all of yourself for your people? She thought maybe it was.

Tierney chuckled again. "No love, I'm not saying that. Believe me, I'm no one to judge who is and who isn't pure of heart."

He caressed her cheek, letting his fingers trail hungrily down her neck. She found herself frozen, caught between the impulse to recoil from his touch and the traitorous increase of her heartbeat.

"What I'm saying is that you are a c'aislingaer. You are a conduit, a vessel to be filled with power. I need you to bind the circle with those to be cured. But, before that, there is the sacrifice."

"Who?" She knew what he was going to say, but she hoped she was wrong.

There was sadness in Tierney's eyes, but she couldn't tell if it was real or an act. He turned, slowly, studying David's sleeping form. "He is more noble than I thought he would be."

"No," Abby said, jerking away from Tierney's touch. "Not him. Eulalia is a c'aislingaer too. She can be the conduit, and I'll be the sacrifice."

"The dowager queen is not as strong as you are," Tierney whispered, almost as though he truly felt bad about what he was asking of her, like he actually cared about David's fate. "And even if she were, she is currently under the Sower's control."

Abby narrowed her eyes. "So free her. Free them all."

Tierney smiled sadly. "I'm afraid I can't do that. Only *he* can slay the Sower. Through the sacrifice."

Abby felt her blood boil with rage and frustration. It was a lie. It *had* to be. Or if he wasn't lying, he was crazy. Only a madman would unleash the Sower with no way to stop him, no plan to end Sholto if things went awry. Well, *more* awry than all the horrible things that had already happened with the Sower in charge. "You're lying. There has to be some other way."

Tierney shook his head. "I'm sorry. I wish there were."

I'll bet. I'll just bet you do. She wanted to scream. Instead, she curled her hands into fists, feeling the sharp bite of her nails digging into her palms. She wouldn't give him the benefit of seeing her lose it. "I *won't* betray him. Don't ask me to do that."

Tierney reached out to touch her cheek again, and she stepped backward, leaving his hand hanging in midair. He frowned and lowered his hand to his side.

"I'm not asking you to betray him. I'm only asking you to deliver a message for me. Tell him about the sacrifice, how he can single-handedly save this world. It has to be of his own free will, so let him decide. He can end this in one of two ways: surrender himself to me as sacrifice, or take his chances fighting. But if he chooses war, he will be battling his own people—his mother, his friends, the people he swore to protect. Tell him I'll be waiting for his answer at Giant's Helmet."

Abby opened her mouth to reply and found herself sitting up, staring at the fire. David was still asleep beside her, and Tierney was gone. Or rather, he had never been there at all.

He was nothing more than a phantom, haunting her dreams, she told herself. But that was a lie. Their conversation had been lucid, just as vivid as her waking life. Tierney's message for David was as real and urgent as if he had been physically present. And, like it or not, she was the one who had to deliver it.

The problem with Tierney's lies was that they were so interspersed with truth, it was impossible to know what to believe. With great trepidation, Abby gathered David and the others around the morning campfire and told them about her dream. To her dismay, David reacted exactly as she had known he would. He was, as Tierney had so aptly noted, very noble.

"I'll do it."

"No!" Abby cried, squeezing David's arm. "You can't. You're playing right into his hands. There *has* to be another way."

David smiled sadly, and Abby could see the decision to sacrifice himself wasn't one he took lightly, in spite of his seeming eagerness to die. "And what if there's not? What if this is the only way?"

Lucia put her hand on David's shoulder. "The girl is right. Tierney has always wanted you dead, and he can't kill you himself. This would allow him to achieve that goal and take the throne with little opposition. It would look like you helped him in an effort to solve Cai Terenmare's problem with the Kruorumbrae. No one would dispute his rule."

"He will attempt to have you killed whether you offer yourself willingly or not," Eoin said. "I do not believe he cares about the state of our kingdom. He will seize the throne, and then things with the Kruorumbrae will be one hundred times worse."

Erela looked from Abby to Lucia thoughtfully, her brow furrowed.

David noticed. "What do you think, Erela?"

The last Daughter of Mercy frowned. "Apologies, Solas Beir, but I would be remiss in advising you if I did not point out that both your betrothed and your aunt have a strong connection to the Kruor um Beir."

Abby clenched her jaw. There it was. The accusation.

Lucia narrowed her eyes at Erela. "And *what* do you mean by *that*?"

The Daughter of Mercy seemed unruffled by Lucia's tone. "Neither of you can deny that Tierney has been a destructive influence in your lives."

"I don't deny it, and I understand why none of you trust me. But how do you know you can trust *her*?" Lucia asked, gesturing to Erela. "The Daughters of Mercy also aligned with Tierney. Very recently, in fact."

"I did not," Erela countered, her voice void of emotion. "I was cursed and cast out long ago."

"So you say," Lucia grumbled, crossing her arms.

As they argued, a thought occurred to Abby. She wanted to ask a question before things escalated further between Lucia and Erela. "Wait. Erela, Tierney believes the Kruorumbrae are sick and can be healed. Isn't that similar to what the Daughters of Mercy believe?"

"I was taught by my elders that the Kruorumbrae are like rabid dogs," Erela replied, "and that killing them is an act of mercy, both for those who are linked to the Darkness and for their victims. The Daughters of Mercy believe that to become a Blood Shadow is to be cursed, to suffer an affliction. And they do suffer."

"Do *you* believe that?" Abby questioned. "That the Darkness is actually an illness? An outside force that corrupts the Kruorumbrae and leads them to kill?"

Erela stared at Abby a long time before answering, and Abby could feel the scrutiny in her gaze. "I used to. Now I believe the potential for Darkness lies in all of us, manifested through our choices."

Abby made no reply, and the Daughter of Mercy turned to David, speaking matter-of-factly. "Nevertheless, I believe the Solas Beir must do his duty for Cai Terenmare. Even if he loses his life."

David sighed and nodded an acknowledgement of Erela's statement. Then he rose and walked over to Cael, who was sitting outside their circle, listening but clearly wrapped up in his own thoughts.

David took a seat on the stone next to the knight. "Please help me, Cael."

Cael looked at David, and the others waited quietly for his

response, but he didn't answer.

"I don't know what to do," David said. "I don't even know what to believe or who to trust. But I know you would never do anything to jeopardize Eulalia or the kingdom."

Cael sighed. "No, I would not. But I cannot advise you as to the best course of action either."

A look of hopelessness crossed over David's features.

Cael gave David a humorless smile. "Remember the one-way portal at the Eye of the Needle? I fell for that trap just as easily as anyone else."

Just as easily as I did, he means, Abby thought. She recalled her dream of Thoth's door and how that vision had followed on the heels of another dream starring Tierney. More of his lies interspersed with truth. She and the others had found the door from her dream and used it as a shortcut in their quest for allies. But when they'd needed the portal most, they found they couldn't access it again.

"I think you need to trust the Light," Cael told David. "It will not fail you. It will show you what to do when the moment comes. But until then, my advice is that we proceed north to the stronghold."

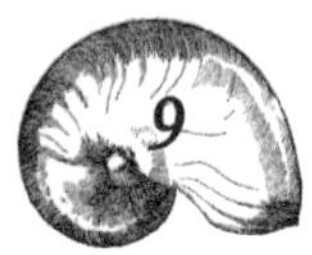

THE NORTHERN STRONGHOLD

As they traded the grassy hills of the southern Highlands for a hike along the rugged ridges of the northern Highlands, Cael described the Northern Stronghold. "It is an imposing stone fortress, situated on the side of a cliff overlooking the northern edge of the Barren. All along the side facing the desert is a balcony with a parapet. From there, one can catch a glimpse of Giant's Helmet in the distance."

"So we'll be able to scope out the place where Tierney has chosen to wait for me," David said.

"Are there giants in Cai Terenmare?" Abby asked, avoiding the subject of David's possible suicide. That was all they needed—Tierney recruiting giants. He seemed to have secured every other advantage.

"No, no," Cael assured her, waving off her fears. "Just someone waxing poetic. Whoever named the rock formation must have imagined it looked like a warrior's helmet. A very large one."

There were three ways to access the Northern Stronghold, Cael explained. All were narrow, meant to bottleneck an army and force the enemy to approach in smaller and more easily dispatched groups.

Two of the paths required travel through the mountains

above the Highlands, via canyons either from the west or east. The other was a tiny trail winding down the rock face to the Barren below. It was this path, Cael informed his fellow travelers, that they would take to meet Tierney on the battlefield.

"The stronghold has never been compromised, though it was built long ago, during the Kruorumbrae wars," he said. "Even now, it retains a troop of fifty soldiers, should the Solas Beir find himself in need of its use."

Now, many days after fleeing Caislucis, what little was left of David's court approached from the western canyon. All but Erela were on foot. Never comfortable with enclosed spaces, she had insisted on flying high above, watching over them, ready to intervene should the Sower's plague be found even here.

Abby grew uneasy as they exited the narrow pathway and approached the tall, iron-clad doors of the fortress. Someone was watching them. She was sure of it.

Suddenly, from one of the turrets, she caught movement, something white gliding toward them. She began to draw her sword, but Cael stayed her hand.

"An ally, I believe," he whispered.

A snowy owl landed in front of David, and then grew taller, dissolving into the shape of the Northern Oracle. "Greetings, Solas Beir," she said, bowing formally at the waist. She wore armor fitted to her petite frame, and her long, black hair was braided. Abby glimpsed the hilt of an elegant sword in the sheath on her back. "I am overjoyed to see you have escaped the long shadow the Sower has cast over our land."

"Northern Oracle," David replied, bowing in return, a smile lighting his face. "You're a sight for sore eyes. I can't tell you how glad we are to see you."

The Northern Oracle returned his smile, and then swiveled around as the door behind her swung open, revealing a dark-skinned figure leaning casually against the doorframe.

"And what about me?" he asked. "Am I a sight for sore eyes as well?"

Abby couldn't contain a squeal of delight at the sight of her friend, the Southern Oracle. Abandoning any sense of formality, Abby ran to his outstretched arms, and threw her arms around his neck.

"Yes," she said, hugging him tightly. "Yes, you are."

A smile lit his handsome face. "Hello, my dear. It is good to see you again too."

Abby and the Jaguar King had bonded when they visited the Blood Altar near his village together. There, Abby had learned of the price Tierney had paid to gain more power—how the river had run red with the blood of his victims, and how the Jaguar King had stopped the carnage with help from David's father.

But the man who became Southern Oracle after Tierney was stripped of his position, had also paid a price for Tierney's crimes. He and Tierney were brothers, and Tierney had never forgiven him for the perceived betrayal.

Because he had lost a brother to Darkness and feared harm coming to the people he had vowed to protect, the Southern Oracle had been reluctant to join David's cause until Abby changed his mind. After that, they had all become friends, trekking through the deadly rainforest the Jaguar King called home.

"Thank you for coming to help us," Abby said.

"I promised I would," he replied, looking, for a moment, uncharacteristically somber. Then he grinned. "I even dressed for the occasion."

Abby laughed, realizing the Oracle was dressed more modestly than she'd ever seen him. "What, no loincloth?" she joked.

"It is, if you have not noticed, a bit colder here than where I come from." He shivered as an icy gust of wind whipped over the face of the cliff.

Abby wrapped her arms around herself. "I *had* noticed that."

"Let us continue our discussion inside," the Northern Oracle suggested, ushering them into the shelter of the fortress.

Erela landed gracefully and peered around suspiciously before following the others. She remained guarded inside the cavernous room, ever vigilant about safety.

The others—Obelia, Eoin, Gorman, Fergal, and even Lucia, seemed at ease. Abby worried at first that the Daughter of Mercy was sensing something she didn't, but chalked it up to Erela feeling protective of David.

Cael seemed to think the fortress was safe enough—he had settled into a chair near the large hearth that dominated the room, which seemed to serve as an armory. Weapons lined the walls opposite the fireplace.

After formally greeting the Southern Oracle, David warmed his hands by the hearth. The roaring fire inside eased the chill they all felt from days of camping. "How did you know to come here?"

"We are oracles," the Northern Oracle stated simply. "We see much."

The Jaguar King looked from the Northern Oracle to David. "After I agreed to help you, my connection with the Northern and Western Oracles became stronger," he explained.

"But not with the Eastern Oracle?" Abby asked.

"Sadly, no," the Southern Oracle confirmed. "And so I knew you had not had success in your mission to make him an ally." He studied Abby with concern. "I lost track of you for some time as well. Are you all right?"

"Yes," Abby nodded. "The Daughters of Mercy herded me into their lair and I ended up in the Wasteland. I was trapped there for a while, but my raven, Brarn, freed me."

The raven was sitting on the arm of her chair. He cocked

his head as if in acknowledgment.

The two oracles exchanged a surprised look and then turned to stare at Abby. The Southern Oracle seemed awed, but the Northern Oracle looked skeptical.

Abby winced, remembering Eulalia's response to her tale. If she told the Northern Oracle about her experiences with Ardal in the Wasteland, would the woman react with belief or doubt? "It's a long story," she stammered, feeling uncomfortable under the Northern Oracle's piercing gaze.

"We shall have time to talk about that later," the Jaguar King assured her, patting her hand. "To answer the question the Solas Beir asked, the bond between the three of us who had aligned was strong, and enhanced our sight. Then, suddenly, the connection with the Western Oracle was severed, and I could no longer see her. I knew something was wrong, but it was as if a veil had been cast over my visions. The only thing I could see clearly was the Northern Stronghold. And so I gathered my people and we journeyed north."

"It was the same for me," the Northern Oracle confirmed. "I foresaw you going to battle with Tierney at Giant's Helmet. We hurried to secure the stronghold before his forces could."

"Have you seen any sign of his army?" David asked.

The Northern Oracle shook her head. "No, not yet. But he is coming soon. I can feel it."

Abby turned to the Southern Oracle. "How about you? Have you seen anything?"

"Perhaps," he responded thoughtfully. "We came by long canoe to avoid the Barren. We traveled around the southern edge of the continent and up the eastern coast to land at Saeran Bay, far north of the City of the Eastern Oracle. Given my inability to see the oracle in my visions, I felt it prudent to avoid his city. Our journey was mostly without incident."

David raised an eyebrow. "Mostly?"

The Southern Oracle nodded. "I was prepared for trouble

when we passed Southport. It is, as you may know, notorious for pirates and slave traders, a scourge that has thrived despite the efforts of past Solas Beirs to bring it under the same law governing other regions of Cai Terenmare. But we saw no one. Much of the town looked as though it had been burned."

"And you saw no survivors?" David asked.

"I did not stop to check," the Oracle confessed. "I sensed no signs of life near the port and dared not risk my people's safety by going inland to investigate further. My priority was to deliver them to the stronghold so we could be of use to you."

David seemed bothered by the Southern Oracle's answer. Abby intervened. "We're very grateful you came. We do need your help." She turned to the Northern Oracle. "Maybe we stand a chance having both of you here."

"I hope so," the Northern Oracle replied. "Let us retire to the dining hall. Now that you have warmed yourselves, allow us to feed you. You must be hungry, and I would hear of the Sower. From what little I have been able to glean from my visions, the fate of our world may be dire indeed."

The stronghold's dining hall was huge, built to serve hundreds of soldiers at once, but the Northern Oracle's three hundred warriors and the Southern Oracle's two hundred had taken to eating in shifts based around their assigned duties, guarding the stronghold and preparing for battle.

Gathering around a long table with food already served, Abby felt comforted by a familiar sense of hospitality, similar to what she'd experienced when visiting the Southern Oracle's village. All that was missing was a warm bath and a soft bed. She planned to make up for too many nights of sleeping on hard ground soon.

As David passed her a dish, Abby shook her head and reached for a bowl piled with rice and vegetables. "No more fish for me, thanks. I've had my fill."

Eoin and David chuckled, and the group fell into easy

conversation until the meal was finished. Then the talk returned once more to the Sower.

Two days later, they were no closer to an answer about how to defeat Tierney and the Sower, and the frustration in the air was palpable. David and Abby had been meeting with the two oracles and court council daily in the dining hall, but the discussion always came down to the same problem: how could they, with a force five-hundred strong, hope to beat an army of thousands?

It was in the middle of this late afternoon meeting that the keeper of the stronghold approached the group. "I am sorry to interrupt, Your Majesty, but a band of travelers approaches from the east."

David rose, concerned. "Kruorumbrae?"

"I do not believe so, Sire. They appear to be refugees and..." the keeper hesitated, his eyes shifting about the room nervously.

David nodded for the man to continue. "Go on."

"There is a young man leading them, Sire. He appears to be riding on a very large bear."

David exchanged a puzzled glance with Abby and took her hand. "Do any of them appear to be infected?" he asked.

"Hard to tell from a distance, Sire," the keeper replied. "I shall have them wait outside the door for your inspection."

"Yes, very good," David nodded. "Thank you, Keeper."

Abby stood by David's side as they peered at the newcomers from the terrace high above the eastern door.

"Hello down there," David called out in greeting.

The boy on the huge, brown bear was wearing a hooded cloak. A bow and quiver of arrows were slung across his back. Behind him stood about fifty men, women, and children, none of them soldiers, precious few with weapons.

At the sound of David's voice, the young man dismounted, pushed back his hood, and grinned. "Well, hello up there."

"Jon!" Abby cried, feeling her heart leap with joy. "It's okay. Open the doors!"

"Wait," David called to the guards, holding up his hand to stop them.

He looked back down at Jon. The grin on Jon's face froze.

"I'm sorry, Jon, but I have to ask," David apologized. "Are any of you infected by the Sower?"

Jon shook his head, looking puzzled. "Infected? No..."

"Thank goodness," Abby sighed.

"How do we know you're not lying?" David inquired.

Beside Jon, the bear shifted into the shape of a man. "He speaks the truth, Solas Beir. The lower mountain villages we passed through and the City of the Eastern Oracle have been abandoned. The only people we found were in the few villages closest to the Northern Stronghold. Tierney and the Sower seem to have overlooked them in doing...whatever it is they are doing."

David nodded, seemingly satisfied by the man's answer.

"We've been looking for someone who can tell us what's going on," Jon explained. He smiled at David. "I guess that would be you."

David laughed. "Guess so." He turned his gaze to the man Abby finally recognized as the Eastern Oracle's former captain of the guard. He looked different, his face thinner and more rugged than the last time she'd seen him.

Apparently David had realized who he was as well, because he said, "Nice to see you again, Hedeon."

"Thank you, Sire," Hedeon replied. "It warms my heart to

see you safe." A worried look crossed his face. "But if you are here, I fear something terrible must have happened at Caislucis."

David nodded, frowning. "Yes, I'm afraid something terrible did. The Sower paid us a visit. Come on in and we'll tell you all about it. Guards, open the doors."

Jon waited with open arms as Abby flew down the stairs. Upon reaching him, she gave him an enthusiastic kiss on each cheek. "I thought I'd never see you again."

Jon chuckled, squeezing his best friend tightly. "I was worried about that myself."

Abby took his face in her hands, looking him over. "You're skinny. Your cheeks are sunken in. Are you okay?"

Jon patted his stomach. "Yeah. But jailhouse diets suck."

"They didn't feed you?" she asked, her eyes wide with alarm.

"Eh, they did, at first. Then they mysteriously disappeared and left me and Hedeon to starve," he replied.

Jon knew how gaunt he looked. He'd gotten a glimpse of himself in a still pool of water when the caravan had stopped to refill their casks, and had been shocked at how much weight he'd lost. It didn't help that he'd grown a scraggly beard. Not his best look. He'd have to rectify that with a shave before he saw Marisol.

He looked around, surprised he hadn't seen her already. "Where's Sol?"

Abby's face fell. "Oh, Jon. You'd better sit down."

"She's all right, isn't she?" he asked, feeling panic thud through his veins.

"She's alive," Abby assured him, guiding him to a bench in the corridor outside the dining hall, "but the Sower has her. Eulalia too. They've been turned."

Jon's stomach clenched; he felt lightheaded. It was hard to breathe. He held his head in his hands. "What do you mean, 'turned'?"

"They're under the Sower's control right now," she explained.

"Did he hurt them? I'll kill him," Jon growled. He hadn't realized he was gripping the hilt of his sword until Abby put her hand on his and gently pried it from his weapon.

"We think they're okay for now. He seems to be using them as hostages, mostly as a slap in the face to David and Cael. I don't think he'll hurt them unless he feels personally threatened." She gazed at him with grave concern. "But Jon, I won't lie to you. They're not the same. He changed them somehow, and he's controlling them like puppets. We don't know if we can change them back."

Jon felt bile creeping up his throat. "How did he turn them?"

"We think it's some kind of parasite, spread through saliva. Gorman calls them sea nymphs," she replied. "I was in the village of Nuren. I saw Yola's infected daughter kiss her, and then Yola turned. The whole village had been infected. We don't know where it started, but it spread fast. Almost everyone in Caislucis was affected, and that's how the Sower seized the throne."

"But *he's* the key," Jon said, more to himself than to her. "We kill him and it stops."

"Maybe. But we don't know anything for sure. We could kill him, and people might return to normal," Abby said. "Or they might not. We just don't know. Except..."

Jon looked up to see her studying him carefully, as if she were afraid to say anything more. Like she was worried about his reaction. "Except...what?"

"I've been dreaming about Tierney again," she confessed. "He said David had to slay the Sower, that he's the only one who can end this. But to do it, David would have to sacrifice himself." Abby grasped Jon's hand tightly. "Jon, I'm so scared and I don't know what to believe." She choked back a sob. "I can't lose him, but I don't want to lose anyone else either."

Jon pulled her into his arms and rested his cheek against her forehead. "What does David think about your dreams?" He hoped, for David's sake, that she had told him and hadn't been keeping things to herself again.

"He's ready to do whatever is necessary to save the kingdom. Even if it means dying." She burst into tears.

Jon held her, rocking her gently like he used to do when they were kids, concerned only with benign everyday problems, completely unaware that Cai Terenmare existed. He desperately wished he could go back in time to before this madness had derailed their lives, to before he had brought Sol into this mess. He wished he had never introduced her to this place. Then she would still be at home, safe.

Except she was never really safe at home either, was she? Jon started. The voice in his head sounded an awful lot like Malden's. *Because* I *was there, and I was part of her life long before you were, boy.*

Jon shook his head, trying to clear it. *You're not real,* he thought. *You're dead. You burned up in that dungeon.*

Did I? Mad laughter ricocheted through Jon's skull. *How would you know? You didn't stick around to make sure. How do you know I'm not on my way to see my lovely* dulce *right now? Who's going to stop me? You?*

And with dawning horror, Jon knew in his heart that Malden's voice wasn't just his imagination, that somehow Sol's personal bogeyman had survived, and he would reach her long before Jon could. If this was what Abby's dreams of Tierney were like, he was surprised she hadn't lost her mind.

He couldn't explain how he knew about Malden—it was just like when he'd felt drawn to travel north into the mountains, toward the stronghold. Maybe Abby's psychic abilities were catching. Or maybe he'd been in Cai Terenmare too long, and the magic of this world was rubbing off on him. He wasn't certain that was a good thing.

While Jon and Abby conversed in the corridor, the guards had escorted the newcomers into the dining hall, where they waited to be greeted by the Solas Beir. He looked different than Hedeon remembered—seasoned, more sure of himself, and even more like his father than he had before. He watched as David went from table to table welcoming the refugees, making sure everyone was given a proper meal.

He was flanked by a muscular, dark-skinned man and a petite woman whose fierce eyes were a sharp contrast to the delicate features of her face. Her black hair was twisted into a long braid. When he reached Hedeon's table, David introduced his friends as the Northern and Southern Oracles.

Hedeon bowed his head in respect. "I am honored to make your acquaintance, oracles, though I wish it were under happier circumstances."

"As do we," the woman replied. She studied the gashes at his chest and shoulder, showing through the torn fabric of his shirt. "You are wounded."

Hedeon shook off her concern. "It is nothing. A fight with one of the Kruorumbrae during our escape from the City of the Eastern Oracle."

His tunic was stained the color of rust on his chest where blood had dried and bright crimson on his shoulder where he had been bitten. He had cleaned the wounds, and the injuries inflicted by Malden's claws were healing, but the bite still oozed blood.

On the long journey, he hadn't had access to proper

bandages, and the laceration on his shoulder kept tearing open. It needed to be stitched; that was all.

The Northern Oracle frowned. "Your injuries have still not healed?" She laid the back of her hand against his forehead. "I am afraid it is *not* nothing. You suffer from fever. Those wounds have festered."

David looked from the Oracle to Hedeon, a pained expression on his face. "I wish I could heal you, Hedeon. But I seem to have lost my abilities as Solas Beir."

Hedeon's mouth dropped open. "How can that be, Sire?"

"I really wish I knew."

"But surely you will get them back," Hedeon insisted. "Else how will you fare in the battle to come?"

David gave Hedeon a sad smile in answer.

"Come," the Northern Oracle said, holding out her hand to Hedeon. "I have treated that kind of wound before. I have healing herbs in my room."

In the oracle's chamber, he watched her work, her small hands busy, mixing a poultice for his shoulder. "Your shirt," she said, her back to him as she ground up various leaves and added a few drops of a pungent-smelling liquid.

He removed his ragged tunic, wincing when he found that the fabric was sticking to his shoulder wound with blood. Removing the shirt ripped the bite open again.

The oracle turned to him and studied the gash. "You were bitten?"

Hedeon nodded, and then pointed to his chest. "Malden raked me with his claws too, but that injury is mostly healed."

She glanced at his chest. "Yes," she confirmed, and then lifted his chin to study his eyes. She frowned.

"What?"

"I fear my herbs will be of no use to you. He poisoned you with his bite." She crossed her arms. "But you already knew that."

Hedeon looked away, avoiding the oracle's penetrating gaze.

"You have already started to feel the hunger, have you not? You hide it well. But you cannot hide much longer. Already I see a ring of scarlet around your pupils. Soon your irises will be red as blood, and then you will turn. You are an assassin sent by the Kruor um Beir," the oracle accused.

"No. I am loyal to the Solas Beir," Hedeon replied quietly, "I was not trying to hide anything, but I did not want to believe that I was turning."

"Why is that?" Her narrowed eyes were cold.

"Because I would rather kill myself than become the thing I hate most."

From the doorway of the dining hall, David watched Jon holding a sobbing Abby, trying to comfort her. He felt a twinge of jealousy at the intimacy between them, and forced it aside. Abby needed Jon now more than ever, both as protector and comforter, since David wouldn't be around to do it. He wouldn't squander what little time he had left with her with something as petty as jealousy over her friend. *His* friend. He had missed Jon too.

David felt terribly guilty that he hadn't been able to make good on his promise to Marisol to free Jon, but he couldn't waste his last hours on guilt either. There just wasn't enough time.

He had so many regrets that if he focused on even one, he'd soon be overwhelmed by them all, buried alive in an avalanche of guilt. That would render him more useless than he already felt.

He stepped into the corridor and walked toward the bench where Jon and Abby were sitting. "I brought you food."

At the sound of David's voice, Jon looked up and Abby

hastily turned away, wiping at her eyes.

David held out a plate to Jon. It was piled with meat, berries, and a slice of bread. "Looked like you and Abby needed a moment, so we got your friends settled in the dining hall. The kids seemed especially hungry."

"Thanks," Jon said, offering a grateful smile as he accepted the plate. "I'll bet they were hungry. We had to ration food on the way here."

"You're welcome."

Jon narrowed his eyes, studying David's face. "Please tell me you're joking about this killing yourself thing."

Abby looked up at Jon and then turned to look at David. Her eyes were red and puffy from crying, and wide with concern.

David choked back the wave of emotion that threatened to buckle his knees. The image of her grieving him already was almost too much to bear. In that moment, he would have done anything to stay by her side, just hand Tierney the kingdom and run away with her, never to look back. But he couldn't do that. He covered his own grief with a nonchalant shrug. "It comes down to this: there are too many of them, too few of us. Even with your recruits."

Jon stared at him, incredulous. "But you've got yourself a perfectly good fort here. Seems like you could make them come to you, and then pick 'em off one by one."

David shook his head. "It's not that simple. Tierney plans to use our own people against us. He'll force Marisol and Eulalia to lead the charge. Just because he can."

Jon winced as understanding dawned on his face.

It was a low-down, dirty play to use Marisol's name in the argument, and David felt no satisfaction about winning the debate. He didn't know if Tierney actually would send Marisol or Eulalia as assassins, but Jon had to have a crystal clear picture of what they were up against. Would Jon really be able to kill

Marisol if he had to? David doubted it. He knew he wouldn't be able to kill Abby if she was the one being used as a pawn. He'd die first. And that was exactly what he planned to do. He felt his resolve strengthen.

"So that's it, then," Jon muttered, his voice bitter and angry. "You're giving up. You're not going to fight, you're just going to surrender."

"I have no other choice," David began, and was interrupted by a strong, authoritative voice.

"Enough!"

David whirled to see Lucia charging down the corridor. He barely had time to grunt an objection before she grabbed his arm and roughly turned him about-face, marching him up the stairs to the terrace.

"Hey!" he heard Abby call out in protest.

"You weren't kidding about her being here either," he heard Jon tell Abby. Then he heard Jon sigh, resigned. "Let them go. Maybe she can talk some sense into him."

Abby watched helplessly as Lucia dragged David out of sight up the terrace stairs. She wanted to follow and rose from her seat, but Jon stopped her. She sat back down on the bench. "That woman," she huffed in frustration.

"Sticks around like gum on your shoe," Jon grumbled between bites of his dinner. "Do you really think she's on his side?"

Abby shrugged. "I don't know what to believe anymore."

Hedeon entered the hallway. He wore clean clothes, and slung across his back was a leather sack stuffed full. Abby couldn't see what was in the bag, but he looked like a man readied for a long journey.

"Hedeon, my friend," Jon smiled. "Did you get dinner?"

The knight didn't return his smile. "I did." He held out his hand to Jon, and Jon shook it, a look of uncertainty on his face. "You were a good cell mate, my friend, but I am afraid this is goodbye."

"What? Why? We just got here."

"I owe you an apology," Hedeon replied. "I have kept something hidden from you, and my staying here puts you all in danger."

Jon just stared at the knight in shock.

"The little wretch poisoned me with his bite. I am becoming the thing that killed my family."

There was pain in his eyes, but Hedeon's face was hard, like stone. Abby could see there would be no changing his mind. Still, she had to try. "Please, don't go. If you become dangerous, we'll lock you up and keep you from hurting anyone."

"No," Jon said, shaking his head, exchanging a look with Hedeon. "You can't put him in jail again. Not after what we went through."

Hedeon smiled sadly. "There will be no prison for me. I must do what is honorable, and end myself."

"No!" Abby cried. "That's not an answer." She rose to her feet and grabbed his hands. "There might be a cure."

Hedeon gave her a long, disbelieving look. "There is no such thing."

"We think there is," Abby insisted. "Tierney thinks there is. If we win the war...Look, you have to stay with us until the battle is over. If we don't have a cure by then, you can leave. You can hold out for that long, can't you?"

Hedeon sighed. "I will fight alongside the Solas Beir." He gave Abby a dark look. "But, if I am still alive after the battle and there is no cure, I *will* kill myself. I will not become a monster."

David wriggled in Lucia's iron grasp. "Stop it! Let me go."

For a moment, he looked just like the little boy he had been back when they lived in the human world and she had gone by a different name. Lucia remembered David voicing similar protests the time she dragged his four-year-old self out of the mud he'd been playing in and into her house. It had rained hard the night before, and her front garden was not yet planted with spring bulbs.

When she had gone from the front yard to the small gardening shed at the back of the house, she accidently left the side gate open. David was playing in the fenced backyard, and when her back was turned, managed to slip away, unnoticed. He found the mucky dirt in the front garden and followed a small trail of it as it dribbled down the front walk, floating in a stream of rain water. He tracked the stream though the open front gate, and when she found him, he was sitting on the curb in front of her house, stirring the water in the gutter with a stick.

The sight of him so close to the road as a car roared past had sent her flying down the front walk. It was only after she'd scooped him out of harm's way that she noticed he was covered nose to toes in mud. "How did you get so filthy?" she demanded.

He had been swimming, he howled, pointing to the large puddle of water that had formed in the center of her garden.

"Swimming!" she huffed, carrying him kicking and screaming to the tub upstairs. She turned the water on and got his dirty clothes off him, and, watching the mud swirl down the drain, they both calmed down.

"If you want to go swimming, you have to do it in a safe place, with an adult watching over you," she explained after she'd wiped down the tub and refilled it with clean water. "And *never* go near that road again." Placing her finger under his chin, she gently turned his small face to hers. "Tell me you understand, David."

"I understand, Aunt Moira," he'd replied meekly, before

going back to playing with the toy boats she kept for him.

Now he was studying her with those same pale blue eyes. Lucia let go of his arm. He rubbed it, an annoyed look on his face. She hadn't hurt him, she knew—the rubbing was just for show.

"I'm sorry if I was too rough," she said.

He brushed off her apology. "Didn't hurt."

Lucia gazed out over the low walls of the terrace. The sun was setting in the west, a blaze of orange tinged with glowing fuchsia clouds. Below her, the golden brown dunes of the desert were fading to a deep grey. "It's time we talked about what you're planning to do."

"I suppose you're going to try to talk me out of it."

She looked at him. "No. I'm not."

David raised an eyebrow in question.

She returned her gaze to the desert, resting her hands on the top of the wall. "It's like you said. You have no other choice. You can't fight them all, not with our low numbers and the fact that you'd be fighting your own people, not just the Kruorumbrae." She gave him a bittersweet smile. "Not to mention you have lost your abilities. Thanks to me."

"Not this again." He reached over and took her hand. "It's not your fault, Lucia."

She looked down at his hand grasping hers and then up at him. "You should have let me die. I was too broken. When you healed me, it sapped both of us of our magic. Now you have no more power than that human boy downstairs."

So many years she'd managed to keep him safe, only to become his undoing. It was her fault. *All* of it. Now he was completely vulnerable. He couldn't fly, couldn't generate fire, couldn't become his spirit animal, couldn't heal.

"You know, if this is your idea of a pep talk, it's not really helping."

She laughed, reaching over and ruffling his unruly hair. He gave her a half-smile. After everything, they were still here together and he was still her boy. Her beautiful boy. It didn't matter who his mother was. He'd always been hers, from the first moment she'd seen him. But she had made so many mistakes, and now he would pay the price for them.

"I can never give back what I took from you," she said. "I made a mistake in siding with Tierney against your father, but at the time I didn't know he wanted you dead too. In spite of how things must appear, I've tried to keep you safe. But it's not enough. The Darkness will take you anyway."

"I know." He squeezed her hand. "But I forgive you."

She felt anguish welling up inside her, and pushed it aside. "There's something you need to know about the Darkness. It's not just within the hearts of those who have chosen it over the Light, or those who have been turned against their will. We all have the capacity for evil. Once you've tasted Darkness, it grabs hold and doesn't let go. Even the Solas Beir is not immune."

He stared at her, puzzled, and then let go of her hand. "What are you saying?"

"Tierney said you have to be the sacrifice because you are pure of heart. But no one is pure of heart." She gave him an apologetic smile. "Not even you, my dear."

David looked taken aback, and then he regained his composure. "And this helps me...how?"

"Where did your power come from? From you? Or from the Light?"

"From the Light," he recited.

"And do you believe that?" She searched his eyes.

He thought about it. "I don't know."

"You *need* to know," Lucia replied. Then she scoffed, muttering to herself more than him. "Your mother taught you nothing of the old magic, did she?"

"Hey now, that's not fair."

"I know. I'm sorry. This is no time to point fingers," she agreed, holding up her hands. She studied his face. "I suspect you've never actually asked the Light for help. You've been relying on your own strength, as though your abilities flowed from some bottomless well of power. But as you've discovered, your well has run dry."

"So what do you suggest I do?" She could hear the frustration in his voice.

"Your father made the same mistake I did. We took matters into our own hands rather than relying on the Light for help. But you don't have to repeat those mistakes. Let go and start relying on the Light. This battle is not yours to fight. You *can't* fight it. But the Light can. Empty yourself of your fears, your pride, and become a vessel the Light can fill," she urged. "Do not submit to Tierney. Surrender only to the Light."

"How?"

"When you take the battlefield, do not think of the battle. Meditate only on the Light," she said, grasping his hand in both of hers. "And *ask* for help."

He looked at her, understanding growing in his eyes. "That's all I *can* do, isn't it? Because there's nothing else."

"I still believe in the Light," she asserted. "I still believe that everything happens for a reason—that all we experience serves a purpose in bringing us to the place we need to be. I believe there is nothing else because you *need* nothing else. If you win this battle, it won't be because of you, because you have nothing to offer. The victory will belong to the Light."

David returned from his talk with Lucia, not in good spirits exactly, but more at peace, like he had accepted his fate. It frightened Abby, but she tamped down her fear and the urge to cry again. If they only had a few hours left together, she wouldn't ruin them with tears. She forced a smile and invited him to share dinner with her on the terrace.

After the meal, they stood next to the wall, hands entwined, looking out at the Barren. Below them the desert was black, and above them the stars were bright. Beautiful. And coldly distant—entirely unaffected by the suffering of those scrabbling for survival under those brilliant, glittering lights.

Abby studied David's face. He was staring at the stars with wonder, a small, reflective smile on his lips. What had Lucia said to make him so serene? "David, whatever happens..."

He drew her into his arms and stopped her with a kiss. She allowed herself to be swept up in the passion of his touch, relieved to let go of her worry for a moment.

But afterward, her fears returned. She pulled away from his embrace. "David, I'm scared."

"Shhh," he whispered, pulling her back to him, his lips brushing her forehead, his arms cradling her against his chest. "I know. I am too. But it's going to be okay. No matter what happens to me, things are going to be okay."

His bizarre serenity was driving her mad with frustration. "How can you say that? If something bad happens to you—"

"You'll be okay, Abby," he replied, in a tone that said he didn't want to spend time arguing with her.

She could see he had already made up his mind, and there was nothing she could do to stop him from whatever crazy plan he'd made with Lucia. Even if it was suicide.

"Let's not think about it tonight. I just want to be with you."

"Okay," she whispered, blinking back tears.

"Let's go back inside," David said.

She let him lead her back down the steps, to his room.

The world was burning.

The stars were gone. All Abby could see above her was a

red sky, scarlet as blood. Around her, a forest on fire, trees blackened, their branches withered like reaching skeletal fingers. Turning lazily on an unnaturally warm breeze, a brown leaf snapped free from the branch arching over her head and drifted down just in front of her nose. Its edges were singed, curling inward. Thick smoke rolled toward her from all sides, filling her lungs.

Then: a shape filled with light, cutting a swath through the black smoke as he padded toward her. The white lion. David. His blue eyes were focused on some point far in the distance, his face filled with that same serenity he'd had on the terrace.

A black shape stalked him from above, in the trees. Abby called out, and the shape, now balanced on a thick branch, turned its gaze to her and growled. Abby waved her arms wildly and yelled, trying to tell David it was a trap. He couldn't see her, couldn't hear her.

She saw the black feline shape fold into a predatory crouch. It was poised to kill, and she could only watch helplessly as it leapt.

Then he was gone.

Abby jerked awake, breathing hard.

David was sleeping peacefully, completely unaware of any disturbance beside him. Just as serene and oblivious as he'd been in her dream. Right before he'd met his end.

Shivering, she slipped out from under the covers and grabbed the spare blanket sitting on the soldier's trunk at the foot of the bed. Wrapping herself in it, she crept out of his room. Without conscious thought, she climbed the stairs to the terrace and then crossed over to the parapet.

The Barren was aglow with light. Enemy campfires, she realized. Thousands of them. Abby felt a sinking feeling in the pit of her stomach.

She looked around, and could make out the silhouettes of sentries standing guard at both the eastern and western corners of the terrace, watching over the two main entrances of the Northern Stronghold. Good. She felt a sense of relief at not being the only one awake to see the fires.

Behind her she heard the soft rustle of fabric and turned to see Lucia stepping out from the shadows. The woman joined her at the wall.

"Bad dreams?" Lucia asked.

Abby narrowed her eyes and wrapped the blanket more tightly around her shoulders. The night air was chilly. She could see her breath. "What did you say to him up here?"

"What he needed to hear." Lucia was silent for a moment, staring down at the campfires. "We're not so different, you know. We both want to protect him."

Abby spun on her, unable to contain her frustration any longer. "Do you *really* want to protect him? Because I'm telling you right now, if you're still in league with Tierney and David gets hurt, so help me..."

Lucia laughed harshly. "I believe I could say the same thing to you, my dear."

"I've *never* sided with Tierney," Abby snapped. "No matter what kind of dreams I've had."

Abby waited for Lucia to respond with another accusation. Instead, she said, "I was trying to protect him—before you got involved. I wanted to give David the best of everything so he never knew what he was missing. I didn't want him to know about Cai Terenmare, because I knew it would someday come to this. One of the oracles prophesied about the conflict between Tierney and David. That one of them would die."

Abby nodded. "The Western Oracle. She said you would be the one to decide who lived. And who died."

Lucia stared at her. "How do you know about that?"

Abby wondered what Lucia would say if she knew it was a long-dead king who had spilled her secret. The king *she* had murdered. "Doesn't matter. A friend told me."

Lucia raised her eyebrows but continued. "I blamed you at first, thinking I had been so close to averting the prophecy. I thought it was your fault for making him fall in love with you."

Abby winced. "You can't help who you fall in love with. You should know that better than anyone."

Now Lucia was the one to flinch. She looked away, avoiding Abby's gaze. "I suppose that's true. But I don't blame you anymore. I blame myself. Considering he grew up under my watch, it's no wonder David defied me and went his own way. We share the same independent spirit."

Abby considered this. She'd never thought of David as being as feisty as Lucia (and, she smiled to herself, certainly not as ill-tempered), but he could be stubborn, that was for sure. Of course, so could Abby. Maybe the three of them had more in common than she had thought.

Abby looked up and found Lucia gazing at her intently, her dark eyes ancient.

"If we're going to protect him, we need to trust each other."

Abby stared back at Lucia. "I know."

"I hope you're not operating under the delusion that Tierney will keep any promises he's made to you," Lucia continued. "Even if David kills the Sower, Tierney won't stop until he gets the throne. David will never be safe until the prophecy is fulfilled. I think perhaps you know that."

Abby thought about all the things Tierney had said, how he acted like he actually liked her but how she never quite trusted him. He could be so charming and yet so ruthless. A sociopath.

Lucia was right. Tierney wanted David dead and he wanted the throne. He would play by the rules until he started to lose, and then all bets were off.

"I think perhaps I do. What about healing the Kruorumbrae, though? Is there any truth to that idea?"

Lucia furrowed her eyebrows. "I don't know. But it doesn't matter right now. First, David must defeat the Sower."

"Do you really think he can beat him?" Abby asked.

Lucia looked worried. "No." Abby felt her heart hitch in her chest, and almost didn't hear Lucia when she said, "He can't, not on his own. But if the Light is with him, he can."

Abby thought back to her dream, and fear gripped her like a vise. What if the Light *wasn't* with him?

"Abby," Lucia began. Then she hesitated, suddenly looking unsure of herself. "There's something I need you to do for me."

"What's that?"

"I too dreamed tonight," Lucia answered, almost shyly. "It involved the prophecy."

Abby gave her a skeptical look. "I thought your dreams didn't come true."

Lucia frowned. "They don't. But I think this one might be different."

"Tell me."

"No. No, I can't," Lucia said, shaking her head. "There's something I have to do, and if David knew about it, he would try to stop me. But if my dream does come true, I might not be around to tell him why I did it."

Abby studied Lucia's eyes. "Why would you not be around?" Was she leaving? Surely she wouldn't abandon David now. Would she? "You can't leave."

"I don't want to," Lucia assured her, "but I will do whatever is necessary to save him. I need you to trust me, and when it's finished, I need you to tell him it was my choice to protect him, and he shouldn't blame himself."

"I don't know..." Abby said. "You're asking me to trust you, but you're not telling me anything."

Something was wrong here. She could feel it in her gut. This was almost as bad as her talks with Tierney.

"*Please*, Abby," Lucia pleaded. "For *him*."

Abby stared at her. There was pain in Lucia's eyes, and she *never* said please. At least not that Abby could remember. It couldn't be easy for her to ask Abby for help.

"Okay," she agreed reluctantly. She hoped she wouldn't regret it. The stress of this discussion was making her head pound with pressure. She could hear ringing in her ears.

Suddenly the terrace rolled like the deck of a ship. Abby let go of her blanket, grasping at the wall to steady herself. She could see Lucia doing the same. Rocks fell below them, sloughing off the cliff face and sliding down the side of the mountain, crashing into each other. Then, just as quickly as the tremors started, they stopped.

Lucia's eyes were wide with alarm. "What was *that*? An earthquake? Here?"

"It may be the Sower," Abby said. "There was an earthquake like this when David and I were on the road to Yakez. And remember how the forests were empty, like all the animals and faeries had fled? We think the two are related."

"If the Sower is that powerful, Tierney's an even bigger fool than I thought," Lucia scoffed.

"And you still think David has a chance against the Sower?" Abby asked. "Even if the Light *is* with him?"

"I hope so," Lucia breathed. "For all our sakes, I hope so."

When Abby returned to David's room, he was sitting up in bed, wide awake, looking panicked. "Where were you?"

Abby smiled apologetically. "I had a bad dream. I didn't want to wake you, so I took a walk."

"You okay?" he asked, reaching for her.

She let him draw her close, relishing his warmth, and nodded. "I'm okay. I was on the terrace when the quake hit. Everyone up there is fine, and I checked in with the guards down here. Everyone seems fine. It was just a tremor—no real damage."

"The Sower," he murmured, scowling.

She brushed his hair away from his forehead. "You should go back to sleep. If that *was* the Sower, we have a big day ahead of us."

Reluctantly, David lay back down on his side, and Abby settled into his embrace, closing her eyes. She didn't know what the day would bring, but she hoped Lucia was right, that this night would not be David's last.

GIANT'S HELMET

Just after dawn, David got his first look at Tierney's army. From the terrace he could see thousands of people below, scattered around the rock formation known as the Giant's Helmet. He couldn't help but think about his own meager troops, and felt despair creep into his bones. But if Lucia was right, he wouldn't need an army at all to kill the Sower.

Still, he had asked Cael to make sure everyone fit to serve had armor. If he couldn't defeat the Sower, they would need it.

David had also made Cael promise to retreat, should he fall by the Sower's hand. "Live to fight another day," he had urged. His face grim, Cael had agreed.

He'd had the same conversation with Jon. He knew Abby wouldn't leave him if he fell. Jon swore he would protect her, even if it meant throwing her over his shoulder and marching all the way back up the hill to the fortress.

"Someday we'll laugh about this," Jon had joked, trying to put on a brave face, his hand on David's shoulder. "We'll say, 'Remember that time Tierney took the *entire* kingdom hostage?' Then we'll laugh."

David wished he could laugh, but he didn't share Jon's sense of humor or optimism. He was grateful, however, to have his friend back and to know that Abby would be okay.

If he *did* defeat the Sower though, and if all those who had been infected were restored, the battle might swing in their favor. That was a lot of ifs to think about. David found he could only focus on the one without risk of paralysis from fear.

He ordered everyone to gather in the dining hall to await final instructions. Alone on the terrace, he took one last look at the battlefield. *Please,* he prayed. *Please help me. I can't do this alone.*

The day was clear and bright, with no wind and excellent visibility all the way to Giant's Helmet, which, to David's mind, looked a little like a skull. Marching down the mountain trail to the Barren, David could just make out a figure standing at its peak.

Around the large rock, Tierney's army had been organized into smaller companies led by Kruorumbrae captains. They stood in perfect formation, ready for battle. It was intimidating, and it was hard to remember that one mind was controlling them all. A mind he intended to crush.

David had nearly five hundred soldiers, between the two oracles and their warriors, some of the guards from the fortress, and his own friends. Abby, Lucia, Jon, Cael, Eoin, Hedeon, and even tiny Fergal were armed and marching with him. Erela and Brarn were watching over them from the air. The thought of losing any one of them terrified him.

He had left over a hundred people in the fortress. Some of them were too young to fight and needed to be looked after, and some remained to guard the fortress in case retreat was necessary.

Obelia and Gorman had agreed to stay to help the stronghold keeper maintain order. Archers lined the parapet, bows and arrows at the ready.

Thankfully, with the clear view, David saw no threat of ambush during the march to the battlefield. He surmised Tierney would hold off on fighting until they were in closer range. He glanced back over his shoulder to see how far they had come.

The Northern Stronghold seemed impossibly high, perched on the cliff face. In case of retreat, hiking back up the mountain could prove problematic.

As he neared Giant's Helmet, David was surprised to see Tierney's forces fall back, moving outside a boundary of large boulders encircling the sandy battlefield. He watched for some sign of a trick, but sensed nothing. He raised the visor on his helmet, and around him, Abby, Jon, and Cael did the same.

From the top of the rock formation, Tierney hailed him with a wave and a grin. "Young Lightbearer! How good of you to join us. And is that Miss Brown I see at your side? How lovely." He gave Abby a conspiratorial smile, and David was pleased to see it was met with a scowl from the lovely Miss Brown.

Cross her today, dirt bag, and you'll lose your head, David thought. The image of Abby cheerfully slicing off Tierney's head filled him with hysterics (and no small amount of pride), and it took some effort to force the mad laughter back.

David cleared his throat and returned Tierney's greeting with equal enthusiasm. "And I've brought two of your other favorites as well! Southern Oracle, Lucia, say hello."

The Southern Oracle raised his visor and gave Tierney a nod. Lucia took hers off and tucked it under her arm before glaring up at Tierney. He looked only mildly surprised to see her standing in front of him.

"My dearest Lucia. I'd heard you were still alive. It's good to see you looking so well," Tierney said, his voice dripping with poisoned honey.

"No thanks to you," she called, giving him an icy smile.

"I've been chatting with your sister," Tierney replied,

unfazed. "I'm sure she and her little friends are anxious to see you."

At that, David heard the rattle of chains. Then, mounting the rock formation behind Tierney, he saw the three of them, bound at the neck and wrists: Eulalia being led by the Eastern Oracle like a dog on a leash; on her right, Aziza, the little girl who'd been kidnapped from Nuren and forced to serve as a courtesan, tugged along by the lamia David had battled in the rainforest; and last, on Eulalia's left, Marisol, being dragged by her hair by none other than Malden.

Beside him, David sensed Jon start, his hand clenching the hilt of his sword. But to Jon's credit, he kept his tongue.

Of the three, only the girl remained unchanged. Eulalia and Marisol were clearly under the Sower's control, their eyes white, staring blindly, as they strained against their chains like feral animals, eager for the taste of blood. David's heart ached for Jon and Cael. It had to be killing them to see the women they loved reduced to this.

Tierney was beaming, savoring his role as ringmaster. The Eastern Oracle, as usual, looked bent out of shape, as if he felt terribly inconvenienced by Tierney's little freak show. Plus, he stood next to the lamia, and was using Eulalia like a shield to keep his distance from the snake woman, making no effort to hide his disgust. With his free hand, he held the embroidered fabric of his flowing robes as far from her as possible. Malden, however, seemed to be having a marvelous time, lapping up all the fear and pain radiating off those around him. He had finally gotten his grimy little hands on his dulce, and this time she was going nowhere.

"So. Getting down to business," Tierney began conversationally, rubbing his hands together. "My forces outnumber yours ten to one. Most of them, of course, used to associate with you, but all that's changed. You'll see it's true, should you engage them in battle. I do hope it won't come to that. It would be rather unsportsmanlike of me to beat you soundly when the odds are so obviously in my favor. I must assume then, that you've come to surrender yourself?"

"No," David said. He sounded calmer than he felt. "I'll never surrender to you."

Tierney clucked his tongue. "Oh come now, boy. Have some sense. If you surrender, only you will have to die. Your friends will be free to leave. Even our dear Miss Brown. Unless, of course, she'd prefer to stay. I wouldn't mind. Perhaps she wouldn't either." He favored Abby with a warm smile, and she huffed, looking disgusted.

David ignored Tierney's attempt to goad him. "Actually," he smiled, holding himself with as much dignity as he could muster, "I have a better idea."

Tierney raised his eyebrows. "Oh? What's that?"

David rested his hand on the hilt of his as-yet-sheathed sword, projecting calm confidence. "A battle between champions to decide the fate of the realm. If your champion wins, you get the throne."

Tierney smiled. "I'm listening. And if your champion wins?"

David looked Tierney straight in the eye. "If my champion wins, I keep the throne, you release all your hostages, and you and your cronies get banished to the Wasteland. Sound fair?"

Tierney looked as though he were mulling it over. "Almost. One condition."

"What?" David asked, not entirely surprised that Tierney would have something to add to his list of demands.

Tierney's gaze bored into him. "If I win, I get the throne, and *you die.*"

David laughed weakly. "Well, if that happens, I'll already be dead."

"And why is that?" Tierney asked, feigning innocence.

David frowned, partly because Tierney was forcing him to

state the obvious, and partly because he was hoping for a more favorable outcome. "Because I'm serving as champion for my side."

Tierney grinned wickedly. "Ahhh. Yes. I was hoping you'd say that. A deal then?"

"Deal," David agreed. "Call your champion."

Tierney's grin stretched wider. "I call upon the Sower."

Of course Tierney was too cowardly to fight his own battle. But where *was* the Sower? David wondered. He had half expected him to be standing on top of Giant's Helmet, gloating with Tierney. But no, that wouldn't fit with the spectacle Tierney had created. The Sower's entrance would have to be much grander than that.

And so it was. David felt the ground began to shake.

On top of the rock formation, the Eastern Oracle lost his footing and stumbled, falling to his knees. He used Eulalia's chains to pull himself back up to his feet. Not surprisingly, she snarled at him in response.

The tremor ran underneath David's feet, fanning out from the center of the battlefield. He could see the sand trembling, and then it began to slide inward, like a sinkhole. Any soldier standing at the quake's epicenter would be swallowed up and buried alive.

"Get back!" he yelled, waving his hands. "Spread out!"

"Run for solid ground! This way!" Cael shouted, directing the soldiers to a point beyond several large boulders defining the northern edge of the battlefield. Tierney's army had all retreated south to a safe vantage point behind Giant's Helmet.

There was a sound, a roaring like a locomotive, and then the sinkhole erupted in a geyser.

"What's happening?" Jon yelled over the noise of the deluge.

"I don't know!" David shouted back.

Cael caught some of the spray on his finger and sampled it.

"It tastes of salt! The undersea caverns!" he yelled in explanation. "Remember the underground river that spans the continent? The Sower is tunneling to the surface from there!"

Seawater continued to rain down, and then, gradually, the chaos abated. The water pooled around the sinkhole, creating a small lake. The abrupt quiet was eerie. David felt the prickle of static electricity in the air. It filled him with a sense of dread and he found himself thinking of storm clouds, laden with lightning. But there wasn't a cloud in the sky.

The silence was broken by another roar, but this one was guttural, and louder than the geyser had been. Abby covered her ears against the sound. She looked terrified, and David couldn't blame her. His stomach was cramped with fear—he could feel his intestines squirming in his gut, and he couldn't seem to still his trembling hands. He slipped his arm around her, and she gave him a grateful look.

Something was rising from the pool, something dark with reptilian scales like armor and a spine ridged in horns. The spikes protruding from the creature's back looked sharp enough to impale him.

David's fear increased tenfold. He'd been hoping to engage in hand-to-hand combat with a *man*, and, worst-case scenario, figured he would have to battle Sholto's spirit animal. But he'd had no idea the Sower would be a leviathan like this.

"Fantastic," Jon breathed. "It's freaking Godzilla."

In spite of his terror, David heard himself bark out a mad laugh. Abby looked at him questioningly, probably wondering if he had lost his mind.

The creature was hunched over as it ascended from the depths of the undersea caverns, but as the rest of it emerged, David could see water gleaming off a ribbon of scarlet scales that lined its flank. Then he noticed its black-and-white paddled tail—there could be no doubt that this sea monster was kin to the former Western Oracle and her sirens.

Gaining solid ground, the beast arched its back and turned around, revealing its face. Or faces, rather, because it had six of them. All of them bobbed on long, serpentine necks, and all of them were filled with gnashing teeth, curved like cutlasses. The heads were crowned in some kind of bony, frilled growth that could have been either gills or horns.

David was far less concerned with the specifics of the creature's anatomy and far more worried about how he could possibly fight the nasty thing. He wondered if, like the hydra of legend, it would grow two heads in the place of every one he chopped off. And how could he get close enough to use his sword without being ripped apart by those awful teeth?

The hopelessness of his situation weighed on him, threatening to bring him to his knees. He had none of the powers of a Solas Beir. He was decent with a sword, but what hope did he have shaking a flimsy silver stick at a giant?

Six pairs of yellow eyes, glowing like lanterns, glared right at him, challenging him to step forward and try his luck. The beast let out another of those ear-piercing roars, and this time belched out half a dozen blue flames, scorching the sand below, turning it to glass. Smoke drifted lazily from its many nostrils, filling the air with acrid fumes.

"Now it's just showing off," Jon muttered.

Of course it breathes fire. Why wouldn't it? David could feel himself bubbling with hysterical laughter again. Maybe by the time this thing got around to ripping his limbs off, he would have gone insane and would be oblivious to the unpleasant experience of being dismembered. *One can only hope.*

He took a breath, regaining his composure, and sighed. Perhaps he should have surrendered when he'd had the chance. Not that Tierney would have granted him a merciful death either. *Too late now.*

He turned to Cael. "Well. Here I go. Wish me luck."

"May the Light go with you, Solas Beir," Cael said, his

hands on David's shoulders. "I am so proud of you. Your mother would be too."

If she were in her right mind. With a whole lot of luck, she would be soon. "If things go badly—" David began.

Cael nodded. "We will retreat. We will find another way to save our people."

David looked at Abby, and she threw her arms around his neck. The expression on her face was strained, and her eyes shone with moisture. It looked like it was taking everything she had not to start sobbing. That was okay. He felt a little like sobbing himself.

"I love you," he whispered. "No matter what happens."

"I love you too," she whispered back, her voice choked with emotion. "Always will." She kissed him hard. "For luck," she said, releasing him. She took his hand in both of hers and squeezed it. But then her eyes went wide with panic and she didn't let go.

David gave her a smile and gently pried his hand loose from her grip, guiding her toward Jon. Jon put his arms around her, partly to comfort her, and partly to keep her from clinging to him again, David suspected.

"Take care of her," he said.

"I will," Jon replied. "Take care of yourself. And come back."

David smiled grimly, watching a tear escape and roll down Abby's cheek. "I'll do my best."

He felt a hand on his arm. Lucia smiled at him warmly. She was the only one who seemed to believe there could be a positive outcome to this. He certainly had his doubts.

"You'll be fine, my sweet boy. Remember: Whoever kneels before the Light can stand before anything."

Abby watched David nod slowly at Lucia, and then the expression on his face changed from sad hopelessness to one of iron determination. He hefted his shield, drew his sword, and marched out to meet his fate.

The Sower, a six-headed sea dragon that had once been a man named Sholto, roared deafeningly again. It graced them all with another fine demonstration of its dominance by scorching a long, sizzling line in the sand. The smoke in the air became thick and heavy. A haze of it drifted over the sun, turning the sky blood red—not unlike the scarlet sky in Abby's most recent nightmare.

Abby fervently wished the beast would choke on its own flames and burn itself to a crisp but figured it was probably unaffected by the heat. Hopefully it would not be immune to the silver in David's sword.

The creature seemed to be waiting patiently for David's approach, not crossing the line it had drawn. *How very considerate.* Or maybe it just didn't think he was worth the effort of a proper attack.

David reached the line, looked up at the beast, and then plunged his sword into the sand. The dragon cocked its heads in unison, studying David with a puzzled expression that might have been comical if not for the fact that those long, yellow teeth were alarmingly close to biting off the head of the boy she loved. *What is he doing?*

Abby watched with trepidation as David dropped his shield. He then began peeling off his armor, first removing his helmet and tossing it beside the shield, then taking off the gauntlets protecting his hands and arms, next doing the same with the heavy armor covering his legs, and finally lifting off his chest plate and throwing it to the ground.

Throughout this ritual the dragon watched, unmoving, as bewildered as any of the spectators until David was standing with nothing but his tunic and leather pants between him and the fire-breathing creature.

Then David dropped down on both knees before the powerful Sower, and bowed his head with his arms open wide. He was completely vulnerable. All the beast had to do was swallow him whole.

Abby clutched at Jon in panic. "What is he doing?" she shrieked.

Jon looked as confused and alarmed as she felt.

Abby started as a strong hand landed on her shoulder. She whipped her head around to see who it belonged to. Lucia.

"Shhh," the woman whispered. "Have faith. Watch."

David's entire body began to glow with white light, becoming brighter and hotter than the flames that had spewed forth from the dragon's many heads. There was a flash like a lightning strike, an explosion so brilliant that, even after it was over, the white image of David's silhouette floated in front of Abby's eyes.

When her vision cleared, he was gone. "What happened?" she demanded. "Where *is* he?"

"I think the Light took him," Cael answered, shocked.

Abby remembered what Eulalia had said once, about past Solas Beirs being taken to join the Light in the world beyond this one. To her ears it had sounded a lot like dying. "Is he...dead?"

"No, child," Lucia said softly, her voice filled with awe. "He is one with the Light now. Look."

Where David had knelt, hundreds of tiny white orbs rose, each glowing with a blue nimbus. They drifted up, slowly at first, circling each of the dragon's heads, bobbing past its eyes, its nostrils. Then, as one, the particles began to vibrate, swirling and picking up speed, before condensing into a swarm of dazzling light that shot forward into the open mouth of one of the beast's heads.

The sea dragon reared back in surprise, and Abby could just make out a soft glow radiating from beneath the dark scales of the monster's neck, as the light descended down its gullet. When the glow reached its underbelly, the creature began to thrash. Violently. The sea dragon roared in agony, collapsing on its side.

From each of its six mouths shone bright light, illuminating the smoky sky. The creature's belly began to swell, growing and stretching with the increasing glow until it looked as though it might burst. Then it did.

The force of the explosion knocked Abby off her feet. As she and the others picked themselves up, smoking bits of blackened flesh rocketed down around them. And where the dragon had been a moment before stood a white lion, glowing with that same white-hot light, blue fire dancing in his eyes.

Jon let out a whoop of joy, picked Abby up, and spun her around. She was laughing and crying at the same time. "He did it!" Jon shouted. "He *toasted* that sucker!"

Around them, cheers erupted from their fellow soldiers.

"That he did," Cael agreed, a wry smile on his lips.

"This victory belongs to the Light," Lucia replied, beaming at David.

The Southern Oracle tapped Jon's shoulder and pointed at Tierney's army. "Look. The hostages are waking up."

Jon scanned the troops stationed beside Giant's Helmet. Those soldiers who had been turned by the Sower were indeed waking up, startled to find themselves among the Kruorumbrae. Most of them were looking around, bewildered.

Jon's gaze shot up the rock face to find Marisol on her knees at the top. Her eyelids were fluttering open and closed, as though she were fighting to regain control of her body and mind. Then her eyes opened wide, and even from a distance, Jon knew they were hers again.

Marisol woke to a nightmare. Her wrists were bound, shackled with chains to a metal collar that chafed her neck. A longer chain was connected to the collar, and holding the chain was the bogeyman who had haunted her since she was a child.

But Malden's attention wasn't on her at the moment. He was focused on the man standing in front of her. A man who looked none too pleased.

Where am I? How did I get here? The last thing she remembered was the queen's wedding, and even that was fuzzy—just flashes of images. What little she remembered felt jumbled together. She couldn't make sense of it. Nor could she understand why Eulalia was kneeling in chains as well. There was someone else in chains, too. A little girl.

Marisol took in her surroundings, hoping for some clues. On the desert floor below her, she saw a white lion. *David.* Her eyes drifted over the crowd, trying to find faces she recognized. Then she saw the person she wanted to see most. *Jon!* Her heart leapt with joy. Unfortunately, her happiness was short lived.

Malden's master fumed at the white lion for a moment, and then he whirled around, his eyes alarmingly wicked with rage. He looked from Malden to the man holding Eulalia's chains before settling on a snake woman Marisol remembered all too well. The lamia from the rainforest. The monstrous thing that had pretended to be her mother and tried to coax her into the waiting jaws of a carnivorous plant.

"*You,*" the man growled.

The snake woman looked frightened enough to jump out of her reptilian skin. "My lord?"

He took a step toward her. "You said the Sower would win." He tapped his own temple angrily. "You said you had a vision. That all we've worked so *very* hard for would come to pass. That the victory would be *ours.*"

"Tierney...my lord..." the lamia stammered, her eyes on the ground. "I apologize...I do not know what went wrong..."

"Western Oracle, indeed," Tierney muttered to himself. He studied her with disgust. "*You*, my dear Meridoris, are no oracle." Then, in a fluid motion almost too fast for Marisol to follow, he drew his sword and lopped off the lamia's head.

The sea hag's decapitated head bounced against the stone once, with a wet smack, spraying the rough surface of the granite with black ichor before rolling over the edge of the rock formation. Marisol heard it thump heavily as it landed on the rocks below. The image of a burst melon came to mind. She felt her stomach heave as bile crept up her throat.

Tierney peered over the edge in fascination before turning back to his horrified audience. He looked from the terrified little girl to the queen, and then at the man in the scarlet robe, holding Eulalia's chains. "Eastern Oracle," he smiled.

"Yes?" the man replied nervously, no doubt worried his head would be the next to roll. His hands were trembling, and his eye had begun to twitch.

Tierney retrieved the chain still tightly held in the lamia's dead hands, and then shoved her headless body over on its side with his foot. "Trade me." He held out the child's chain, offering it to the Eastern Oracle.

The oracle accepted it reluctantly and handed Tierney the chain that bound Eulalia.

"On your feet, my queen," Tierney ordered. Eulalia glared at him, and he yanked her up roughly. She stumbled, and he steadied her, smiling coldly.

"Get your filthy hands off me," she snapped, whipping her shackled hands out of his grip.

Tierney clucked his tongue and pulled her closer to him using the chain at her neck. "Now, now, my dear. There's no need to be rude. Look," he pointed to the white lion staring up at them, "that's your son down there. Aren't you proud of him?"

The queen kept her tongue.

"I see your new husband too," Tierney continued, undeterred by her defiant silence. "And what's this? Your *sister* is standing right next to him." He stroked her cheek, and Eulalia jerked away from his touch. "How nice. Wouldn't you like a little family reunion?" He grabbed her by the arms, and held her teetering over the edge. "I wonder how fast your son can fly?" With that, he let go.

Eulalia cried out, and Marisol gasped in shock, watching the queen fall. David changed from the white lion to his human shape and leapt into the air. But he wouldn't be fast enough.

Luckily for the queen, someone else was. Rocketing down from the sky above, Erela caught the queen in her arms and carried her to safety, setting her down next to Cael. Eulalia threw her shackled arms around Cael's neck and he held her tightly.

Marisol felt a warm smile creep to her lips, and then froze when Tierney turned his gaze to *her*. But it wasn't her he was looking at. It was Malden.

"I *really* hate that winged woman. Let's kill her." Malden chuckled gleefully in response, and Tierney grinned. "Let's kill them *all*."

With that, Tierney retrieved Marisol's chain from Malden and tossed it to the Eastern Oracle, who managed to catch it despite his shaking hands.

Then Tierney took on his animal form, a black tiger with vicious fangs like sabers. He raced down the back of the rock formation with Malden running at his heels.

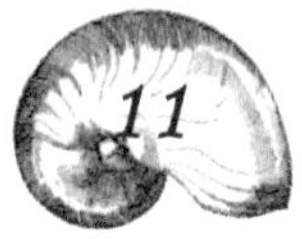

THE PROPHECY

With the scourge of the Sower now ended, David hovered above the creature's remains, rallying his troops. He raised his sword. "Now, my friends! For the Light!!"

A collective roar rose up from the army of the true Solas Beir. Some of them, like the Southern Oracle and Hedeon, morphed into large beasts. Others drew their swords and charged into battle, skirting the pool of seawater created by the Sower.

With his army on the offensive, David signaled to Erela. Together they flew over the hostages, now freed from the Sower's plague, encouraging those who could fight to turn on their captors.

The Kruorumbrae fought back, killing those hostages who were too slow in recovering their minds. Among the fallen were citizens who had never been trained for war, but who had nonetheless been swept up in Tierney's madness and continued to pay the price.

David and Erela began to carry those who weren't fighters to safety, while Cael and his troops helped the other hostages fight the Kruorumbrae. Now that alliances had changed, the Kruorumbrae found themselves surrounded, challenged by multiple attackers.

Jon's priority was freeing Marisol while Malden's attention was elsewhere. He tapped Abby's shoulder, beckoning her to follow him. Together they fought off Kruorumbrae, hacking their way to the rock formation where Marisol was struggling to wrench her chain out of the Eastern Oracle's grasp. He was a frail-looking man, but apparently much stronger than he appeared.

Jon couldn't help but grin when he overheard the verbal lashing Marisol was giving the man. The Eastern Oracle looked aghast. Remembering the oracle's strict rules about women remaining veiled and silent in his presence, Jon was pretty sure being thrashed by a girl was a novel experience for him. Jon couldn't have been more proud.

Marisol unleashed another string of colorful curses and screamed in frustration, kicking the oracle in the shins before driving her knee into his stomach. The man grunted and doubled over in pain, but stubbornly kept his hold on her and the little girl's chains, as if it were a matter of personal pride not to be bested by a mere woman. "Let us go, you self-righteous coward!" Marisol yelled.

Jon sidled up behind the oracle while he was trying to catch his breath and slid his sword under the man's chin. With the feeling of cold metal pressed against his skin, the oracle froze. Jon held out his hand. "Keys. Now."

For a moment, Jon wasn't sure if the oracle would comply. His face grew red with rage, and his grip on the chains tightened. Jon grabbed a fistful of the man's short, dark hair, yanking his head back. He dug the sword into the oracle's neck, not hard enough to break the skin, but with just enough pressure to convince the man he wasn't messing around.

"The keys," Abby repeated, moving in beside Jon, her sword pointed at the center of the oracle's chest.

"My right pocket," the Eastern Oracle spat. His eyes were filled with anger, and one of them was twitching. He dropped the chains.

Jon nodded to Abby, keeping his sword pressed tightly against the oracle's neck while she rifled through the deep pocket in the man's robe. With a jangling sound, she fished out a set of rusty skeleton keys.

Handing off her sword to Marisol, Abby went to work unlocking the shackles at her friend's wrists and neck. As the iron collar unlatched and fell to the ground with a loud, metallic clang, Marisol rubbed her neck and stretched it out.

"Ahh," she sighed. "I can't tell you how good it feels to get that thing off me." Raw, red lines encircled her throat and the insides of her wrists.

Jon fought to control his rage. Steering the oracle toward the back of the rock formation, he spoke in a barely contained growl. "Touch either of these girls again, and I'll slit your throat. Now go, before I do something I *won't* regret."

Giving Jon a reproachful look, the Eastern Oracle skulked off, down the gently sloping back of the Giant's Helmet. When Jon was sure the man wouldn't come back, he turned to Marisol, Abby, and the girl.

Jon sheathed his sword and embraced Marisol. "I was afraid I would never see you again."

She tightened her grip around his neck and kissed him hard. The sounds of the battle around them disappeared as Jon crushed her to him.

"I love you," she breathed in his ear.

"I love you, too," he grinned. "Let's get out of here."

"Guys? We have a problem," Abby said. She was on her knees, working to get the chains off the little girl.

Aziza's wrists were freed, but the hinge on the collar was rusted, making it look even more barbaric than Marisol's collar, and much more difficult to remove. Abby was having trouble getting it off without scraping the vulnerable flesh of the child's neck. She whimpered in pain.

"I'm so sorry, Aziza," Abby said. "I'm trying to do this without hurting you."

"My kingdom for some grease," Jon frowned. "Here. Let me try." He knelt down and inspected the collar. It was unlocked, but would only open a few inches. He tried to wrench it open with his hands, but to no avail. "We're just going to have to slide it off her. Very carefully."

"You're going to hurt her," Abby objected.

Jon took in the alarmed look in Aziza's eyes. "I'll be as gentle as I can," he assured her. "I'm going to have to do something really gross. Okay?"

The little girl nodded, smiling a little.

Holding her gaze, he smiled back and ceremoniously removed his armored glove. Then he stuck out his tongue and proceeded to lick his palm and fingers like a cat.

Aziza giggled, and Jon didn't think he'd ever heard a more wonderful sound. Marisol and Abby exchanged a look of puzzled amusement. Once his hand was covered in saliva, Jon slathered Aziza's neck with it.

"Eeewww!" she cried, giggling some more.

Marisol and Abby started laughing too. Jon grinned at Aziza and began to slowly slide the metal over her now slimy skin, squeezing her neck through the opening.

"Yes!" he cried, relieved his idea had worked.

The lubrication, though disgusting, prevented the metal collar from digging into the girl's bare flesh. He felt bad enough that the kid had suffered bruises and lacerations on her arms. He suspected it wasn't just the shackles on her wrists that had done the damage, but the toady hands of the snake woman. He didn't feel at all sorry the lamia had lost her head.

The saliva on Aziza's skin was almost dry, and all but the back of her neck had been freed. "Almost there," Jon smiled.

"One sec."

He gathered all the spit at the back of his throat and hawked it into his palm, intending to grease the girl's neck one more time. Then her eyes went wide and she started shrieking in terror.

Things are going surprisingly well, David thought. In between incinerating a hulking Kruorumbrae soldier and running his sword through a leaner one that leapt at him with the agility of a simian, he ran through a checklist in his head.

First on his list was gratitude to the Light for his still being alive and feeling stronger than ever. He had his powers back and the Sower was dead. His mother was safe, and he and Erela had cleared the battlefield of any hostages who weren't strong enough to fight.

Slowly but steadily he and his forces were overpowering what remained of Tierney's army and, last he'd looked, Abby and Jon were working on freeing Marisol and the little girl. If he could just put an end to the Kruor um Beir, David's victory for the Light would be complete.

But where *was* Tierney? David couldn't imagine he'd scuttled off like a coward, not after the look of indignant rage he'd seen on the Kruor um Beir's face after David killed Sholto.

Tierney would want to make him pay. Dearly. Of that, David had no doubt.

Seeing Aziza's eyes suddenly widen in fear, Marisol looked up to see Malden crouched in his feline form on the rock a few feet away. He had returned silently, and his red eyes were full of hate, staring at Jon's turned back.

As the child screamed in terror, Marisol felt her own fear slip away, replaced by purpose and a sense of everything around her slowing down. Seeing the scene before her in vivid detail, she noted the look of shock on Jon's face as he turned around, and saw his hand drop to the hilt of his sword, trying to unsheathe it as Malden launched himself at Jon's face.

Still grasping Abby's weapon, Marisol stepped in front of Jon and thrust the sword deep into the monster's hairy chest. He glanced up at her with hurt in his eyes, a mixture of indignant surprise and rejection, before sliding off the end of the blade in a pile of twisted, twitching limbs. Black fluid oozed from the gaping wound, pumped out from his dying heart.

And then Marisol began stabbing him. Again and again she plunged the sword into Malden's body, unaware that she was screaming until Jon gently placed his hand on her shoulder.

She quieted, looking from him to the wide-eyed little girl Jon had somehow finished freeing in the chaos. The expression on Aziza's face was one of shock—and possibly horror at what Marisol had done. She hadn't meant to traumatize the kid. She slowly lowered the sword.

"It's over," Jon whispered, carefully wiping off the blood on Marisol's face, ichor that had sprayed back up at her during her rampage. "It's done. He'll never haunt you again."

She studied Malden's prone corpse. *La Malogra*, the monster that ruins, the bogeyman that had haunted her dreams and cursed her mother with a sickness that was making her waste away to nothing. Now he was dead, and both she and her mother would finally be free to heal.

Marisol held out the sword, hilt first, to Abby. "Thank you," she managed weakly when Abby accepted it, before letting herself be enfolded in Jon's waiting arms. He held her as she cried softly, emotionally spent.

Abby silently wiped her sword clean and scanned the battlefield. She had a clear vantage point from the top of the Giant's Helmet. The fighting below continued, although incredibly, it seemed they were winning—something that had seemed impossible when she'd surveyed the Barren the night before and discovered thousands of enemy campfires.

She spotted David. He was battling in his human form, alternating between shooting blue fireballs with one hand and using his sword in the other. He was fighting brilliantly, but she realized with concern that he had somehow gotten separated from Erela, Cael, the Northern and Southern Oracles, and other, more seasoned fighters.

Then her concern changed to alarm as she saw a black shape slinking between the boulders that lined the battlefield. The black tiger was shadowing him, stalking him. David had no idea he was about to be blindsided.

She called out to him, waving her arms madly, but just like in her dream, he could neither see nor hear her. Taking on her raven form, she swooped down from the top of Giant's Helmet and flew toward him as quickly as she could.

David had just run his sword through another Kruorumbrae when he heard a primal roar that chilled his blood. He wrenched his sword free of the goblin's corpse and looked up to see an enormous black tiger flying straight for him, deadly fangs bared.

He raised his sword to protect himself, and then, from the side, a dark feline shape collided with the tiger mid leap, tackling the beast. The two large cats rolled around on the sand, alternating between their human and animal forms as they wrestled, before one gained the upper hand.

Settling into his human form, Tierney jerked Lucia to her

feet and held a dagger at her throat. Lucia had managed to draw her sword but now held it limply at her side.

The white raven landed beside David, becoming Abby once again. She glanced at David, and then, assured he was unharmed, turned to Tierney and Lucia. Holding up her hands, she approached the madman.

"Abby," David cautioned, reaching for her.

She took a careful step closer. "You don't want to do this, Tierney. Let her go."

Tierney eyed Abby, and twisted Lucia's long blond hair into a knot around his fist. He yanked her head back, exposing her neck to the edge of his knife. "Maybe I do."

Lucia kept her tongue, refusing to show any sign he was hurting her. But David could see the pain in her eyes.

Abby held Tierney's gaze. "You loved her once."

"Once," Tierney agreed. "But she has betrayed me one too many times."

"Please, Tierney," Abby pleaded. "I know you. You're better than this."

Tierney laughed bitterly. "That's where you're wrong, love. My heart is as black as my hide." He raised the dagger.

David stared at Lucia, wracking his brain for a way to help her. He couldn't blast Tierney with fire without hitting her too.

Lucia stared back at David as though she could sense what he was thinking. Then the strain on her face smoothed into a serene expression. *I'm sorry,* she mouthed. Lucia grabbed the hilt of her silver sword firmly with both hands, and drove it through her abdomen, impaling herself and Tierney.

"No!" David cried out. He rushed across the sand to his aunt, Abby by his side.

Tierney released his grip with a gasp, and his dagger fell to the sand. He studied the sword pinning him to his former lover with wide-eyed astonishment, and then looked up at Abby. *Can you believe this?* his eyes seemed to say.

Abby broke eye contact with him and turned to David. "We have to help Lucia. Pull out the sword, and I'll ease her to the ground."

"Be careful of him," David warned, afraid to take his eyes off Tierney.

Abby nodded and slipped her arms around Lucia to catch her once she was free of the sword. David gingerly pulled out the blade, and as soon as Abby and Lucia were clear, he thrust it back into the bloody gash in Tierney's gut. The dark lord fell to his knees, and then collapsed on the sand.

Abby dragged Lucia away from the Kruor um Beir and laid her gently on the ground. She cradled the woman's head in her lap. "I'm so sorry, Lucia."

Lucia gave her a wan smile. "Not your fault."

Others began to gather around them. Cael and the Southern Oracle stood guard near Tierney, swords drawn in case he attempted to get up, and David retrieved Tierney's dagger, tucking it into his own belt.

Erela landed softly beside David and rested her hand on his shoulder. David acknowledged Erela and then went to Lucia and knelt down, inspecting her wound. "I can heal you." He moved his hands over her abdomen.

"No," Lucia croaked, her voice dry. She pushed his hands away. "Not this time. A wound like this would kill you."

"She speaks true, Solas Beir," Erela agreed, standing over them, her winged shadow shielding them from the sun. "You must let her go."

Lucia coughed, and then laughed and gave David a wry smile. "I knew that man would be the death of me."

David laughed bitterly, his voice hitching.

Lucia grabbed his hand, her grip surprisingly strong. Her eyes were serious. "I have to tell you something, David. When I took the silver mirror from the nixie, my intention was to go into the Wasteland and kill Tierney, not free him. But I was weak. If I were a stronger person, I could have ended this much sooner."

"Shhh," David said. "You're the strongest person I've ever met."

Lucia shook her head. "I made terrible mistakes. The worst was falling in love with him."

Abby looked over at Tierney. "He's fading. There's something I have to ask him before he goes."

David raised his head and studied the dying man, before returning his gaze to Abby. "Be careful," he cautioned. None of the Kruorumbrae had come to Tierney's aid, but that didn't mean he wasn't still dangerous.

Abby nodded. "I will. Erela, can you hold Lucia's head?"

The former Daughter of Mercy traded places with Abby and she walked toward the man who had haunted her dreams.

With his eyes closed, Tierney looked boyishly innocent. Not at all like the sociopath Abby knew him to be. He had lost, and now he was dying.

Abby didn't want to feel sorry for him, but she couldn't help herself, not with him lying there pinned to the ground like an insect, powerless and bleeding out. There was no one left who cared enough to mourn what he once was, before the Darkness had taken hold, or to acknowledge that there might still be some good in him.

He was an evil man. He had proved that time and again, she knew. But Abby also knew that he hadn't always been bad, and she'd seen a side of him no one else had, with the exception of Lucia. But had the Tierney she'd seen in her dreams only been an illusion?

As she stood over him, he opened his dark eyes. Seeing her, he smiled weakly and nodded toward Lucia. "She killed me."

Abby knelt beside him. The physical agony he was experiencing was eclipsed by the grief of dying alone. She could feel his emotional pain acutely, coming off him in waves. She wished she couldn't.

She wished she could be more like Erela—decisive, acting based upon a strict paradigm of right and wrong, good and evil, black and white. Simple. Clear. None of the muddled grey muck she felt now. This was the part about being an empath she hated. Feeling like an emotional train wreck. "I'm sorry."

Tierney studied her face. "You really are, aren't you? Well then, you're the only one." Ichor bubbled to his lips. He twisted away, coughing, and then turned his head back toward her to look into her eyes. "We could have been happy together, you and I."

She remembered the dream where they'd sat together on the edge of a cliff, watching the ocean. She felt overwhelmed as another wave of emotion crashed over her—a confusing mixture of anger at him and sadness for him, and a realization that there was some truth to what he said. If she had never met David, and if Tierney had never been touched by the Darkness, things might have been different.

"I know." Abby looked at the sword plunged deep within his abdomen. It looked obscene buried in his flesh like that. An ugly, hateful thing. She reached over to pull it out.

He followed her gaze and smiled, shaking his head as he stopped her, gripping her outstretched hand in his. "No, Abby. If you care for me at all, don't do that. If you freed me, I would hurt you. I wouldn't be able to stop myself."

She could feel her eyes grow pinched as she tried not to cry. *Stop it,* she told herself. *Pull yourself together. This is the same man who wanted David dead.*

He closed his eyes and shuddered, changing to a black tiger, his hand becoming a large paw grasped in hers. For a mere second, his form flickered, his fur turning white and then back to black before he became human-shaped again.

She gasped. "You're changing!"

He opened his eyes and gave her a sad smile. "No. I'm not."

"But I saw your fur turn white...in my dreams you said the Kruorumbrae could be healed. Was that a lie?"

"No," he replied. "It's true. But it's too little, too late for me. The others still have time. You could heal them." He glanced over at David. "You and him."

"We will," she promised. She wanted to press him for more information, but he reached up and caressed her cheek.

"Goodbye, love. You could have made me whole." Then the King of Blood and Shadows closed his eyes for the last time.

With that, she could no longer hold back the sadness she felt, and a single tear rolled down her cheek.

When Abby returned to kneel next to David, his expression was guarded, unreadable. How much of her conversation with Tierney had he overheard? Had she hurt him again?

The guilt Abby felt was almost unbearable—guilt that she couldn't save Tierney, and guilt that David would feel betrayed by what she had said and felt.

"Did you get what you needed?" he asked quietly.

She nodded and took his hand, sure he would pull away and relieved when he didn't. "He confirmed that we could heal the Kruorumbrae—change them back to what they were before they were corrupted by the Darkness. But I'm still not sure how we're supposed to do that."

"What about the sacrifice?" David asked. "I thought I had to surrender to make it work."

Lucia reached up and placed her palm against David's cheek. "You already did, my dear, sweet boy. When you surrendered to the Light."

She was fading fast, and Abby finally understood what Lucia meant by not being around anymore. Her body started to flicker and she changed into her animal form. Like Tierney, her fur turned white. Unlike him, it stayed that way.

David looked at Abby in surprise. Then, David's shirt began to glow, lighting his face, and he fished out the sigil he was wearing around his neck underneath his clothing. The Sign of the Throne was glowing brighter than Abby had ever seen—radiating white light.

Lucia changed back into her human form, and then her body started to look less solid, more like particles of bright light held together by some unseen force.

She gripped David's hand. "The Light is calling me."

"I don't want you to go," he said.

"I wish I had more time," she whispered. "But we'll meet again in the world beyond. I'm finally clean." With her other hand she took Abby's and smiled. "Take care of each other."

The Sign of the Throne grew brighter, and Lucia's form began to glow brighter as well. Abby and David watched in awe as she dissipated into tiny white orbs that floated into the sky, twinkling like fireflies.

Hands interlocked tightly, David and Abby walked to the top of the Giant's Helmet, with Marisol and Jon close behind. Cael had directed the troops to round up any remaining Kruorumbrae, and now they stood at the base of the rock formation, surrounded by the Solas Beir's soldiers.

David scanned the prisoners. "Where's the Eastern Oracle?"

"He fled," the Northern Oracle replied from below, sheathing her sword. "The coward."

Marisol and Jon exchanged a meaningful look with each other and then with Abby, which David did not miss.

He raised an eyebrow. "Something you want to tell me?" he murmured to Abby.

"Later," she whispered, hiding a smile. "Suffice it to say the Northern Oracle is correct."

The Southern Oracle stepped forward and addressed the Solas Beir. "In light of his crimes against the realm, I must recommend the Eastern Oracle be removed from his position." He looked at the Northern Oracle. "Given my own history with my brother, you know I would not suggest such a thing lightly."

The Northern Oracle nodded gravely. "I understand." Then she looked up at David. "And I agree. Such action is regrettable, but necessary and in the best interests of Cai Terenmare."

"Very well," David said. He held up the Sign of the Throne in both hands as the two oracles clasped hands and bowed their heads. "Let it be known that, as of this moment, the Eastern Oracle is stripped of all authority and power pertaining to his post, and another shall be appointed to serve."

In his hands, the sigil glowed again. A breeze picked up, stirring the sand, gathering strength and whirling until everyone was forced to shield their eyes against it.

Then, as suddenly as it had appeared, the whirlwind was gone, and David knew that the man formerly known as the Eastern Oracle had received the message. He wondered if, like Tierney, the man would someday retaliate, but he doubted it. Though David hated to admit it, the old Eastern Oracle was half the man Tierney had been.

David surveyed what was left of Tierney's army. When the Sower's captives had been freed, the Kruorumbrae had been overpowered. Some had fled, more had died. All that were left were encircled by soldiers serving the Light.

Of those that remained, a few still looked fiercely defiant, their heads held high. The majority, however, looked lost, rudderless without their leader. These Blood Shadows shrank before David, their thoughts apparent by the fear in their eyes. The Solas Beir's army had them surrounded; they were dead, and they knew it. Or they would be if Tierney were still in charge and they had crossed him.

David studied them one by one, feeling pity well up in his heart. He cleared his throat. "Now. As to those of you who sided with Tierney..."

"Kill us, for we will never side with you!" one of the Kruorumbrae called out—a large and rather nasty-looking goblin in the defiant camp. Around him, a handful of others nodded, murmuring in agreement, while others looked on in horror.

David could see his own soldiers gripping their swords, ready to thwart a rebellion. He eyed the Blood Shadow who had spoken. "That is one option," he said calmly. "There are others—like spending the rest of your life in the Wasteland."

This was met with more resistance than the threat of death, and as the grumbling grew louder, Cael signaled for the soldiers to step forward, tightening the circle.

David held up his hand to silence the Kruorumbrae. "There is a third option, however." At the front of the crowd, one of the smaller Shadows perked up his large bat-like ears. "I am aware that not all of you had a choice in becoming Kruorumbrae. Some of you were forced to serve the Darkness, and you have suffered for it. I'm offering you the chance to end that suffering, to be healed by the Light."

"Impossible!" the Kruorumbrae who had spoken earlier thundered, raising his fist to rally his comrades. "It cannot be done. He lies!"

"He's telling the truth!" Abby shouted back at the goblin. "Tierney himself believed it could be done!"

"And you killed him," the Kruorumbrae argued, glaring up at her.

"His choices killed him," David countered. "You don't have to make the same mistake." He looked around, making eye contact with any of the Blood Shadows who dared return his gaze. "Your choice is to submit to the Light. It has to be done of your own free will. If you won't, I can't make you. I'll allow you to leave and no one here will harm you." David turned back to the Shadow who had appointed himself leader. "But know this—if you use your chance at freedom to harm someone else, there will be consequences. Either the Wasteland or death."

The new leader grumbled something David couldn't quite hear and then leaned down, consulting with a smaller Blood Shadow. Around them, other Kruorumbrae seemed engaged in a similar discussion.

In the outer circle, the soldiers watched anxiously. David wondered what his troops thought. By the looks on their faces, some of them weren't too happy about the idea of the Kruorumbrae running free again.

David glanced at Abby, who was also observing both the prisoners and the soldiers. Were they making the right decision, offering the Kruorumbrae a choice? And would they really be able to heal these monsters? After witnessing the change in Lucia, David had felt certain they could, but staring out into the crowd, he began to have doubts. Still, he had to try, for Hedeon, if not for those who had already turned.

He thought back to the moment he'd stood before the Sower, completely defenseless, with only the Light to protect him. He'd given himself over to the Light, and it was the Light that had won the battle. He had to trust that a force strong enough to vanquish a six-headed dragon was powerful enough to heal these creatures' hearts. "All right," David called. "Decision time. Who among you will surrender to the Light?"

The silence among the Kruorumbrae was palpable, and for a second, David was sure that none of them would submit. Then he'd be forced to let them all go, only to round them up later, after they'd killed again, to be herded into the Wasteland. Or executed, in which case, he'd have to serve as executioner, a role he dreaded.

Then the bat-eared Shadow hesitantly raised his hand.

"Okay," David said, nodding. "Good. Anyone else?"

Around the first Shadow, others started to raise their hands, tentatively at first, and then, as courage caught like a flame and began to radiate across the crowd, more and more joined in.

David smiled. "Good! Good." Now only the outspoken Kruorumbrae remained, with a few others who looked around sullenly. "Last chance," David warned. "Will you yield?"

"Never," the Kruorumbrae growled, his red eyes glowing dully in sunken sockets.

"All right, then. You've made your choice," David replied. He held up his finger. "Just remember, harm anyone, and justice will be swift."

"But what will we eat?" a smaller Shadow whined.

"You'll have to learn to survive as we do," David answered her. "It won't be easy, fighting your cravings. But if you change your mind and want to be healed, come to me. I will help you."

The creature nodded, looking as though she longed to stay, but cowered when the largest Kruorumbrae growled at her. He held out his hand, and she took it with a hand that was almost delicate in the way it trembled, if not for its long talons. The new leader looked up at David expectantly.

"You are free to go."

In response, the giant goblin began to push his way past several soldiers who stared at David in disbelief, unable to accept that their king was simply allowing these monsters to go.

"Let them pass," David commanded.

The soldiers lowered their weapons, clearing a path.

Once the rebel Kruorumbrae were well on their way, walking south into the heart of the Barren, David took Abby in his arms and they flew into the midst of the remaining Shadows. Both the creatures and the soldiers seemed surprised. It occurred to David that no one in his right mind would land in the center of a mob of bloodthirsty monsters.

While Solas Beirs past had executed Kruorumbrae without a second thought, David had just made history. He had shown mercy to creatures who didn't deserve kindness by giving the rebels a second chance. He sincerely hoped he wouldn't regret it. He hoped he could make history with those that remained.

"All right," he said, setting Abby on her feet. "I need all the Kruorumbrae in a circle around us, holding hands." The monsters looked at each other, and then slowly complied. "Hedeon, you too," David instructed.

The knight hesitated, giving the Kruorumbrae a long look before joining them. This had to be hard for him, David thought, given what had happened to his family.

"Everyone else, form a circle around them and join hands."

Cael nodded, taking Eulalia's hand and Marisol's. Marisol took Jon's, and he took the Southern Oracle's, who took a soldier's hand—before long, the circle was complete, and David was standing with Abby in the center.

"Good. Now, for the next part." David slipped the Sign of the Throne off his neck and placed it in Abby's open palms, covering her hands with his.

She smiled at him. "This is familiar," she said.

Not so long ago, they had used the power of the sigil to repair the portal in Newcastle Beach, the one that had allowed them access to Cai Terenmare so David could claim his throne.

"I just hope it works," he whispered.

"Me too," Abby replied.

David looked around the circle. "The Solas Beir has no power," he declared in a loud voice. "He is only a vessel for the Light to fill, just like this sigil. Alone, he can do nothing, but with the Light's infinite power, anything is possible." *Please help me,* he thought. *Help us all.*

With this, the Sign of the Throne began to emit a soft, beating light. The glow grew steadily stronger, pulsing into a bright beacon that shot upward and pierced the sky before radiating across the inner circle and spreading outward in a rush of warmth.

The Kruorumbrae began to change, the red of their eyes fading as they looked more like humans and less like goblins. Their bodies shifted into those of their spirit animals, twisting at first into monstrous black renditions before settling into a menagerie of animals that would have been at home on a number of continents on Earth. Most of them bore the regular stripes, spots, and colors of earthen animals, although David could see a few cast in the trademark white, indicating noble blood.

When they regained their humanoid forms, all traces of the Darkness were gone. Cheers erupted from those who had been healed and the soldiers alike. David and Abby found themselves swept up in the celebration.

Hedeon knelt before David and Abby. "Thank you, Solas Beir, C'aislingaer. You have given me back my life. My sword is yours for the rest of my days." He seemed overcome with emotion as he added, "I only wish my family could have been here to see this day."

"Thank you for your pledge," David responded, gesturing for the knight to rise. "I hope, however, your days will be filled with peace. After your faithful service today, you deserve a rest."

"Thank you, Sire." Hedeon bowed and then went to join Jon and Marisol, who each greeted him with an embrace.

The creature with bat ears turned out to be a young man whose ears weren't quite so large. He approached David shyly, and then said, "Thank you, Solas Beir. To be free of the gnawing hunger that has been my curse—I cannot express my gratitude for this gift."

"Don't thank me," David replied, grinning. "Thank the Light. Come—we'll have a feast at the Northern Stronghold. Spread the word."

Before he began the long walk back to the stronghold, David took one last look at the battlefield. His eyes were drawn to the place where Lucia had gone to the Light.

"I think she knew she was going to die," Abby said quietly, beside him. "But she saved you anyway, because she really did love you."

David gave Abby a bittersweet smile and took her hand. "I loved her too."

With all the newcomers, the Northern Stronghold's pantry had become seriously taxed. Luckily the fortress's keeper had squirreled away enough food to make sure everyone was fed, and David promised to send supplies to restock. The keeper didn't seem vexed to prepare a feast. Rather, he looked delighted to witness so many happy reunions as those who had been held captive found their families, and those who had been thought lost to the Darkness were welcomed.

David was surprised to learn that most of his court council was present. Two of the other members, Navit and Rodas, had been captured when the Sower seized Caislucis and made Eulalia, Marisol, and nearly everyone else into puppets. The third, Fedor of the Great Plains, had been killed while trying to protect his fellow council members from becoming infected.

Claiming one of the tables in the dining hall before the feast, David held an impromptu meeting with the council, the remaining oracles, and his closest friends.

"Although we're celebrating a great victory for the Light, we can't forget about those who lost their lives to this war. There were a number of sacrifices. My aunt, Lucia, lost her life saving mine, and in doing so ensured the end of Tierney's reign as Kruor um Beir. We also lost our friend Fedor, a valued member of our council. When we return home to Caislucis, I want to honor these sacrifices and many others." Around him, David heard murmurs of approval. "We also can't forget about the work ahead to rebuild what we've lost. We know there were fires in Southport and in the City of the Eastern Oracle, but we don't know the extent of the damage. And it's not just the physical destruction that concerns me. We have a long way to go to rebuild communication throughout the kingdom and to help those who were healed reenter society. More than ever, it's important that we work together." David looked at each of the council members in turn, studying them, and then turned to the Northern and Southern Oracles. "It also seems we have job vacancies for the roles of the Eastern and Western Oracles."

"Indeed," the Southern Oracle agreed. "Although I mourn the loss of Nerine, I cannot say I am sorry about the former Eastern Oracle. Or the sea hag."

"Good riddance," Abby muttered, and the Jaguar King smiled in response.

"Any suggestions on who should fill the posts?" David asked.

The Northern Oracle spoke up. "You will need a strong leader in the East, someone with experience to handle the challenges there." She looked at Obelia and put her hand on the dark-skinned woman's arm. "I suggest the head of your court council."

David grinned. Although Obelia had earned it by being a tremendous resource to him in learning about the politics of Caislucis, the thought of a woman replacing the stodgy Eastern Oracle and eliminating his archaic policies was also too satisfying to pass up. "I love that idea. What do you think, Obelia?"

Obelia's golden-brown eyes twinkled as she smiled

warmly. "I would be honored to serve, Solas Beir."

"Excellent," David said, reaching over and squeezing her hand. "From what Jon and Hedeon told me, the palace may have burned, but Hedeon has promised to get the new oracle settled into the Hall of Solas Beirs until it can be rebuilt—assuming, of course, that the hall survived the fire."

"I am not at all worried, Your Majesty," Obelia replied.

"Good," David said. "What about the Western Oracle?"

"Traditionally, the Western Oracle has been someone with a connection to the sea," the Southern Oracle explained. "Do any of your council members possess such a link?"

David nodded. "Actually, yes. And in the time I've known him, I've come to respect his passion for service and courage to speak his mind. He taught me that even a small fishing village like Yakez is worthy of a Solas Beir's attention. What do you think, Eoin?"

Eoin blinked in disbelief. "But Sire, I have only served on the council for a few short years."

David chuckled. "And I've served as Solas Beir for less time than that. But when you dove into that bay, you risked your life to protect your people by looking for evidence of the Sower. I respect that. I should add, however, that there's been high turnover with the job. It may be cursed."

Eoin laughed. "I shall take my chances. Thank you, Sire. I have never dreamed of such an honor."

The Southern Oracle clapped Eoin on the shoulder. "Welcome, brother."

"Thank you, Southern Oracle," Eoin said. The Northern Oracle took his hand and smiled, and Eoin returned her smile, beaming.

"So now we have three vacancies on the council," David announced. "I'd like to ask my mother, the dowager queen, to head the council."

"Of course," Eulalia exclaimed, delighted, as Cael proudly

slipped his arm around her shoulders.

David acknowledged her with a nod, but worried someone might cry favoritism since she was family. Just in case, he thought it prudent to share his reasoning. "Eulalia has worked closely with you all during her time as queen, and I value her advice. Any objections?" David waited a moment, looking around the table. Seeing there were none, he continued. "Okay, good. The second vacancy is Fedor's. He sacrificed himself in an effort to save his friends, Navit and Rodas. As far as his place on the council, I can think of no better candidate than Cael, who is well-acquainted with sacrifice."

"I agree," said Obelia.

"Thank you, Solas Beir," Cael replied. "I look forward to serving in this new role." Eulalia kissed her husband's cheek.

David placed his hand on Cael's shoulder and gave him a solemn nod, and then turned back to the council. "I also think it's high time we had a faery representative on the council. Fergal, would you be willing to serve?"

The tiny green faery bowed. "It would be my great honor, Sire, to serve as a voice for my people. Thank you."

"You're most welcome. Now," he addressed the council, "once we've concluded our meeting, we'll gather the people in the hall to honor our lost with a feast and officially appoint you all to your new posts. I know we handle these things with more formality at Caislucis, so I beg your forgiveness for my haste and the lack of ceremony."

He turned to Abby and took her hand, and the naidyris stone in her ring sparkled up at him. "There's one last thing I wanted to discuss with you, my friends. As you know, Abby is my betrothed. When we return to Caislucis and put things to rights, I intend to marry her." He hesitated, suddenly feeling self-conscious. He'd gotten more comfortable taking a leadership role, but he still hadn't gotten used to the idea of his love life being so public. "So…it seems we'll be having another wedding. And a coronation."

"Long live the queen!" the Southern Oracle declared, and Abby favored him with a shy smile. He rose from his chair as the first of many to offer their congratulations.

After David swore in the new oracles and council members, Jon pulled Abby to the side. "Can we talk?"

"Sure," she said, leading him down an empty corridor. "What's up?"

He hesitated, shifting his weight and looking at the floor as though he felt uncomfortable about something. "Marisol and I…well, you know we've been through a lot recently, right? Me in prison, and her ordeal with the Sower…"

Abby nodded slowly. She felt guarded, wondering where this was going. "Things have been less than ideal. For all of us."

Jon looked at her as if stung, and she felt guilty for acting defensive.

"I'm sorry. I didn't mean that how it sounded." He looked away, and she slipped her hand in his, waiting for him to continue.

Jon stared at Abby's hand. "We've been talking about leaving Cai Terenmare."

"What? No—you can't," she stammered, her grip on his hand tightening. "I know things haven't been easy, especially for you two, but you can't just leave—not now that things are getting better." She searched his eyes. "We won." Abby realized she was squeezing his hand too hard and relaxed her grip, letting her hand drop to her side.

Jon shook his head. "You and David won. This is your world. Sol and I *survived*. We just…we need to go home—we need a sense of normalcy. No magic. No monsters."

Abby's eyes widened. "But you'll come back, won't you? At

least for the wedding?"

Jon leaned forward and kissed her forehead. "I wouldn't miss it for the world. You know that."

Abby threw her arms around his neck, burying her face against his chest. "Are you sure you want to leave?"

"Abby, you have to let me go. I need to check on my mom, and Marisol wants to make sure her mom is okay, too, now that Malden is dead. And we want to finish school. We've missed so much, I'm not sure we can even graduate on time..."

Abby looked up. "Cassandra will help you. There are tests you can take. An independent study, maybe."

In her old life, before coming to Cai Terenmare, Cassandra Buchan had counseled Abby on college and had become both her mentor and friend. Cassandra and her family had even stayed in Cai Terenmare for a time.

Jon nodded. "I've thought about that too. Cassandra mentioned a few options before she went back to Newcastle Beach, when we realized I wouldn't be finishing her psychology course. We had a long talk after I decided to join you and David in visiting the Southern Oracle." He gave her a bittersweet smile. "I may have to attend summer school."

Abby laughed. "Juvenile delinquent."

He stuck out his tongue. "High school dropout."

She scowled. "Ouch. A little harsh, don't you think?"

"Only kidding," he said, and did actually look sorry. "I'm just jealous you're going to be queen."

She cocked her head to the side and raised her eyebrows. "You're saying *you* want to be queen?"

"Uh...no," he laughed, shaking his head. "I'm saying I think it's great you already have your life figured out."

"But I don't have it figured out. Not at all."

"Yeah you do. Maybe not all the details, but you know who you are and what you want. You always have. And this world? It was made for you. You'll be a great queen."

Abby frowned. "I'll be an uneducated queen."

Jon shook his head. "No you won't. You'll learn everything you need to know from Gorman. He'll make sure you know the history, the customs..."

Abby sighed. "I guess. I'll miss out on college, though."

Jon chuckled and took her shoulders. "I don't think the people of Cai Terenmare put any stock in human education. You're much better off learning at Caislucis. But for Sol and me, things are different. We need to live in our own world, figure out what we want out of life."

"So that's it then," Abby said, holding back tears. "You'll live in your world, I'll live in mine." She looked up at him. "I'll never see you."

Jon smiled and lifted her chin. "Yes you will, you dork. I'll be a portal away."

EPILOGUE: THE CEREMONY

In the last days of summer, Jon made good on his promise to return to Cai Terenmare, along with Marisol, his mother, Blanca, Abby's family, and the Buchan family.

Jon had gone to summer school, but not to finish high school. With Cassandra's help, he had managed to graduate on time and take two college courses with Marisol, getting a head start on their freshman year at the University of Santa Linda.

Abby's mother had made several trips to Cai Terenmare, working with Eulalia to plan the wedding and coronation. Abby and David had spent the time learning as much as they could about their new kingdom, in between the work of rebuilding it. With the death of the Sower, the faeries had slowly begun to come out of hiding and return to Caislucis, along with the animals. For Abby, this was a sign the kingdom was healing.

Now Abby stood under the same archway where she had waited for a different wedding to begin. This time, Eulalia and Cael were seated in the front circle with Abby's mother and brother, along with Blanca Reyes and three of the four oracles. In the circles behind them, the Buchans were in attendance, along with all of the people Abby had come to love in Cai Terenmare.

David was standing at the dais with Jon, who was serving

as best man, and Obelia, who would once again lead the ceremony, this time as the Eastern Oracle.

The dais and courtyard looked gorgeous, arrayed in flowers in a myriad of colors, and the air smelled like jasmine and the sea. A feast was waiting in the banquet hall, the tables covered with more flowers, colorful silken cloths, and candles.

David had had only one request: that Abby's dress be blue. "To complement your eyes," he'd said.

She hadn't minded. "Blue is my signature color, you know."

"I know," David had grinned, kissing her hand. "That's why I chose this ring for you."

For her dress, Abby selected a fabric that mirrored her ring—cerulean variegated with shades of peacock blue and emerald, shimmering like the colors in an ocean wave. The blue dress she had worn at the Autumn Ball a lifetime before paled in comparison to the majesty of her wedding gown.

Abby was waiting for the ceremony to begin with her dad and Marisol. She and David had decided to incorporate traditions from both of their worlds, one of them being that the bride would be escorted down the aisle by her father.

"You look beautiful, sweetheart," he murmured, taking her hand.

"Thanks, Dad," Abby whispered, giving his hand a squeeze. Emotion welled in her chest, and she had to blink, fighting to hold in happy tears.

Her father beamed with pride and turned to Marisol, who was holding her bouquet in one hand and adjusting the flowing skirt of her gown with the other. He gave her a bright smile. "You look beautiful as well, Marisol."

"Thank you, Mr. Brown. I'm honored your daughter included me in her special day."

"I had to!" Abby gave Marisol a hug. "It wouldn't be special without you. I've missed you and Jon so much."

"We missed you too," Marisol said, hugging Abby back.

"And thanks for not dressing me funny."

"You're welcome," Abby laughed. Another tradition she and David had chosen to adopt was including a maid of honor, and blue suited Marisol too. As had been the case in Eulalia's nuptials, the other members of the wedding party were dressed in colors coordinating with the bride's gown—shades varying from emerald to sapphire—but for this ceremony, there would be no sowing of seeds and flowers.

Abby turned her attention back to the courtyard. Hidden from view, she smiled as she watched David standing on the dais, waiting for his first glimpse of her. He looked anxious for the ceremony to begin, but not at all nervous.

Jon said something to him, probably making a joke to ease the tension, because David laughed. He looked unbelievably striking, more handsome than ever. Her signature color complemented his eyes too, and around his neck he wore the Sign of the Throne.

The silver diadem balanced on David's head made his dark hair look regal. She didn't care that, as always, his hair was somewhat unruly. It was endearing, and she loved it. She loved everything about him. Abby couldn't believe that in a few short moments, she would be marrying this amazing man.

As the sun began to set, streaking the sky with orange and fuchsia, the music started, and Abby watched Marisol walk up the aisle. Then it was her turn. Her father held out his arm and she took it. Passing under the arch, she caught David's eye and her heart leapt. His smile lit his entire face.

He was all she saw. Everyone around her disappeared. Only the two of them existed.

Her father walked her up to the dais and shook David's hand. "Take good care of her."

"I will," David promised. "Thank you." He took Abby's hands in his, beaming.

They turned to face Obelia, and she began the ceremony.

"Today we bear witness to the joining of two souls..."

Abby barely heard the words. *I love you,* she mouthed, and David's smile grew brighter.

I love you too, he mouthed back.

"...forever bound by their love," Obelia was saying, "David Corbin, Solas Beir of Cai Terenmare, and Abigail Brown, cai aislingstraid of Santa Linda. David, will you speak your vows?"

"I will," David replied. "Abigail Brown." He looked into her eyes, and she found herself entranced by his gaze. "Abby," he smiled, repeating her name softly. "You are beautiful beyond words. You are my best friend and the love of my life. We've found each other, lost each other, and come back to one another again. Nothing, not even a six-headed, fire-breathing dragon, can keep me from you."

Abby giggled and heard laughter coming from their family and friends.

"I promise you that I will always love you, this day and all my days, in this world and in the worlds beyond." With that, he slipped the naidyris ring on her finger.

"And Abby," Obelia said, "will you speak your vows?"

Abby nodded and looked at David. "I will." He smiled, and she felt her heart beat faster. She looked into his pale blue eyes. "David, I do believe I loved you from the first moment I saw you."

He grinned, and someone in the audience sighed loudly and longingly. Everyone let out a short burst of laughter again.

"And I've loved you every day since. You are my best friend and the person I love most in the world. I promise you that I will always love you, this day and all my days, in this world, and in the worlds beyond." She slipped a simple silver ring on his finger, one that matched the circlet he wore on his head.

They turned back to Obelia, who nodded and solemnly recited, "With vows spoken, you are bound in the Light, husband

and wife." Then she smiled. "Solas Beir, you may kiss your bride."

David's face lit up again. He took Abby's face in his hands and kissed her tenderly. She wrapped her arms around him and held him tight, kissing him back. Around them, their family and friends cheered and applauded.

When they turned to face their guests, Obelia announced them. "May I present to you, David and Abigail Corbin of Cai Terenmare!"

The audience applauded again, and then, after a moment, Obelia quieted them, raising her hands. "One matter remains."

From the small ceremonial table behind her, she retrieved an object. David squeezed Abby's hand as Obelia held out a delicate silver tiara.

"Solas Beir, would you do the honors?"

David accepted the crown. "Of course." He turned to Abby. "Abigail Corbin."

Hearing her new last name from his lips, Abby smiled, and David grinned as though he liked the sound of it too.

Then he recited the words she'd heard at his coronation. "Do you promise to serve the Light, to protect your people against the Darkness, and to use your throne and your power for the benefit of your people, as long as you shall rule?"

She nodded. "I promise."

"Then, as Solas Beir, I crown you Queen of Cai Terenmare, with this diadem as representation of your authority." He lifted the tiara and placed it on her head as she bent forward. "May your rule be wise and long, and may there ever be peace in your kingdom."

The crowd erupted into an enthusiastic ovation.

Someone, the Southern Oracle, Abby suspected, shouted, "Long live the queen!"

David raised Abby's hand to his lips, kissed it, and then raised her hand high, clasped in his own. When the guests quieted, the sky was dark, and the first stars were making an appearance.

David assumed a serious expression. "You may have noticed that we did not include a sowing ceremony in our wedding. Given recent events, I hope you'll understand why we broke with tradition."

"I'll say," Jon muttered, causing the crowd to laugh once more.

David chuckled. "Instead, Abby and I wanted to introduce a new tradition, something to honor the Light and our triumph over the Darkness. The battles we fight belong to the Light. The Light is infinite power, not belonging to the Solas Beir alone, but to all of us, no matter who we are, or where we're from."

David took Abby's hands in his, and around his neck, the Sign of the Throne began to glow.

"The Light binds us with love," he said.

From between their entwined fingers seeped cerulean light. It became an orb that hovered over their hands, burning bright white at its core and encircled by a nimbus of blue.

"Love," he continued, "that we share with each other and with all of you."

David took the orb in his open palm and it split in two. Abby took one half, and he kept the other, and then they each divided those spheres of light in two. Abby passed an orb to Marisol while David gave one to Obelia, and then split his again to pass to Jon.

As Marisol and Jon divided their spheres and passed them on, David spoke again. "Love that never falters, but continues to burn brightly as we share it."

Azure light began to radiate across the courtyard as people split their orbs and passed them to their neighbors.

When the entire courtyard was alight, David spoke one last time. "It is the power of the Light and the power of love that ensure peace and prosperity for all in our kingdom."

He turned to Abby, and as one, they let their orbs go, guiding them gently into the air with their hands. Around them, everyone released their cerulean spheres.

Together they watched the shimmering orbs float up into the night sky until they were indistinguishable from the stars.

CHARACTERS
(in alphabetical order)

Abigail "Abby" Brown: a girl with the ability to see the future and communicate with others through dreams. The daughter of Frank and Bethany Brown and sister of Matthew Brown, she was born and raised in the human world.

Ardal of Caislucis (AR-dahl of KASS-loo-sis): the father of David Corbin and the previous Solas Beir, also called the Great Bear King. Ardal was assassinated shortly after David's birth and before his kidnapping. (In general, people in Cai Terenmare use their city or region of origin as a surname.)

Aziza (ah-ZEE-zah): a young girl abducted from the village of Nuren, forced to serve as a courtesan, and given to Meridoris as a reward for her service to the Kruor um Beir.

Brarn (rhymes with barn): the raven who guides Abby and is a friend to Queen Eulalia.

Cael (kayl): Queen Eulalia's champion and first knight of the castle, Caislucis, he is charged with ensuring the safety of the Solas Beir and the royal family.

Cai Aislingstraid (KIGH AY-sling-stride): a soul who sees, a person with the ability to see the future and communicate with others through dreams.

C'aislingaer (KIGH-sling-ahr): the slang term for Cai Aislingstraid.

Cassandra Buchan (BYOO-can): Professor of Psychology and Statistics at the University of Santa Linda, she's married to Riordan Buchan and is the mother of their children, Ciaran (KEER-ahn), Siobhan (sh'-VAWN), and Rowan (ROH-un).

David Corbin: the new Solas Beir (king) of Cai Terenmare, he grew up in the human world, and prefers his human name over his birth name, Artan. His adoptive parents, the Corbins, were murdered by two of the Kruorumbrae, Calder and Malden.

Eastern Oracle: one of the four Oracles ruling the outer realms of Cai Terenmare, who work in concert with the Solas Beir to keep the balance between the Light and the Darkness. He governs the City of the Eastern Oracle, perched on the cliffs above the east coast of Cai Terenmare. The other Oracles are the Northern Oracle, the Southern Oracle, and the Western Oracle.

Eoin (OH-en) **of the North Forest:** a man from the small fishing village of Yakez, who serves on the Solas Beir's court council.

Erela (eh-REL-lah): a winged woman and warrior, who also serves on the Solas Beir's court council.

Eulalia (YOO-lahl-ee-ah): dowager queen of Cai Terenmare, widow of the last Solas Beir, Ardal, and birth mother of Artan (David Corbin), the new Solas Beir.

Fergal (FER-gahl) **the Valorous**: a shape-shifting faery, loyal to the queen. His spirit animal is a frog.

Gorman: a small indigo man who serves on the Solas Beir's court council and is the historian and librarian for Caislucis.

Hedeon (heh-DAY-on): head knight charged with the security of the City of the Eastern Oracle.

Jonathon "Jon" Reyes: Abby's best friend, neighbor, and the son of Blanca Reyes.

Kruor um Beir (KROO-or um BAIR): the King of Blood and Shadows, and the one who rules those who serve the Darkness.

Kruorumbrae (KROO-or-um-bray): evil shape-shifting creatures who feed on others, often referred to as Blood Shadows or simply Shadows.

Lucia (loo-SEE-ah): Queen Eulalia's sister, she assassinated Ardal and kidnapped Artan (David Corbin), betraying her family for Tynan Tierney, the Kruor um Beir. While living in the human world, she disguised herself as an old woman named Moira Buchan.

Malden (MAHL-den): a sadistic shape-shifter loyal to Tynan Tierney, who has historic ties to Newcastle Beach.

Marisol (mah-REE-sol) **Cassidy**: daughter of Marcus Cassidy, a wealthy businessman, and Esperanza Garcia, a former supermodel. She is friends with David Corbin and grew up in Newcastle Beach.

Meridoris (MEER-ee-dor-ess): a sea hag and vile sorceress from the depths of the ocean.

Nerine (NEER-ih-nee): a mermaid and daughter of the Sea King, she is the newly appointed Western Oracle, replacing the former oracle, a sea monster destroyed by Cael.

Northern Oracle: one of the four Oracles, she governs the Gauntlet and the Ice Mountain Territories.

Obelia (oh-BEEL-ya): head of the Solas Beir's court council. The other members of the council are Gorman, Erela, Eoin of the North Forest, Fedor of the Great Plains, Navit of the South, and Rodas of the East.

Phelan (FAY-lan): a knight, and Cael's second in command, charged with the security of Caislucis.

Sholto: a member of the Sea King's court. Nerine is his betrothed.

Solas Beir (SO-lass BAIR): ruler of Cai Terenmare. In representing the Light, the Solas Beir is endowed with great power and is meant to be a servant to the people. Solas Beir can be translated literally as Lightbearer, but this less formal term is used to refer to a future ruler who has not yet ascended to the throne. The term Lightbearer can also be used as an insult, referring to a ruler who is weak.

Southern Oracle: one of the four Oracles, he governs the Rainforest.

The Sower: it has been foretold that this mysterious creature will herald the destruction of Cai Terenmare.

Tynan Tierney (TIGH-nan TEER-nee): the leader of the Kruorumbrae, creatures of the Darkness. He calls himself Kruor um Beir and seeks the throne of the Solas Beir. He is often referred to simply as Tierney.

Western Oracle: one of the four Oracles, she governed the seas and was mother to the murderous sirens. She, her daughters, and her island temple were destroyed by Cael.

Yola (YOH-lah): a woman from the village of Nuren, whose brother, Daudi (dah-OO-dee), was abducted along with five other villagers, including a young girl named Aziza (ah-ZEE-zah).

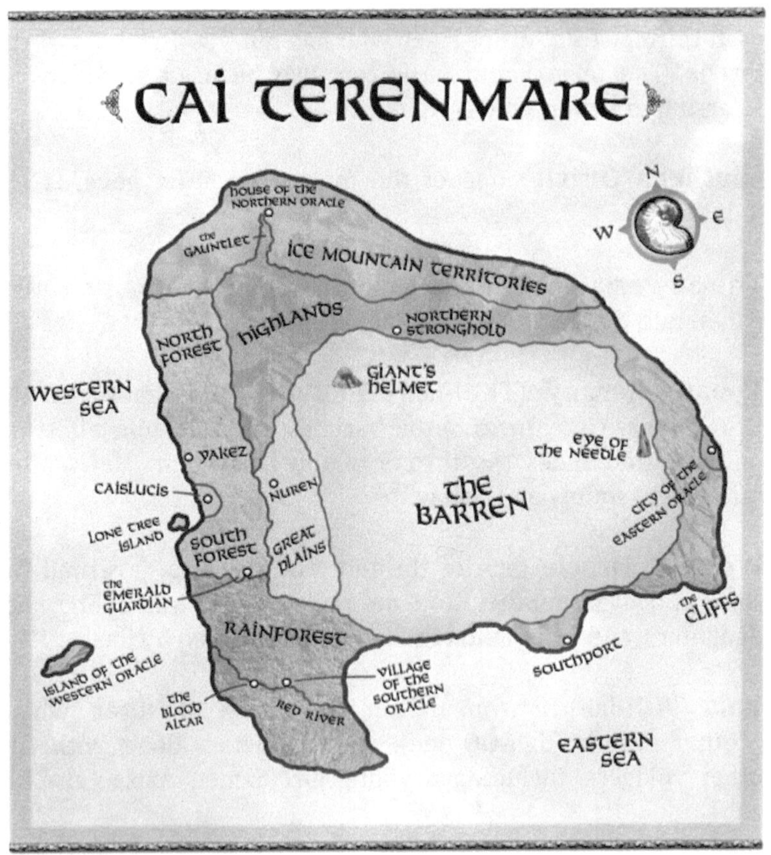
CAI TERENMARE
N
E
S
W
HOUSE OF THE NORTHERN ORACLE
THE GAUNTLET
ICE MOUNTAIN TERRITORIES
HIGHLANDS
NORTHERN STRONGHOLD
NORTH FOREST
GIANT'S HELMET
WESTERN SEA
EYE OF THE NEEDLE
YAKEZ
CAISLUCIS
NUREN
THE BARREN
CITY OF THE EASTERN ORACLE
LONE TREE ISLAND
SOUTH FOREST
GREAT PLAINS
THE EMERALD GUARDIAN
THE CLIFFS
RAINFOREST
SOUTHPORT
ISLAND OF THE WESTERN ORACLE
VILLAGE OF THE SOUTHERN ORACLE
THE BLOOD ALTAR
RED RIVER
EASTERN SEA

PLACES AND TERMS
(in alphabetical order)

The Barren: the vast desert in the center of Cai Terenmare, spanning from the Great Plains to the Eye of the Needle.

Cai Terenmare (KIGH TAIR-en-mahr): a parallel world to Earth filled with magic, shape-shifters, mythical creatures, and blood-thirsty monsters.

Caislucis (KASS-loo-sis): castle and city of the Solas Beir, perched on the cliffs above the Western Sea.

City of the Eastern Oracle: a large, bustling, walled city governed by the Eastern Oracle.

Eye of the Needle: a rock spire near the City of the Eastern Oracle.

Giant's Helmet: a rock formation in the Barren near the Northern Stronghold.

Newcastle Beach Inn: a mansion built by Thaddeus Buchan as his home, and later deeded to the Newcastle Beach community. It sits across the street from his brother Samuel's mansion, which was damaged in an earthquake and is in ruin.

Northern Stronghold: a fortress built into the cliffs that serve as the border for the northern edge of the Barren.

Nuren: a small village on the Great Plains.

Pool of Healing: a sacred pool within Caislucis that can heal almost any wound.

Sigil: a seal, signet, sign, symbol, or image with magical power.

Sign of the Throne: the sigil of the Solas Beir and an object of great power belonging to the Light. It is used to open and close portals from Cai Terenmare to other worlds.

Silver Hand Mirror: an object of power also used to open and close portals, but created and corrupted by Darkness.

Southport: a coastal town notorious as a haven for pirates and slave traders.

Village of the Southern Oracle: governed by the Southern Oracle, this tiny village stands in the center of a dangerous rainforest.

The Wasteland: a parallel world to Cai Terenmare that serves as a prison. In this desert where time is frozen, prisoners are compelled to count scarlet grains of sand for all eternity.

Yakez: A small fishing village on the coast of the North Forest region.

ABOUT THE AUTHOR

Melissa Eskue Ousley is the award-winning author of *The Solas Beir Trilogy*, a young adult fantasy series. Her first novel, Book One, *Sign of the Throne*, won a 2014 Eric Hoffer Book Award and a 2014 Readers' Favorite International Book Award.

Melissa lives in the Pacific Northwest with her family, a piranha, and their Kelpie, Gryphon. When she's not writing, she can be found hiking, swimming, scuba diving, or walking along the beach, poking dead things with a stick.

Before becoming a writer, Melissa had a number of jobs that contributed to her education and enlightenment, ranging from a summer scraping roadkill off a molten desert highway, to years of conducting social science research with an amazing team of educators at the University of Arizona. Her interests in psychology, culture, and mythology influenced her writing of *The Solas Beir Trilogy.*

www.MelissaEskueOusley.com

www.goodreads.com/MelissaEskueOusley

www.facebook.com/MelissaEskueOusley

www.twitter.com/@MEskueOusley